DOCTOR WHO

ISLAND OF DEATH
BARRY LETTS

BOOKS

DOCTOR WHO:
ISLAND OF DEATH

Published by BBC Books, BBC Worldwide Ltd,
Woodlands, 80 Wood Lane, London W12 0TT

First published 2005
Copyright © Barry Letts 2005
The moral right of the author has been asserted.

Original series broadcast on BBC television
Format © BBC 1963
'Doctor Who' and 'TARDIS' are trademarks
of the British Broadcasting Corporation

ISBN 0 563 48631 7

Commissioning editors: Shirley Patton and Stuart Cooper
Editor and creative consultant: Justin Richards
Project editor: Vicki Vrint

This book is a work of fiction. Names, characters, places
and incidents are either a product of the author's imagination
or are used fictitiously. Any resemblance to actual people living
or dead, events or locales is entirely coincidental.

Cover imaging by Black Sheep © BBC 2005
Printed and bound in Great Britain by Clays Ltd, St Ives plc

For more information about this and other BBC books,
please visit our website at www.bbcshop.com

Twenty grand! More than four times what she earned in a year! It was no good. He was well and truly hooked.

'Off you go,' she said, seeing his almost panicky glance over his shoulder as he realised that his new brothers and sisters had all disappeared.

'I want to have a word with his nibs,' she added grimly. 'I'm not going to let this one get away.'

Jeremy's shadow of a frown at her disrespect was wiped away by the sunny grin of the new-born zealot. 'Please yourself,' he said. 'You'll join us in the end. Everybody will. Honestly, Sarah, I've never been so happy in all my bally life!'

And off he went.

She turned to speak to the guru – who had been wiping the ceremonial cup and replacing it in a little cupboard – only to find that he was staring at her with a slight frown on his face.

Had he heard what she'd been saying?

When he caught her eye he turned away, taking a key from his pocket, to unlock the double doors underneath the sacred icon.

'Excuse me!' called Sarah.

He turned back – but not before he'd re-locked the door. 'You're missing all the fun,' he said, with a charming smile.

She definitely knew him. In the mould of the traditional Hollywood star – literally tall, dark and handsome – you'd think he would be hard to forget. And the voice... that was like an actor's too.

Had she seen him around Hampstead? In Tesco's or something?

'Could I ask you a few questions? I'm Sarah Jane Smith – from *Metropolitan*. The magazine, you know? We're doing a feature on –'

His smile abruptly vanished. 'A journalist... Ah yes, I remember you now. *Metropolitan*. And can I expect you to do as efficient a hatchet job on me now as you did last time?'

Eh? Oh Lor'! Of course. He looked so different with his long hair and his white robes.

'We only reported what the committee said.'

Alex Whitbread. Shortened his name from Alexander to woo the masses. Alex Whitbread, the charmer – until you got on the wrong side of him. The farthest right member of a right-wing government, thrown out for blatant corruption – and more than a touch of racism. Better be careful, though. He was as sharp as he was good-looking. Tipped for prime minister in his early days.

This was a story in itself! If she could grab a photo...

Her hand was creeping towards her shoulder bag. After the foul-up at Space World, she never went anywhere without a 35mm camera and a Polaroid back-up.

'Why should I submit myself to the smears of the gutter press?' he asked.

Gutter press! Clorinda would love that. As editor of the glossiest of the glossies...

'Look, Mr Whitbread –'

'Brother Alex, if you don't mind.'

'Okay. Brother Alex. It's obvious that you've moved away from your old life. And anyway, we want to write about your... your movement. Not you personally.'

He relaxed slightly. 'Mm. Nonetheless, you infiltrated this meeting by pretending to be a new disciple. That's hardly likely to inspire my trust.'

'But that's just it. Why the secrecy? Why can't anybody just walk in and join up? And what's it all about?'

'The criteria for becoming a disciple – even a guest – are extremely strict. Mother Hilda insists that...'

'Mother Hilda?'

For a moment, Whitbread looked as if he'd let out too much. 'Ah yes... Mother Hilda. Mother Hilda is the founder of our order. It was through the revelation vouchsafed to Mother Hilda that the divine message of the great Skang was given to the world. Skang – may his name be blessed – Skang deserves, nay *demands*, only the most perfect representatives of the human race as his initiates. All the vitality of supreme bodily fitness; superlative intelligence...'

Superlative intelligence! Jeremy?

'...and a dedication and a devotion which will merit the ultimate reward.'

'And what's that?' Sarah asked.

'The reward of Skang's incomparable love.'

Incomparable codswallop, more like. 'I thought they were asking rather a lot of questions when I applied. I'm flattered that they let me in.'

'I gather that you didn't partake of the... the communal cup?'

Couldn't bring himself to say communion, could he!

'No,' said Sarah. 'I just wasn't thirsty.'

'Once you've experienced the at-one-ment of the family of Skang, you'll understand – and be eager to learn the esoteric truths of our teaching.'

'I believe you,' said Sarah, drily. 'So where does this Mother Hilda hang out?'

Again the hesitation.

'In Bombay,' said Whitbread. 'It's no secret. The ashram was the first Skang centre in the entire world.'

'You mean... you mean there are places like this in other countries? How many? How many kids have got caught up in this?'

Whoops. Not the most tactful way of putting it! She'd blown it.

'I've said enough,' snapped Whitbread, turning away. 'Print what you like.'

She pulled out the small camera. 'Oh, Mr Whitbread... Brother Alex!'

He turned back. 'What?'

Got him!

His reaction was extraordinary. With the speed of a cobra's strike, he lunged towards her and whipped the camera from her hand; and all in one movement he took out the film, pulling it from the cassette, letting it fall into useless curls.

Dropping the open camera at her feet without a word, he turned back to the door, taking a key from his pocket.

The bastard! He wasn't going to get away with that!

'One last question, Mr Whitbread. What's through that door? Why do you keep it locked?'

But his only answer was a resounding slam.

CHAPTER TWO

It was Jeremy's mother and, indirectly, his Uncle Teddy (who just happened to own about thirty per cent of the company that published *Metropolitan*), who had been the prime cause of Sarah's incursion into the further reaches of the New Age.

'Here,' Clorinda had said, tossing a letter with an impeccably engraved letterhead towards Sarah. 'You'd better look into this. I've just been glad to see the back of the little creep.'

Jeremy hadn't come into work for something like three weeks. Since his absence had little or no effect on the output of the editorial department, it was hardly noticed, apart from giving rise to the occasional brief sigh of relief.

When, however, Sarah reluctantly went to see his 'Mama' (as he always called her), it appeared that she looked on the matter somewhat differently.

'The poor boy is so trusting,' she'd said to Sarah, dabbing at her eyes with a scrap of a handkerchief. 'I'm just afraid that somebody's got wind of his trust fund. And he's generous to a fault, as I'm sure you know.'

Generous? The last time he bought a round, there were riots in Fetter Lane. Well, not quite, but Sarah wouldn't have been surprised.

'Trust fund?' she asked.

'A legacy. Granny Fitzoliver left him a few shares. And when he turned eighteen...' She'd dabbed at her eyes again and taken a sip from the half-filled tumbler in her other hand. The aroma of Chanel No. 5 had mingled with a whiff of neat gin.

'He moved out, you see. Slumming it in Knightsbridge...'

Compared with Eaton Square, y-e-e-ss, I suppose you could say that, Sarah had thought.

'... and the last time I saw him was about three weeks ago. Popped in to get his cricket togs, he said. Cricket? He hated cricket at school!'

'Paid three months' rent in advance and took off after a week,' said the caretaker of the block of flats in Knightsbridge where Jeremy had been living. 'Here, I've got a forwarding address somewhere... Not that he's had any post...'

And it had transpired that he'd gone even further down market than Knightsbridge (or so Mama would have thought) – to Hampstead. Number 115 South Hill Park Square, NW3: a stone's throw from the Heath and, for that matter, from Sarah's own little attic bedsitter (dignified by the name of 'studio flat' because it had a bath in a box next to the kitchen sink). And when Sarah had put the new address under surveillance, having had no joy with a direct approach at the front door, sure enough there he was, resplendent in his cricket flannels, having slipped out to buy some fags.

'You won't have to wear white as a guest,' he'd said (as if she was worried!), after he'd told her the glad news of his own acceptance into the bosom of the great Skang. 'It's all a gas. Chanting and stuff... and... and things. You'll love it, Sarah, honest. And you're only just in time!'

'Just in time? For what?'

Jeremy's happy expression had disappeared. For a moment, he'd looked like a naughty little boy – a guilty little boy. 'Oh... er...' His face had cleared. 'In time for today's celebration, of course. What did you think I meant?'

Jeremy had always been easy to read. So what had all that been about? Sarah had filed his obvious slip away in the 'To Be Dealt With Later' section of her brain and followed him into the house.

* * *

14

One of the advantages of the temple room of the ashram... the commune... whatever... being on the second floor of the lofty terrace of houses that made up the north side of South Hill Park Square, was that there was a ledge, at least eighteen inches wide, between the little balconies outside the front windows. And until Sarah had got halfway to the window of the room with the locked door, she'd thought it would be a good idea to edge along it.

Then she looked down.

And froze.

It was at that moment that it started to rain. And the low rumble of distant thunder promised a downpour. For a moment her nerve failed her and she was on the point of turning back. But whether it was her professional pride, or just the plain stubbornness of a true Liverpudlian, her curiosity had to be satisfied. She had to know what the locked door was hiding.

Inch by inch, her fingertips clutching vainly at the smooth wet stone behind her, she made her way to the ornamental railing of the next balcony, and, after a few convulsive breaths, managed to loosen her grip and climb over.

But the curtains were drawn. Utter frustration...

Hang on! There was a crack between the curtains, and if she pushed her face really close to the glass she could just see enough to be able to scan the room from the double door on one side to the other door in the far wall. It was an ordinary room, with chairs and a big table. And there in the middle: the Skang!

It was a shimmering bronze statue (an idol?) the height of a man and roughly of the same dimensions throughout, save for the head, which was at least twice as big, with great eyes. It patently represented the same being as the one in the painting. It was sitting cross-legged on the floor, holding a large bowl in which the tip of its proboscis was resting.

As detailed as a rococo carving, the thing seemed to be a cross between a reptile and a giant insect. But in spite of its grotesque features, there was something about it that Sarah found strangely beautiful.

She pulled the Polaroid camera from her bag and, blinking the raindrops from her eyes, took as good a shot of it as she could manage. She'd just have to hope that the automatic flash would take care of the lack of light.

She'd got what she wanted. This was going to be quite a story.

But as she stuffed the camera back into her bag, ready for the terrifying journey back along the ledge, she heard a sound – and the curtains were flung back. She threw herself flat against the wall as the world was bleached by the first lightning flash of the coming storm.

Whitbread! He must have still been in the room, and seen the flash!

Not daring to move, Sarah held her breath, waiting for the window to open and the humiliating confrontation. But the thunder broke the heavens apart, the rain sheeted down, the lightning danced around the rooftops of South Hill Park Square – and the curtains were closed again.

She'd got away with it.

'No,' said Clorinda.

'But I've checked, and if I go by Garuda – that's the Indonesian airline – it'll only cost me... er, *you*... two hundred and fifty pounds return, and I –'

'No,' said Clorinda.

'But if I join this Mother Hilda's ashram –'

'No,' said Clorinda. She peered into a small mirror from her handbag. 'India's swarming with kids dressed up in white or orange or sky-blue-pink, thinking they're going to save the world. One, the world probably isn't worth saving, and two, they're not going to do it with my money.'

She sucked at her front teeth, but whether this was an expression of her contempt for Sarah's project, or an attempt to remove a smear of lipstick, Sarah was uncertain.

'And while we're on the subject of what I'm paying for, where's your think-piece on fish? It had better be good. I've waited long enough for it.'

'Yes, well... It's nearly finished. I've had to do a lot of research... Honestly, Clorinda love, this Skang thing could be really big! And it all started in India, so –'

'Why are you so fired-up about it, anyway? They're doing us a favour, aren't they, getting Jeremy off our back?'

There Sarah had to agree. But still... This needed to be approached from a different direction. She took a deep breath and launched into Clorinda-speak. 'Tell you what, we could plan a whole campaign! "*Is the New Age old hat?!*" "*All you need is love? We say no!*" "*Will meditation give you a fat bum?*" That sort of thing. And I could go out to Bombay and –'

'No,' said Clorinda.

Why *was* she so fired-up?

The whole Skang set-up was on a par with most of the other new cults that had been springing up over the past few years. Why did she feel there was something there that was fundamentally wrong – evil, almost?

It was then that she thought of the Doctor.

This was right up his street, surely? A strange alien-looking creature; kids being brainwashed by a shady politician... If anybody was on the side of the good guys... And, after all, in spite of his being attached to the United Nations Intelligence Taskforce, he was his own man. (Would you call a Time Lord a man?) Surely she could get in to see him after all that they'd been through together?

But there was something she had to do first...

'I went back, you see Doctor, and applied all over again. But I thought that Whitbread might have banned me, so I went as somebody else...' She giggled at the memory.

Her mother, the ultra genteel daughter of a Harrogate vicar, used to be teased by her dad (Liverpool born and bred) calling her 'the foreigner from across the border'; and her mum had responded with traditional Yorkshire aphorisms, like *Wheere theere's moock theeres brass!* or *Niver do owt for nowt!*, all in the broadest possible accent.

So, with her hair slicked back, a pair of outrageous horn-rimmed spectacles and her mum's even more outrageous Yorkshire accent, Sarah had called herself Daisy Peabody – and nearly got caught. She'd claimed that she was a champion chess-player – almost grandmaster level – on the grounds that they wouldn't know much about it, and it would prove her 'superlative intelligence'. But her interviewer had turned out to be a club player herself; and had only grudgingly given her the benefit of the doubt.

And all to get a sample of the happy drink.

'I pretended to swallow it, you see, and then nipped off to the loo and spat it into an aspirin bottle. And here it is!'

Sarah looked at the white-haired figure, dapper in his velvet jacket, and felt a sensation so familiar to her when dealing with the Doctor – a sort of affectionate exasperation. Had he even been listening?

Every so often as she had spun her tale, he had grunted. But, at the same time, he seemed to be aiming a piece of apparatus – which looked like the inside of a doorbell connected by some sort of electronic circuit to a pocket flashlight – at a fish tank that contained a sleepy-looking goldfish.

'Excuse me,' he said, and disappeared inside the TARDIS, which was standing in the corner of the cluttered lab. Sarah's affection almost extended to the old police telephone box as well. Without it (or should it be 'without *her*'?), she'd have been stranded in medieval England, or on the planet of Parakon on the other side of the Milky Way, or... On the other hand, without the TARDIS, she wouldn't have been in either place to begin with.

The Doctor returned with a minute silver button (or that's what it looked like), which he carefully fitted into the middle of his lash-up.

'Stand clear,' he said and flicked a switch.

A swoosh, a flash, a fountain of bubbles, and the goldfish shot out of the water like a leaping dolphin.

'Doctor!' said Sarah. 'Are you experimenting on that poor fish?'

'Certainly not,' he replied. 'It's an on-going project. Inter-species communication...' And turning to the tank, he stuck his lips out, and wiggled them, pouting like a goldfish blowing bubbles.

What on earth?

'What on earth are you doing now?' said Sarah.

'Asking him if he's feeling better.'

The goldfish came to the front of the tank, nuzzling the glass, and waggled its tail vigorously.

'Good,' said the Doctor. 'Gary's a friend of mine,' he went on as he started to dismantle the equipment, 'and he was a bit under the weather. So I gave him a re-charge. A quick shot of coherent bio-energy waves. Analogous to the laser.'

'But he looks just like an ordinary goldfish!'

'For the very good reason that he is an ordinary goldfish.'

'But...'

'Well now, I suppose I'd better have a look at this photo of yours,' said the Doctor, obviously changing the subject.

So he had been listening!

The moment she handed it to him, his whole manner changed. 'I owe you an apology, Sarah,' he said. 'I thought you were indulging in the usual journalistic hyperbole.'

Cheek!

'Do you recognise what it's supposed to be then?' she asked.

'Never set eyes on the creature. Where's that aspirin bottle?'

It was on occasions like this that Sarah had the feeling that investigative journalism was rather like trying to sprint across

a soggy ploughed field in gumboots. The Doctor was interested, certainly, but he didn't seem to see the urgency of the
matter any more than Clorinda had.

'Come back in the morning,' he said, unscrewing the cap and
giving the little bottle a sniff.

Ah well, she thought as she made her way back to the office,
at least it would give her time to think about Clorinda's ridiculous fish article – a supposedly topical subject, the peg being
the quarrel with Iceland. She hadn't even started the piece
yet and Clorinda had now demanded it for the next morning.

But she sat at her desk all afternoon and found no inspiration
at all. Her mind just wouldn't get into gear. Why couldn't the
Doctor have analysed the stuff straight away? Surely it couldn't
be all that difficult for somebody like him?

It was no good. Every time she tried to concentrate, the
monstrous (but somehow fascinating) image of the Skang
floated into her mind.

Bloody fish! At six o'clock she gave up. She'd have to write
it at home, even if it meant sitting up half the night.

'I don't understand, sir,' said the young constable behind the
reception desk at Hampstead Heath police station. 'Are you
reporting some sort of incident?'

'It's a clear enough question, I should have thought,' said the
Doctor tetchily. 'I'll ask it again. Have there been any bodies
found near here – on the Heath, perhaps – which give the
impression that the person concerned starved to death?'

The PC hesitated. 'Er... I won't keep you a moment,' he said,
and disappeared.

CHAPTER THREE

'So why do you want to know?' said Detective Constable Willard, after the Doctor had repeated his question yet again.

'That, Officer, is my business.' The Doctor's mood had hardly been improved by his being forced to wait in the bleak interview room for over twenty minutes.

'I think you've made it ours as well, sir. You can't expect us to reveal all our info to any Tom, Dick or Harry who wanders into the nick, now can you?'

'My name is neither Tom nor Dick. And do I look like a Harry?' The Doctor's words were clipped, as he tried to keep his temper.

'Well now,' said the CID man, taking a fountain pen from his pocket, 'that's as good a place as any to start. What *is* your name?'

'I am known as the Doctor.'

'Your name, I said.'

For a moment the Doctor was tempted to give this plodding oaf his original, Gallifreyan name, just to watch him wrestle with the spelling. But then he sighed, and produced the pseudonym that had served him so well in the past. 'My name is John Smith. Now, can we get on with it?'

'John Smith? Is that so? Well, well, well...'

As Sarah left the path with its reassuring lights to trudge across the muddy grass – her usual short cut over the Heath from the tube – she glumly tried to find a fishy angle.

Fink Yourself Fin!

Get real...

She could go to the library tomorrow and look up demonic figures. If the Skang was part of Tibetan folklore, for instance...

She wrenched her mind back to the matter in hand. Eating fish was supposed to boost intelligence, wasn't it? What about... something like... *Brains, Boobs and Beauty...*? Bit downmarket for Clorinda, perhaps. But maybe there was a smidgen of an angle there. Intelligence... The intelligence of fish gravely underestimated... After all, look at the Doctor's goldfish...

She stopped dead. What was that noise? A rustle... She peered into the little thicket of evergreen nearby.

Nothing. It must have been some sort of creature: a dog or a cat; or a fox.

She resumed her gloomy trek up the hill, and her gloomy cogitations. Something a bit raunchy perhaps? *The Fishy Way to Fulfil Your Feller...* Oh, for God's sake!

It might even be Japanese, the Skang. Some of their demons were pretty peculiar. Though the name didn't sound particularly Japanese. But then it didn't sound like anything she'd ever heard of before.

Sarah Jane Smith, lost to the world, walked into the autumn darkness.

Unaware.

The Doctor's lip-reading skills had often proved as useful as a diploma in advanced telepathy. Although the detective constable was a good thirty feet from him as he talked to a stern-looking colleague, the Doctor could see him through the partition, and could make out his words as clearly as if he were a yard away.

'...a right nutter. Obviously a false name – and he *does* seem to know more than he should about the bodies...'

Bodies! So he was right. And more than one!

He stood up as the door opened. 'Thank you, gentlemen,' he said, still tight-lipped. 'I'll be going.'

'You're not going anywhere, mate,' said the newcomer. 'Sit down.'

'And who might you be?'

'DS Harrap. There are a few more questions I'd like to ask you.'

The Doctor's eyes narrowed. He moved towards the door – only to find his way blocked by Willard. 'Will you get out of my way!'

'Best do what the Sergeant says, sir.'

He turned back. 'This is intolerable! Let me go at once!'

'Please sit down, sir.'

The Doctor didn't move. 'I have no intention of staying here. You'd have to arrest me.'

'If that's the way you want to play it.'

The Doctor gave a little laugh. 'On what charge?'

'Oh, I'll think of something... Obstructing the police in the performance of their duty? That'd do nicely. Don't you agree?'

It was becoming obvious that he would have to play their ridiculous game. He sighed. 'Oh very well,' he said, and sat down.

'That's better,' said the sergeant. 'Now then, let's try again. What's your name? Your real name.'

'I've already told your colleague.'

'Yes, sir. John Smith. Have you any means of identification?'

An image of the Doctor's UNIT ID pass flickered briefly across his mind's eye; tucked behind Gary's tank along with the stack of official rubbish (income-tax returns and the like) that he habitually ignored. 'If you don't believe me,' he said, 'I suggest you ring your Commissioner at Scotland Yard. He'll vouch for me.'

'Friend of yours, is he?'

'You could say that. I was able to put in a good word for him when the appointment came up.'

The sergeant lifted an eyebrow to his partner standing by the door. 'I'm sure you did, sir. Very well, I won't insist. John Smith it is. And maybe Mr John Smith would like to explain how it is that he knows so much about these bodies...'

The last stretch of the short cut led through a little spinney up a track that had been worn into the grass by the feet of the small army who shared its secret with Sarah.

Sarah could see the lights of the paved path that led to the gate glittering through the leaves some fifty yards away and hastened her steps slightly. Even the thought of her typewriter sitting on her desk awaiting fishy words of wisdom couldn't detract from what was uppermost in her mind.

She could murder a cup of tea.

But then she heard them, the footsteps. She stopped, and so did they.

There was nothing behind her, save the darkness, and the distant lamps of the proper paths and the streets beyond. And silence, apart from the far-off traffic, and the faint barking of a dog.

Come on! She wasn't a child, to be frightened of the dark. It was just her imagination.

She turned and hurried on, trying not to break into a run. The hill was quite steep now, and she soon found herself gasping. But when she paused for a brief moment to get her breath she heard it again, the sound of running feet, abruptly coming to a halt.

She looked despairingly around. She could see nobody to whom she could appeal for help. The only thing to do was to escape from the darkness. She turned off the track and plunged into the trees, aiming for the sanctuary of the lights.

Now she was running, running, running for all she was worth, the pounding of the following feet sounding ever nearer. Another fifteen yards... ten... five... and then the root of an aged tree caught her toe and she plunged headlong into a squashy carpet of long-dead leaves. Rolling onto her back, she automatically put up her arms to protect her face – but not before she caught a glimpse of the black shape that was her pursuer, not a dozen feet away.

And now, no longer was she Sarah Jane Smith, investigative journalist, the bright secure product of thousands of years of civilisation. Instinct took over. Even her panic retreated into a white blankness as her body crunched itself into a primeval foetal ball to await the inevitable attack.

Time vanished.

Then a shout – 'Oi, you!' – and the footsteps again; but now they were retreating, at speed.

Still she could not move – until a touch on her shoulder awoke the terror inside. 'No!' she cried. 'Get away!' She opened her eyes, shrinking back, her hands held out in futile defence against an attack that no longer threatened.

'Are you all right, miss?'

She recognised him then. She'd seen him often, the old codger with the ancient bull terrier. She sat up, trying to find herself in the turmoil of feeling that came flooding back.

'Yes... yes. I'll be all right. Thank you...'

'Just happened to catch sight of him in time. Best to stay in the light, you know. Shall I call the police?'

Sarah clambered to her feet, unthinkingly brushing the leaves from her skirt, the nondescript blue skirt she'd thought a Daisy Peabody might wear. 'No point,' she said, 'thanks all the same. He'll be miles away by now, whoever it was.'

Whoever it was. Or whatever it was.

'Very gratifying, Doctor,' said Brigadier Alistair Lethbridge-Stewart. 'Taking notice of me at last! Rather overscrupulous, in fact. I can't see that security would have been breached by your contacting UNIT earlier.'

'Nothing to do with your precious security, Brigadier. If we'd had Detective Sergeant Plod and his friends trampling all over something as sensitive as this...! I needed the information, but the situation called for the utmost tact.'

The Doctor found it hard enough to admit even to himself that things had actually gone from bad to worse at Hampstead Heath police station.

It was when the sergeant had utterly misunderstood him to be claiming acquaintance with Sherlock Holmes that his credibility sank to absolute zero. In spite of his irritable attempts to explain that he'd actually been referring to Holmes's creator, Arthur Conan Doyle – 'He latched onto a few little tricks of observation and deduction I showed him, you see. Said that I'd given him an idea for a short story for the *Strand Magazine*.' – he was still escorted firmly to a cell. And when he caught the words 'Colney Hatch' as the detective sergeant's voice receded down the corridor, he'd decided that enough was enough and persuaded the police to let him make a phone call. He had no intention of letting them cart him off to the local 'loony bin', as Sergeant Benton would no doubt have called it.

'Sorry I couldn't come myself,' said the Brigadier. 'Previous engagement. I'm sure Benton handled it very well.'

The Doctor grunted, trying to put out of his mind the image of the barely concealed grin with which Benton had greeted him as they'd unlocked his cell the night before.

'So... what's it all about?'

Sarah arrived at UNIT HQ as hot and bothered as a sunny but sharp September day would allow.

When she'd eventually got away from her typewriter with a scant fifteen hundred words under her belt – she couldn't even *start* on the fish story until she'd had a really good look at the Skang Polaroid and written up her notes about the cult – she'd fallen straight into an exhausted sleep, only to wake up half an hour later, shivering, her heart pumping, convinced she was being attacked by the fearsome creature she'd seen at the commune. She'd pulled the bed-clothes over her head and curled up small, just as she used to as a six-year-old plagued by nightmares, so long ago.

And then, like Alice finding that she wasn't in the sheep's shop but in a rowing boat, Sarah had found herself in a Technicolour paradise, surrounded by a full complement of Indian dancing girls. An all-singing, all-dancing Bollywood dream – with the image of a golden Skang looking on benignly and oh-so-lovingly – that had lulled her into a deep slumber that more or less wiped away the horror of her encounter on the Heath.

After all, she thought as she closed the window the next morning – why had she left it open to that cold north wind? – the old man would have said if he'd seen some sort of monster, wouldn't he? It must have been her obsession with the Skang that made her think... oh God, she hadn't set the alarm! It was gone half past nine!

Her usual morning routine: the jog around the Heath, the leisurely breakfast of wholemeal toast and banana – or a real fry-up, if she was feeling bolshie – and the skim through the *Guardian* and the *Mail* (to get a balanced view); all had to go by the wayside. There was barely time for the essential cup of coffee.

What did come back 'in the morning' mean? About ten o'clock, probably. But by the time she'd finished tidying up the cobbled-together fish article (inspired by Gary the goldfish: *Would You Eat Your Best Friend?* – a plea for stricter vegetarianism) and delivered it to the office, it was getting on for eleven-thirty when she walked into the Doctor's lab... to be greeted by what seemed to be some sort of row.

'I'm sorry, Doctor,' the Brigadier was saying, 'I've just spent the best part of a month trying to prevent Geneva from cutting my budget by twenty-five per cent. I just can't afford a wild-goose chase. If we went after every wacky cult in the country, UNIT UK would be broke in a fortnight.'

Here we go again, thought Sarah. They seemed to respect

each other – almost to be friends – but they could never agree on the best thing to do.

The Doctor held up the little screw-top aspirin bottle. 'This tastes like fruit juice, mixed fruit juice – exactly what it is, no doubt. Nevertheless, it contains some three per cent of an extremely powerful drug. One that I don't recognise, but judging by its structure it's probably psychotropic.'

'Drugs? LSD and all that caper? Just what the police are for, I should have thought.'

'And how well did the police cope with the Yeti? Or the Autons? Or the Cybermen for that matter?'

'Are you saying...?'

'Show him your photograph, Sarah.'

The Brigadier, giving her a suspicious look, took the Polaroid print and inspected it. 'Ah... See what you mean.' He cleared his throat. 'Wouldn't do any harm to take a look, I suppose...'

But they were too late. Frustrated by the unanswered bell, the Brigadier resorted to thumping on the door.

'No good making that racket,' said a hoarse voice from beneath their feet. 'They've gawn.' A craggy little man had emerged from a door in the basement area.

'Gone? Gone where?' said the Doctor.

'Don' ask me. Piled into a coach just after seven o'clock this morning. The whole shooting match, including the high and mighty Brother Alex. Good riddance. Rahnd the bend, the lot of them.'

With a little persuasion, aided by a discreetly folded note, the caretaker let them in to have a look round.

Mary Celeste time, thought Sarah. Well, not quite. There were no half-eaten meals, or abandoned, unmade beds. On the contrary, everything was clean and neat and ordered. The food in the kitchen was tidily put away – but there were seven loaves of sliced bread, one of them three-quarters eaten; four and a half dozen eggs in the larder; several pints of milk in the fridge...

It looked as if they'd just gone off for a day trip to the seaside.

'If you ask me, they've gone for a picnic,' said the Brigadier, coming down the stairs to rejoin the Doctor and Sarah in the hall. 'They're obviously coming back.'

'Handed me the keys, didn't he?' said the caretaker. 'To give back to the estate office. Nah, they've gawn for good.'

CHAPTER FOUR

'You're eating a ham sandwich!'

A startled Sarah looked up from her desk drawer, where she had been searching for her passport.

Clorinda, a tiny woman whose dyed hair (tending towards the pillar-box end of the spectrum), bright make-up and primary-coloured garments normally gave the impression of an escaped parakeet, now had the air of an angry macaw.

'Er, yes... I didn't get any breakfast,' said Sarah, puzzled.

'I knew I was right. My office! Now!'

Oh Lor', thought Sarah, as she followed her irate boss, it must be that wretched fish...

It was, too. Clorinda tossed the manuscript towards her as if she'd like to toss it into the nearest dustbin. 'Research? Don't make me laugh. Every word tells me that you know zilch about being a vegetarian. If I wanted candy-floss I'd go to Southend pier!'

'I must admit...'

'It's an angle, certainly. But it reads like a filler for a teenager's weekly. What do you think you're up to?'

'Well, you see...'

But it was a rhetorical question. Clorinda was on a roll. 'If you want to convince me to be a vegetarian, I want to know all that jazz about one cow versus ten fields of corn... And how a nice juicy steak *au poivre* fills my arteries with axle grease... and so on and so on... Yes, and I want it backed up with the latest facts and figures. And I want it now! We go to press tomorrow, as you very well know.'

Sarah took a deep breath. 'Yes well, I was going to come in and see you anyway. I'm going to take my holiday, you see, and...'

'You what?'

'I'm due four weeks, what with missing last year's because of the Space World thing and...' Her voice trailed away. Hardly the most tactful way to approach the subject, Sarah suddenly realised. The Space World story, having had a D-notice slapped on it by the Brigadier, had had to be spiked.

Clorinda looked at her for a long moment. 'You've had a holiday. You went to Sicily.'

'That was due from the year before. Oh please, Clorinda! I promise to tell everyone how kind you are, how generous, how unutterably lovely you are in every possible way...'

'And completely ruin my reputation?' said Clorinda. Then she sighed. 'Oh Sarah, Sarah, what are we going to do with you? Once you get a bee in your bonnet...'

Cliché! thought Sarah automatically.

'It is this Skang affair, I suppose?' Clorinda went on.

Sarah nodded eagerly. 'Yes. Apparently the centres all over the world have closed down. And the devotees are all going to Bombay!' The UNIT network had quickly supplied the Brigadier with the information – and much to his disgust, Geneva had given him the responsibility of finding out exactly what was going on.

'Well, I suppose I can't stop you.'

'Clorinda, you're a doll!'

'Just as long as you don't try to swing it on your expenses.'

'That I can promise you. It won't cost you a penny!'

It wouldn't cost anybody a brass rupee. They were going in the TARDIS.

It seemed a little strange to be lugging her backpack through the door of the old police box, for all the world as if she were catching the so-called Magic Bus to Kathmandu with the rest of the hippy throng. Though the Brigadier's own luggage was a smart hide suitcase, he evidently had similar feelings.

'I'm not sure if this is a good idea, Doctor,' he said. 'Wouldn't we be better off with British Airways?'

'Time is of the essence,' replied the muffled voice of the Doctor, whose top half was deep inside the central pedestal of the TARDIS control column. 'If we don't stop this thing before it really takes root, the world could be facing one of the biggest disasters in the history of *Homo sapiens*.'

The Brigadier sighed. 'I seem to have heard that before.'

'You have indeed,' said the Doctor, emerging. 'And was I ever wrong?'

'So what is "this thing",' said Sarah. 'What *is* going on?'

The Doctor was peering with a slight frown at a dial on the console, where a needle flickered to and fro. 'Mm...' he said. 'The relativity circuit of the temporal balancing governor has been playing up a bit... Oh well! In for a penny...'

The doors closed, the centre of the control column started to move up and down (albeit a little shakily), and the TARDIS started to sing the song with which it always started and finished its journeys, like the desperate cry of some alien elephant in agony.

It stopped.

'Bombay!' said the Doctor, tuning in the monitor that would show them what awaited them outside. 'That's odd,' he said, as a wide landscape of dried-up grass appeared, punctuated by a twisted tree. 'I programmed in the co-ordinates of VT, as they call it.'

'VT?' asked the Brigadier.

'Victoria Terminus Station. Think of St Pancras filled with a Wembley football crowd. Some people live their whole lives there. Nobody'll notice us tucked away in the corner.

'Come on then,' he added, striding towards the opening door. 'No sense in hanging about.'

Sarah waited for the Brigadier to go out in front of her. Let *them* find out where the TARDIS had landed! But before she'd gone two steps, she heard a shout of alarm and the pair of them erupted back through the door, the Doctor making a dive for the controls.

The door slammed shut, and the entire TARDIS lurched as something – what, for Pete's sake! – hurled itself at this intruder into its domain.

Sarah, thrown to the floor by the shock, cast a look at the monitor. 'That's a lion!' she said.

'A very large lion,' said the Brigadier, grimly picking himself up.

'But there aren't any lions in India.'

'Of course there are,' said the Doctor impatiently. 'We must be in Bombay Zoo.'

'Rubbish!' said the Brigadier.

'Aha! Got it! The temporal governor's stuck again. We're still on the Greenwich Meridian!'

Sarah's mind did a quick flick through her admittedly small stock of geographical facts. 'So we're in Africa?'

'Well of course we are!' said the Doctor, busy checking the relevant sections of the errant circuit. 'As far as the time dimension was concerned we haven't moved at all. Didn't they teach you anything at school?'

And there she was thinking she'd been so clever!

'Just let me know when we get there,' said the Brigadier, parking himself in the only chair in the control room, stretching out his legs and closing his eyes.

'No need to be sarcastic, Lethbridge-Stewart. We'll be at VT Station in two shakes of a sluggerlug's tail.'

I'm just not going to ask. I wouldn't give him the satisfaction, thought Sarah, as the TARDIS started trumpeting again.

Jeremy had often been abroad. Even before his father died (when he was only six), they used to go to his flat in Cannes every summer; and Mama had kept up the custom, even though, as she said, it was more like Margate these days.

But this time a flight of over fifteen hours was followed by a jolting, sticky coach ride from the airport, which took them through acres and acres of shanty town. The 'houses' seemed to be custom-built out of cardboard and scraps of corrugated iron, and the atmosphere stank of fresh poo! He longed for Hampstead. He'd been so happy there! Well mostly. Especially after the daily celebration and the love-in. Why did they have to leave?

'Pretty idle lot, the natives,' he said to Paul, the long-time Skangite with hair down to his shoulders and a thin straggly beard, who sat next to him on the coach. 'You'd think they'd want to smarten the place up a bit, wouldn't you?' he went on.

His remarks were met with a slight frown. 'They do their best, chum,' said Paul. 'And if that's your idea of loving kindness for our brothers and sisters, strikes me you've missed the point.'

'What did I say?' thought Jeremy glumly, as Paul turned away and looked out of the window again. They were all the same, this lot. Self-righteous bunch. He never seemed to do anything right.

He slumped down in his seat, and tried to comfort himself with the thought that Paul, who had a strong Brummy accent, probably only went to a secondary-modern... or at best a grammar school. No wonder he was a bit of an oik, in spite of having oodles of cash.

Even arriving at the ashram didn't cheer Jeremy up. A high wall protected a complex of white stone buildings – offices, living quarters, conference buildings and an expansive open-sided celebration hall in the shade of an ancient tree. A bubbling stream, which ran alongside the main path, and the occasional cry of a foreign-sounding bird completed the scene.

Certainly, the turmoil of hooting and shouting that had accompanied the latter part of their journey from the airport was a strong contrast to the low murmur of the crowds of white-clad disciples in the ashram. But it all seemed to Jeremy as cold and functional as a newly built car park; and the people, glancing at him with ill-concealed hostility, as alien as a bunch of Martians.

He was given some sort of chopped up veggies for his dinner – no potatoes, no meat – and then, to top it all...

'Here's where you London lot will be sleeping. Yours is number nine,' said Brother Dafydd, who wore the long robe of a 'teacher' like Brother Alex.

Horror! It was worse than the dormitory at Holbrook. He'd thought all that was behind him when he left school. Twelve people crammed into one small room – and to be expected to climb a ladder to the top of a tower of three bunk-beds, squashed in the middle of the others...!

Once, on a February holiday at a five-star hotel in Tenerife, he'd seen Mama go into full *grande dame* mode when she wasn't satisfied with her room. 'You expect me to pay your preposterous rates for this garret?' she'd said to the quaking manager. 'My husband used to be Master of the Ferney. His hounds lived in a better kennel than this!' And so on and so on. She and Jeremy had ended up in the owner's suite.

Jeremy wasn't quite so successful.

'You're lucky you're not sleeping under the kitchen sink, boyo,' said Brother Dafydd. 'We've got to find room for nearly two hundred of you.' He ticked off Jeremy's name on his clipboard and turned to the next on his list.

Well really! Twenty thou for an iron bedstead and his nose touching the ceiling? He'd see about that! A word to Brother Alex...

'If that's a railway station, they must have had a power cut,' said the Brigadier, staring at the monitor, which was totally dark.

'Really, Lethbridge-Stewart, is it necessary to be so negative?' said the Doctor as he set the controls to 'stand by'. 'I programmed the TARDIS to arrive in an inconspicuous corner.

I expected the screen to show us exactly what it is showing us now.'

The Brigadier was unconvinced. 'One way to find out,' he said.

'Indeed,' said the Doctor coldly, putting out his hand to the door control.

'Stop!'

The two men turned in surprise at Sarah's yell.

'I don't think it would be a very good idea to open the door,' she said. 'Look!'

They both looked up. Filling the monitor screen was the face of a curious and very large shark.

The TARDIS was at the bottom of the sea.

Jeremy had a pretty good idea where Brother Alex would be found. He'd gone on at length about the purpose of their flight from Hampstead. They were going to get their reward – and that meant first joining Mother Hilda in Bombay.

Mother Hilda! Next to the Great Skang himself, the very centre of their devotion. Brother Alex would have gone straight to her.

But it wouldn't be so easy for somebody like Jeremy. Her bungalow had a fence round it even taller than the massive helpers (known as guards, he'd learnt on the introductory tour) who stood glowering either side of the gateway.

For a moment he was tempted to forget about it and accept that he would have to be crammed in with all the others, no matter how *common* – as Mama would have said… though he'd learned by bitter experience not to use the word himself.

The thought of his mother stiffened his resolve. She wouldn't give up so easily. On the other hand, *she* would have put the fear of God into the guards and talked her way in. She wouldn't have found a convenient tree and scrambled up it, crawling along a projecting branch, only to slip off and fall heavily into the bushes on the other side of the fence.

It just wasn't fair, he thought, as he pushed his way through the shrubbery into the open. Somebody like him ought to have been given a good room automatically – not the best, necessarily, he wasn't unreasonable – but a decent sort of room, with a proper bed and stuff. What was the point of paying out all that lolly otherwise?

His internal grumbling was interrupted by voices. There was the bungalow, different from the rest of the ashram buildings, a remnant perhaps of the prosperous days of the Raj. Sitting on the extensive open veranda, under a lazily turning fan, were three people: a thick-set man who looked too tough to be a Skangite (where had Jeremy seen him before?); next to him, Brother Alex; and on the other side of the bamboo table, a small woman with white hair.

Mother Hilda.

'There's only one possible answer,' said the Doctor. 'The relativity circuit has overcompensated. We're on the reciprocal arc of the meridian great circle...' He dived back under the control column.

'So where exactly are we? In English.'

'I just told you. The latitude is Bombay's – round about twenty degrees north, but the longitude is one hundred and eighty degrees – exactly opposite the longitude of London.'

The Brigadier dug deep into his memory. He'd managed to scrape a pass in Geography, but he hadn't had occasion to consider such matters for years. 'In the middle of the Pacific Ocean. Right?'

'Well done,' said the Doctor, coming into view and setting the TARDIS on its travels once more. 'And because there was no land in sight the TARDIS naturally made the assumption that we wanted to be on the ocean bed.'

'It doesn't seem to want to take us to Bombay,' said the Brigadier, 'that's for sure.'

'Nearly there,' said the Doctor, unruffled. He leaned forward to inspect the dials. 'Good grief!' he exclaimed, and seizing the signal-red handle of a large lever, he yanked it down to its full extent.

After a short pause, the TARDIS started her song of arrival.

'What's up? Are we there?' asked the Brigadier.

The Doctor turned from the control console. He didn't speak. His face was ashen.

'Are you all right, Doctor?' said Sarah, putting a tentative hand on his arm. She'd never seen him like this before.

The Doctor shuddered. He took a deep breath.

'We're safe now,' he said.

'What on earth...?' said the Brigadier.

The Doctor turned back to the control panel and restored the emergency lever to its normal position. 'The temporal governor had cut out completely; and the back-up circuit hadn't kicked in. Our acceleration into the past was increasing exponentially. If our speed had reached six and a half googol years per metasecond – and we weren't far off it – it would have been irreversible. We'd have shot straight through the singularity of the Big Bang and out the other side!'

The Brigadier cleared his throat. 'Before... before Creation, you mean?'

'Before time itself, if there's any meaning in that. No time, no space, no change. We'd have been stuck in the TARDIS with nowhere to go for... for eternity? For an infinite number of years? And with no possibility of death... There are no words to express it.'

Sarah found she was holding her breath.

The Brigadier frowned. 'Mm. Beyond me,' he said. 'So I take it that we're not in Bombay?'

The door of the TARDIS opened. Brigadier Lethbridge-Stewart came out, and strode across to the phone on the laboratory desk.

'Switchboard?' he said. His voice was tight, controlled. 'Get me British Airways...'

CHAPTER FIVE

Now what?

Jeremy's plan, if that's what it could be called, had been to march straight up to Brother Alex and demand to be given what was clearly his due. He'd made his way across the billiard-table lawn, which looked as if it had been clipped with nail-scissors, pretending to himself that he was walking round the edge to avoid the spray, but really trying to keep out of sight for as long as possible. By the time he had reached the other side, his courage, never very great, had all but vanished.

Mama would have had no qualms at all in interrupting a private conversation. But even she might have drawn back when she realised that there was a row going on. Brother Alex was getting really ratty.

'But I tell you, she thought she'd seen an idol of the Skang!'

'And how, may I ask, do you know that?'

'I found out where she lived and...'

'That was most imprudent!' Mother Hilda's voice was stern, like Nanny's when Jeremy had forgotten to wash his hands before tea.

'It was bloody stupid!'

At the big man's intervention, Mother Hilda raised a hand. 'Thank you, Brother Will. Leave this to me.'

Of course! That's who the other man was. Will Cabot, the boxer, who'd won a gold medal in the Munich Olympics and then turned professional. What was he doing here?

Alex changed to a more placatory tone. 'Do you think I didn't take precautions, Mother? I promise you, she couldn't have had any idea that I'd been there. But I found the photograph, and I read her notes. It was quite clear.'

'Mm. Well, if you're sure...' Her voice was a little gentler.

Why didn't he say sorry?

'I do see now that it was foolish of me. Please forgive me.'

That was the way. It always worked with Nanny.

But the big man wasn't going to let him off so easily. 'And have you nothing more to tell Mother Hilda?'

A long pause.

'I don't know what you mean,' Alex replied at last.

'It's no good denying it,' said Cabot. 'See for yourself. It's even made the headlines in *The Times of India*.'

As Alex picked up the paper, Jeremy shrank into the shadows, creeping under the floor of the veranda. What did he think he was doing? The boxer fellow looked dangerous – and what about the guards? What if he were to be handed over to them? Nobody knew where he was. He could just disappear...

His paranoid musings were interrupted by Brother Alex speaking in a very different tone to the one he'd used to address Hilda. It was the way Mama would speak to an impertinent servant. 'And why do you think that I'm responsible, Cabot?'

Will Cabot laughed. But he didn't sound amused. 'Come off it, Alex!' he said. 'Three of them – on Hampstead Heath? The next nearest centre is in Cardiff, for God's sake.'

But Alex was not going to give in easily. 'Even if you could lay these incidents at my door, it would be irrelevant. You know very well that I have never agreed with Mother Hilda's basic strategy. From the very first...'

The boxer's voice was harsh. 'And you know very well that she has the authority to overrule your stupid suggestions!'

'And, what's more,' broke in Hilda, 'my way forward has the consensus of the group.' Her gentle voice couldn't have been more different from that of the boxer.

'That remains to be seen,' said Alex. 'Things can change.'

There was some sort of creepy-crawly climbing up Jeremy's leg. He could feel it under his trousers. What was that thing... like a sort of prawn that had a curly tail with a nasty sting at the end of it? He tried to roll up his trouser leg without making a noise, but found he couldn't stop himself from letting out a tiny whimper of fear.

He became aware that none of them had spoken for quite a long time. Now he was for it!

Then Cabot spoke again. 'Mother! We can't let this go!'

She sighed. 'I'm afraid you're right.'

They hadn't heard him...

'Meaning?'

'What do you think she means?' said Cabot. 'You've blown it Whitbread. It's about time you got what's coming to you.'

'Now, look here, Cabot...'

'The whole question – and your crass behaviour with the journalist girl – will have to be brought to a full meeting.'

'I'm afraid he's right,' said the little old lady.

'I hardly think that will be necessary,' replied Alex.

'I do. And that's my final word on the matter.' The gentleness had quite gone.

'But...'

'You can come out now,' she went on, raising her voice – though it had quickly lost its steely tone. 'Yes, you under the veranda. Let's have a look at you.'

Jeremy, only too pleased to be able to move, scrambled out onto the lawn and did a stamping, stomping dance to dislodge the scorpion he was convinced was poised to stab him in the calf. A small beetle (about half an inch long) fell to the ground and scuttled away. Jeremy, still panting with fear, looked up, awaiting his fate.

'Don't look so scared,' said Mother Hilda, with a little laugh. 'We're not going to eat you. Come and have a drink. You must be thirsty in this heat.'

He went up the steps and sat down where Mother Hilda indicated. She clapped her hands, and an Indian bearer appeared.

'Bring the young sahib a glass of fresh lime and soda – the special soda – with ice.'

'At once, memsahib.'

Jeremy breathed a sigh of relief and settled back into the cushions. This was a lot better. Five-star stuff. She'd obviously spotted that he was a bit different.

Sarah discovered that one of the advantages of travelling with Brigadier Alistair Lethbridge-Stewart, the Commanding Officer of UNIT UK – and, indeed, being a temporary member of his staff – was that you found yourself in First Class.

Not that it made all that much difference. As it happened, they were the only passengers in the curtained-off area at the front of the plane. The seats were marginally more comfortable, and they were offered a free drink as soon as the seat-belts sign went off, but that was about all.

'Better bring a bottle,' said the Brigadier, after the smart air-hostess had brought him his second dram of Scotch in a miniature.

'Sorry, sir,' she replied, 'it's regulations. We have to monitor your drinking.' And she disappeared.

For a moment the Brigadier was speechless; and the Doctor looked as if he was struggling not to burst into laughter. Not a good start, thought Sarah.

The flight was going to be a difficult one. The Brig was not in any sort of mood to chat, especially after a couple more drams. And the Doctor, almost as soon as they were on their way, had pulled something out of his pocket that looked like one of those old-fashioned silver cigarette cases you saw in black-and-white thirties films. This was fatter, though, and had some push buttons and other knobs and dials on the outside. When he opened it, she saw that it was filled with parts so minute that it was impossible to make out whether they were electronic components or mechanical cogs. And as he worked at it with what seemed to be a long metal tooth-pick, the parts moved and sparkled, and it emitted a tiny noise like a fairy music box.

He noticed that she was watching him. 'Fair wear and tear,' he said. 'But if I don't get it working, the TARDIS will be about as much use as a car without a gear-box.'

The Brigadier gave a snort. It wasn't a snort of laughter.

The Doctor looked across the aisle at him. 'I didn't quite catch that, Lethbridge-Stewart,' he said icily. 'Would you mind repeating it?'

Oh God! If they were going to behave like a couple of kids from the infants' class, it was going to be a swinging journey.

'Doctor,' she said hastily, before the Brig could react, 'forgive me, but you've been awfully cagey so far. Won't you tell us what you think is going on?'

Her diversion worked.

'Quite right,' said the Brigadier. 'Here we are setting off to go halfway across the world, and you haven't yet deigned to explain exactly what particular breed of wild goose we're chasing.'

'Oh, very poetical,' said the Doctor. 'I should have thought it was obvious, even to the meanest intelligence.'

Oh dear! You could hear the irritation in both their voices.

'Evidently not,' snapped the Brigadier.

The Doctor grunted and turned to Sarah. 'Did you do Biology at that school of yours?'

The Doctor never seemed to have much opinion of human education.

'Some. Not a lot. It was part of General Science.'

'Entomology?'

'Bugs and things? Well, I suppose we touched on it. Yes, the bees and... and fertilisation and all that,' said Sarah, pushing down the memory of a hilarious session on sex given reluctantly – and incomprehensibly – by the elderly Miss Prosser, popularly known as Old Prodnose.

'Then I expect you're familiar with the family of *Asilidae* – the robber flies.'

'Er... not so you'd notice.'

The Brigadier, who had already finished his fourth Scotch, broke in. 'Are you trying to tell us that... that thing is an insect?'

'Not exactly...' The Doctor paused as if to marshal his thoughts.

Must be like trying to explain trigonometry to a couple of toddlers in nursery school, thought Sarah.

'All physiological details of the body, with very few exceptions, show their evolutionary function in their shape, or their position, or both. Sometimes the development of an organ is so fitted to its purpose that it seems to be teleological – but no doubt you'd agree with me, Lethbridge-Stewart, that such a way of looking at it is erroneous.'

'Oh, absolutely. Couldn't have put it better myself,' said the Brigadier, reaching for the bell to summon the stewardess.

'Teleological?' asked Sarah.

'The idea that evolution is mediated by a preordained future purpose.'

Sarah thought for a bit. 'You mean... like... like evolution had no way of knowing that we were going to wear glasses, yet look where it put our ears?

'Sorry,' she added. The look on the Brig's face told her that this was no time for joking. But the Doctor didn't seem to mind.

'In a way, that's just what I do mean. It was a very popular view before Charlie came up with the obvious answer.'

'Charlie who?' said the Brigadier, as the air-hostess arrived with several more miniature bottles and an air of resignation.

'Charlie Darwin. Bit of a plodder old Charlie, but he got there in the end.'

The biggest name-dropper in the universe, the Doctor! Sarah was still not used to somebody like him caring about such things. Or perhaps it was the other way round – he just didn't care...?

'So what's that got to do with the price of turnips?' she said.

'The asilid has the habit of stabbing its prey – another insect; it might be one of your friends, Sarah, a bee perhaps – stabbing it in the neck with its proboscis. Though perhaps it should more properly be called its hypopharynx...'

'Oh, for Pete's sake...' said the Brigadier, whose glass was nearly empty again.

'Quite right, quite right. What it's called hardly matters to the poor old bee. You see, the asilid injects its saliva into the body of its prey; and the saliva has proteolytic enzymes in it which... all right, all right... It has what you might call digestive juices, which liquefy the bee's innards. And then all the asilid has to do is suck out its dinner. Simple.'

The Brigadier had lost his air of irritation. He was leaning forward, listening intently. He said, 'I see what you mean. Those bodies...'

'As soon as I saw Sarah's snap, I realised the creature's physiognomy could have only one function. And I'm sorry to say that I was right.'

While the Doctor was speaking, Sarah had pulled the Polaroid print out of her pocket. The Skang looked as if it were drinking from the bowl with its trunk thing, but...

'You mean it's not a statue – and it's going around sucking out the...' She could hardly finish the thought, let alone the sentence.

And where was the Skang now?

Jeremy tried to remember why he'd gone looking for Brother Alex, without success. It didn't seem to matter, though. After all, he'd met Mother Hilda, and had a whizzo drink; and that nice fellow who'd brought him back to the dormitory (one of the guards, wasn't he?) had been so kind; and then there were all those lovely people they'd met on the way, who'd smiled at him as if he was their bestest friend in all the world...

Smashing idea, putting all the London brothers and sisters together in one room. He was sleeping just above one of his closest friends, Brother Paul – it was quite an adventure, having to climb a ladder to go to bed! All in all, much better than being in a five-star hotel. More fun.

Jeremy Fitzoliver snuggled down into the featherbed comfort of the thin kapok mattress on the utilitarian springs of his iron bedstead, and fell into a slumber of deep content.

CHAPTER SIX

First class in the air, just for PR, thought Sarah, but once we're out of sight... How hypocritical can you get, Brigadier Lethbridge-Stewart?

They obviously couldn't stay in the ashram; but when the Sikh taxi-driver (all the taxi-drivers seemed to be Sikhs) took them straight to the Taj Mahal hotel on the seafront, the Brigadier took one look and condemned it as being unnecessarily luxurious.

Huh! Thirty rupees a night per person, that's what the hotel they'd ended up in cost UNIT. About a couple of quid! At least it was clean. And, to be fair, it was just down the road from the ashram.

It was run by an expatriate Aussie by the name of Ron (with a flowing ponytail and a kaftan), which was just as well... In spite of their élite status, the food on the aircraft had been as plastic as ever, and Sarah was in no mood to experiment more than she had to with Indian food, which had never been a favourite.

She fancied a hamburger.

'Sacred cows, duckie,' said Ron. 'No beef here. But I can do you a simply delectable buffburger.'

'Buffburger?!'

'Buffalo meat. We can get away with that. How do you like it done?'

He was right. It was delectable, she thought as she sat chumping away, listening to the Doctor and the Brigadier arguing the toss. They hardly seemed to notice that their omelettes were getting cold, they were so irritated with each other.

'I shall contact the UNIT liaison officer in the morning, and we'll make an official visit. This has to be done by the book.'

'And frighten them off? What possible advantage is there in going in bull-headed? Once the china has been broken, I would defy even you to stick it back together again.'

'It's all very well for you, Doctor, but I have to answer for my actions. Your hare-brained schemes – that is, if you have one at all...'

'Hare-brained! You don't even know what I'm proposing.'

'Tell me, then.'

The Doctor took a sip from his glass. 'Surprisingly good, don't you think?' he said. 'Not unlike a small wine of Burgundy.'

'Ha! I thought as much. You have no idea what to do, now have you?'

Sarah, sitting between them, found that her head was swivelling from side to side like that of a tennis fan at Wimbledon.

'If, as we suspect, these people have something to hide...' started the Doctor.

'If! You yourself said that this creature must be an alien life form!'

'If, as I say, they want to conceal what's going on, they'll have built themselves a defensive wall to hide behind. That's what the cult must be. We need to find a crack in that wall.'

'And in the meantime, people are being slaughtered.'

'I doubt it. Has UNIT had any similar reports from the other countries where the cult has been established?'

'Well, no.'

'I think you'll find that the Hampstead bodies were an aberration. Indeed, that may be the very thing which will betray them.'

And so on, and so on, back and forth. Sarah found her jet-lagged eyes starting to close, and left them to it.

After all, it was the story she was after. And that was inside the ashram. She could get up early tomorrow and follow her original plan. She could become a devotee herself.

'But I've come all the way from London!'

The large man in white, in the little lobby to the right of the main gate, shook his head.

'I'm sorry,' he said, in a soft Germanic voice.

Austrian probably, thought Sarah automatically.

'You should in London have joined, perhaps. It is now too late.'

'Oh, but I did! I just haven't had time to get some white things to wear, and...'

'Then what is the password, please?'

There'd have to be a flipping password!

'Well, I didn't exactly join. Not in so many words. But I...' She stopped as she saw him shaking his head. 'Oh, *please*! I've dreamed of being a Skang... er... disciple... follower... whatever. For yonks! That's why I've come all this way!' She could see that she was getting through to him.

'I shall tell you what. Go into the shop, over there. Ask Sister Helga. She could say yes, I don't know.'

'Oh, thank you, thank you! You've no idea what it means to me...' Steady girl, don't go too far, she thought.

On the left side of the massive gate was a small hut with a shop window, which had obviously been full of books and coloured images, almost like icons, of Mother Hilda and of the Skang itself. But at this very moment, Sarah could see that somebody was taking everything out from the back, leaving the shelves denuded.

'I heard what Brother Dieter has said,' said the tall blonde woman in teacher's robes.

Swedish, I'd guess, said the little categorising, journalist voice in Sarah's head.

Even as Helga spoke, she went on with her job, packing

everything neatly into cardboard boxes on the floor. 'There are no vacancies. We have to limit our numbers. At the moment only. It will be different, maybe, in a few months...'

'But I want to join now!'

'It is not possible, my dear.' She dived into the window again.

'Well...' Sarah was thinking fast. 'At least let me buy a book... You know, with information about it all, and the rules and so on.'

And maybe the password?

Helga reappeared. 'I have cashed up. I cannot take your monies. But... here, I give you Mother Hilda's book. No, no, no – it's a present. It has brought many to the Great Skang.' She held out a thinnish hardback, with a portrait of Hilda on the dust jacket.

And with that Sarah had to be content.

The Doctor's mind was not on the TARDIS's relativity circuit. Yes, he had to get it fixed; but that was only a matter of testing each connection and sub-system in turn. Probably it was nothing more than an electron entanglement that had snapped.

As he sat in the dusty, dry excuse for a garden at the back of the hotel, he was quite aware that his fiddling was a displacement activity. He had no plan, it was true, and he couldn't think of one. Lethbridge-Stewart seemed determined to go through official channels, and unless that was handled with the utmost care, it could be the very thing that frightened them off. It was essential that they should get more information; more information about the cult, and by extension, the Skang itself...

He heard the door of the hotel sitting room slam. Was the Brigadier back so soon? Hm. He mustn't appear too eager. The Brigadier was too full of himself already.

So first he finished checking the calibration of the chronon scale; always a tedious job. Only then did he close the silver case, put it in his pocket, and make his way to the French windows.

She'd occasionally caught sight of one. She'd seen the word on menus. But she'd never tasted one.

It's just about impossible to eat a mango like a well-brought-up young lady unless you've been shown how to by an expert – especially if you've been told that, for safety's sake, all fruit in India should be peeled.

'Oh my God!' exclaimed Sarah, as the sloppy, slippery, squishy thing shot from her fingers, to be neatly fielded by the Doctor as he came in. 'Sorry, sorry, sorry!' she continued, as he politely handed it back to her. 'I missed breakfast, you see, so I... Thanks...'

The Doctor smiled distantly as he fastidiously wiped his fingers on the immaculately laundered linen handkerchief he produced from his sleeve.

'Is the Brig about?' she went on. 'I went out on a bit of a recce, and I've got some info.'

'He's gone to find his Indian colleague – the person you would no doubt describe as his "oppo",' replied the Doctor drily. 'Unfortunately, I've not been able to bring him round to my way of thinking.' His measured tones suddenly disappeared. 'You'd think a military man, of all people, would realise that going off at half-cock is likely to lead to your shooting yourself in the foot!'

Neat, thought Sarah. A perfectly valid mixed metaphor. She looked at the orange pulp in her hand. There was no way of eating it that her mother would have approved of, it seemed. Oh well, in for a penny...

Blimey! So that's what a mango tasted like. Food of the gods, that's what!

'So what is this info?' the Doctor asked. 'I freely admit, even though I castigate Lethbridge-Stewart for his methods, I've yet to come up with an alternative.'

That was one of the things she liked about the Doctor. Arrogant at times, yes, but always honest.

'Well done,' he said, when she'd told him her story, right up to Helga and the packing up of the books. 'It's possible that they are preparing to decamp even from Bombay. In which case, where are they going? And why?'

'Oh yes,' said Sarah, 'and there's one other thing. Hang on...' Wiping her fingers surreptitiously on the hem of her tee-shirt (it hardly mattered, the front being already soggy with mango juice), she delved into her shoulder bag and produced the book she'd been given – '*The Way of the Skang*' by Mother Hilda. She pushed it across the table towards the Doctor. 'There may be something in it that might help. I glanced through it, but I didn't see anything...'

No password, anyway. Too much to hope for, perhaps.

'Good grief!' said the Doctor, as he picked up the book and gazed at the portrait on the jacket.

'What?'

'That's Hilda Hutchens!'

'Who she?'

'Hilda Hutchens. Emeritus Professor Dame Hilda Hutchens. 1970 Nobel Prize for Philosophy. Wrote *Quantum Qualia*.'

That should be a sparkling read to take on the beach.

'Thank you, Sarah. Thank you very much. You may have provided me with the very thing I've been looking for. The chink in their armour!'

He looked up at her, beaming – and quickly averted his gaze. Nobody would want to dwell on the sight of Sarah Jane Smith avidly slurping on a nearly naked mango stone.

Alex Whitbread had, whenever possible, worked to make himself popular with his fellow teachers. He had been both admired and despised by those in the political know, during his time in government, for his behind-the-scenes twisting and turning, which – harnessed to the election of the previous leader of the party – had earned him his ministry. But his populist (and handsome) public face had been badly marred by the sordidness of the scandal that had finished him.

Though he was respected in the Skang group as one who had made a fresh start, he'd found few so far to join him in his schemes to replace Hilda. In spite of knowing that the ultimate prize could be for a far bigger game than the present one, the majority clung to the built-in loyalty of the Skang community. It was as if they had guessed his plans, he'd thought after the fateful meeting with Hilda. The one thing he needed was time – time to charm, to cajole, to threaten...

There were a few, a disaffected six or seven, but he'd been unable to contact any one of them the day before. As the time for the meeting drew near, he could be seen in search of his missing supporters, almost running, casting hither and thither through the clusters of devotees blissfully and aimlessly wandering through the groves and lanes of the ashram. And then at last, standing by a group in the shadow of the great pipal tree...

'Dafydd! Thank goodness! The very man...'

Brother Dafydd, a recruit from the ranks of the modern Druidic revival – and a former bard, renowned for his evocations of the more romantic gods of nature – turned from his task of briefing his small cadre of helpers about the coming evacuation, and greeted Alex with some concern.

'Brother Alex! Is it true?'

'What have you heard?'

'A moment...'

He turned back to dismiss his group of lieutenants and watched as they hastened away. Only then did he turn to Alex once more. 'They say that...'

Alex raised a hand to stop him, and taking him by the arm, led him behind the massive trunk, out of sight and hearing; and still he lowered his voice. 'What do they say?'

'That she means to go the whole way.'

'Exclusion?'

'Worse. Excision.'

For a moment, Alex's face betrayed him. The fear of total loss, the ultimate despair, that lurked behind his grandiose plans was all too plain to see.

'What have you done to make her so angry?' Dafydd went on.

Alex at once slipped back behind his political mask. 'Nothing. It's a ploy, a pack of lies to discredit me. She knows full well that if I had the chance to make them understand the full extent of her treachery, I wouldn't be the one to suffer.'

Dafydd nodded as if this were too obvious to be said. 'What are you going to do?' he asked.

Alex paused and shook his head. 'She'll have Schwenck on her side... and the two from down under. We stand our best chance with the Pakistani and the Balkan two. And Moskowicz is teetering on the edge, certainly.' He took hold of Dafydd's shoulders; his unblinking stare seized Dafydd's eyes. 'It's up to us. We must find the others and spread the word. If we believe it, and believe it utterly, through to our very bones, we can make it come true. Hilda will be out.

'This could be our last chance!'

CHAPTER SEVEN

Brigadier Lethbridge-Stewart had, of course, sent a message from London to Major Chatterjee of the Indian Army, the UNIT liaison officer in Bombay, to let him know that he was coming; and he'd followed it up with a phone call as soon as he had settled in to the hotel. Though this had been somewhat protracted, as he was passed from extension to extension up the ladder of command, he had eventually been able to make an appointment.

He'd been a little taken aback to find that the UNIT office, which was situated in a large suburban mansion badly needing a lick of paint, was little more than a store-cupboard behind the lifts on the fourth floor, and that the entire staff consisted of the Major himself.

'My dear chap,' he said when he'd been told why the Brigadier and his two assistants had come, 'of course I am understanding the urgency of the matter. I shall be very delighted to accompany you on your visit to this strange lady.'

'Good,' said the Brigadier. 'Then I suggest that we waste no more time. The authority of your uniform should guarantee us access.' The Brigadier, being officially on a private visit, was of course in mufti.

The young major stroked his Errol Flynn moustache and nodded his agreement.

He was evidently very proud of his uniform, thought the Brigadier. The knife-sharp creases in his shorts would have done credit to an officer in the Grenadier Guards.

But he showed no sign of urgency.

'Are you free now?' the Brigadier went on, getting up from the rickety bentwood chair that was provided for visitors.

Chatterjee raised his hands in apology. 'My dear fellow, we cannot be importunate. These things take time, you know. I can clear it with the police in a phone call or two. Perhaps. But the politicos... I am sure I can be getting an answer by the day after tomorrow. Or the next day, without a doubt. Maybe.'

'What!'

'I have to send a memo, in triplicate, to the Secretary of the Under-Secretary in Delhi, who will consult with the Permanent Secretary, who will decide whether to involve the Minister, you see. And then we must await for the answer to come back along the line. In triplicate.'

The Major grinned at the sight of the Brigadier's appalled face. 'We have a saying here, you know. The British invented bureaucracy – and the Indians perfected it.'

'This is ridiculous!' said Lethbridge-Stewart.

'Not to worry, sir,' said the Major. 'After all, they aren't sailing for a while yet.'

'Sailing? What are you talking about?'

'You didn't know? They have a ship, a small cruise ship, or an extremely large yacht – I suppose you might be categorising it as either one – which used to belong to the billionaire Papadopoulos, you know? Before his imprisonment? To be honest, Bombay will be glad to see their backside. We have heard such tales, you know.'

Ah! More horror stories! Now they were getting somewhere.

'Such as?' the Brigadier asked.

The Major tutted. 'Naked revels. Dancing by moonlight, etcetera, etcetera. And worse!'

No Skang stuff then.

'But where are they sailing to?' said the Major. 'That we shall be learning when they are submitting their intentions to the appropriate authority. Until then, one can only be asking the question.'

'Nobody knows,' said Jeremy cheerfully to Sarah. 'At least, I suppose somebody must know, otherwise we'd never get there, would we? But they haven't told us.'

Sarah was now dressed in a short tennis frock (as the shop assistant had called it), the only totally white garment she had been able to find in her hurried shopping trip. Its pristine freshness was marred by a long green smear, the unfortunate result of her clambering over the wall behind the pipal tree.

'Sorry, Sarah,' the Doctor had said that morning. 'I know it seems unfair, but I really think I should go alone. Or maybe with the Brigadier, if he comes back soon.'

Which had been the reason for her shopping trip.

'You're all leaving?' she said to Jeremy. 'Er... I mean, we're all leaving, are we? All of us?'

'Oh yes. We're going to get our rewards, you see.'

Reward for what? Coughing up twenty grand? Oh no, she remembered now. Devotion to Skang. And he got to love you back. Big deal. So why did they have to sail off into the sunset?

'I'm so glad you decided to join us, Sarah,' went on Jeremy. 'Fancy coming all this way! They must have been really impressed!'

'Yes, well... they were in an awful hurry, because they're so busy, packing up and stuff. I mean, I didn't even catch the password when they told me. But I don't suppose it matters if we're leaving.'

They were strolling down the crowded main pathway under an avenue of palms, with Sarah, even as she talked, keeping a surreptitious eye open for Brother Alex, in case he recognised her.

'Oh, but we're not sailing yet. They haven't told us when. And you might want to go out to the shops. To be honest...' Jeremy lowered his voice and looked round to make sure nobody was listening, '...I nipped out only this morning to get some fags. They're not exactly banned, but everybody *looks* at you! You know?'

'Mm. There are a few things I need. But I expect I'll manage.'

Jeremy casually looked up into the fronds of the trees above their heads. 'Open your heart!' he said, without moving his lips.

'What?'

Jeremy looked at her in irritation. 'Open your heart!' he hissed. 'That's the password! Or three of them, I suppose. I can't be too loud. We're only supposed to say it coming in at the gate, and then we only murmur it.'

'Jeremy, you're a poppet!'

It would have been difficult to judge whether Jeremy was more surprised by the epithet, or by the kiss Sarah planted on his cheek.

After all, Sarah was pretty surprised herself.

Twenty-one different nationalities, with skin-colours ranging from freckled blush-white to deep brown, and a spectrum of gender identities nearly as diverse. They were unified only by their human shape and the long white robes that marked them out as Skang teachers or organisers. They filled the drawing room of Hilda's bungalow as if they were the ghosts of the former residents' cocktail-party guests.

But there was no chatter, no tittle-tattle, no bemoaning the shortcomings of their Indian servants. They were there for a very serious purpose: the trial (for that's what it was) of one of their number for just about the most serious offence possible.

At first things seemed to be going Alex's way. Having had a metaphorical arm twisted, Dafydd had begged Hilda to be allowed to speak on Alex's behalf before the charge was heard; and there were three others – including (surprisingly after the row in Rome) Eduardo from Venezuela – who joined Dafydd in expressing their dismay that he should even be under suspicion.

Alex kept an eye open as they spoke. Many others were nodding. Some even gave him an encouraging smile. He'd been worrying unduly. With any luck, the whole thing would be thrown out without a hearing.

Unfortunately, he hadn't made clear to his supporters the extent to which the evidence itself condemned him. They'd taken his word that it was political; but when they heard what Will Cabot had to say, they fell silent. In spite of all his efforts to woo them, the faces around the room were grave. Many now avoided his eye, like members of a jury who had found a murderer guilty.

'But I don't understand,' said a small dapper man, who, as ex-editor of one of Tokyo's leading broadsheets, was not likely to find much beyond his comprehension. 'Why did you not follow the practice of the group? This journalist woman could have been recruited, surely? To make her an enemy was not only foolish, but exposes us all to the utmost danger.'

Brother Alex found it hard to hide his irritation. The wretched little man had too much influence. He was losing the battle. He'd been stupid even to mention Sarah to Hilda and Cabot, whose account of the story in the *The Times of India* had already alienated the majority of the group.

It was time to stop trying to placate them and start fighting back.

'Why? She made me lose my temper, that's why,' he said. 'She was the usual muck-raking hack who was only interested in stabbing the notorious Alex Whitbread in the back. But she was deprived of the chance. As it happened, we were leaving the next day. We'll hear no more from her, mark my words.'

'But...'

'Thank you, Brother Shunryu,' said Mother Hilda. 'I think we have heard enough. Brother Alex, the time has come to...'

'I haven't finished what I have to say!'

Hilda clearly wasn't used to being interrupted. She looked at Alex over the top of her glasses, as if he were an uppity student challenging her views on Wittgenstein. 'Very well. Continue.'

Alex glanced round the room, looking for his allies. There was Brother Ali from Pakistan, and Igor and... but only Dafydd would catch his eye, and he was frowning. 'I do not recognise the authority of this kangaroo court. I have made quite clear in the past my belief that the strategy of the present leadership is not assertive enough. Mother Hilda has abrogated any right to...'

But he could not continue. The murmur of dissent had become a growl, and the growl a clamour that drowned his words. He looked towards Dafydd once more, only to see a little shake of the head, before he too dropped his eyes.

'The sense of the meeting is overwhelmingly apparent,' said Hilda. 'Please lock the door, Will.'

Alex's aggressive air vanished. 'No! Please, no! I beg you!'

Mother Hilda stood up. She looked at him with compassion in her eyes. But then she shook her head.

'It's too late,' she said.

At first, as she travelled through the leafy suburb where the ashram was situated, Sarah rather enjoyed sitting in her bicycle rickshaw, playing at being a memsahib from the days of the Raj, when merely to be British was to be one up on the world. This was the life!

But when she found herself in the middle of Bombay's rush-hour – which included double-decker buses that seemed twice the size of London's, vans and lorries of every description, a multitude of out-of-date cars, three-wheeled taxis, and even an elephant loaded with greenery, all hooting at once (except the elephant, who kept himself to himself) and making for the same gap in the traffic – she began to have second thoughts. And the sight of the pitifully skinny legs in front of her losing their struggle to pedal her up a mildly steep hill finally decided her.

She paid the owner of the legs the six rupees he had quoted, much to his delight, and walked the rest of the way to the docks.

On leaving the ashram that morning, Dieter, at the gate, had recognised her at once, in spite of her attempt to change her face by pulling in her cheeks and adopting a sultry pout. But, thank goodness, he seemed thoroughly pleased.

'So she has said yes! I wish you very well with us.'

'Thanks,' she'd said, with a quick glance at Helga's shop, which, to her relief, had an empty window and a firmly closed door.

The critical moment would come when she tried to use the password to get back in, she thought to herself as she arrived at the quayside.

The place was full of ships, of all types and sizes. And quite a number were anchored out in the middle of the big harbour, including, she recognised with a curious pang, a British warship of some sort. Not a destroyer; it was much smaller than that. More a tubby spaniel of the sea than a greyhound. But it was the usual sort of grey and it was flying the White Ensign. Her fling with Sammy had finished nearly five years ago, but the sight of anything to do with the Royal Navy still gave her a little nostalgic glow.

How was she ever going to find the Skang ship? She didn't even know its name.

And then she saw it. Very modern and streamlined, and painted brilliant white (of course). Not all that large. It would be a bit of a squash if it was going to house the entire community. But it must have cost a bomb, which just showed that there were plenty of other clots like Jeremy. It was flying the Indian flag, and on its bow it proudly bore its name, in big capital letters: *SKANG*.

It made a sort of sense. But wasn't it odd, this mixture of openness and secrecy? Still, if the Doctor's suspicions were justified – and how could they not be? – that's exactly how it would appear: the New Age cult open to the world on the one hand; and on the other, the hidden mystery known only to the elect.

The thought produced a shudder of sudden fear. For surely, somewhere in the bowels of this shining vessel, concealed from all but the chosen few, must be the Skang itself. And what would it be living on?

Hilda Hutchens had experienced many different types of meditation. Even before going to university, where her introduction to the rigour of philosophical thinking led her to lose her rich Anglo-Catholic faith, she had practised a deep contemplation that was surely first cousin to her later experience of Hindu Samadhi.

But now, as she sat in focused concentration, observing the feelings that had arisen in her breast at the sight of the limp body of Brother Alex being carried out, she recognised that she no longer identified with them in any way. Compassion was there, yes, and an iron determination that the project should not be jeopardised, but they were not *her* feelings. It was not even Mother Hilda, herself, who was concentrating on them. What had to be done, was done. What had to be felt, was felt. And that was all.

'Mother Hilda...' The rough voice of Brother Will brought her back to the bungalow.

'Where is Doctor Smith now?' she said, after she had scanned the note he handed her with a wryly raised eyebrow.

'At the main gate. Brother Dieter was concerned that...'

'Of course I must see him.'

'But Mother, are you sure that's wise? We've been so careful not to let anybody get a sniff of...'

'He would think it very strange if I refused. At this time of all times, we can't allow the slightest suspicion. Show him in at once.'

CHAPTER EIGHT

Dame Hilda glanced at the note in her hand. She smiled. 'How could I resist, Doctor? It reminded me at once of our delicious arguments in Oxford. Do you think I shall end up thumping the table this time?'

'One or two emphatic taps, perhaps, or would even that be beneath the dignity of an emeritus professor? Not to mention a Dame of the British Empire.'

Hilda's laugh was a delicious gurgle, like the bubbling of a mountain beck. 'Oh, I've dropped all that nonsense,' she said. 'It would hardly go with the teachings of the Skang. That is why we wear white, you see. As I'm sure you know, it's the colour they wear at funerals in India. We are celebrating the death of the personal self.'

The Doctor nodded. 'So I've gathered,' he said. He'd filled the time he'd spent fruitlessly waiting for the return of the Brigadier by absorbing the information in the book that Sarah had given him. 'It must have been nigh impossible not to have been blown away by the winds of change that have swept through the universities, I can see that,' he continued. 'It is, after all, the *Zeitgeist*, the spirit of the New Age. But Hilda Hutchens of all people! I had to come and ask why.'

'You're not the first, Doctor,' said Hilda. 'Most of my friends have expressed their astonishment.'

'It seems a world away from the logical positivism of the young don who published *Empirical Epistemology* – twenty years ago, was it?'

'Twenty-two. No, twenty-three. And not so young, I'm afraid.

Are you sure you won't have a drink? A small sundowner, as they used to say out here?'

'Thank you, no,' replied the Doctor. It would be wise to avoid drinking anything that could contain the substance he'd found in Sarah's aspirin bottle. If its effect was anything like her description...

'And it hardly ties in with the rigorous approach of *Quantum Qualia*,' he continued.

'You never came across my subsequent study of consciousness, then,' said Hilda.

'Indeed I did,' replied the Doctor. '*The Emptiness of the Busy Mind*.'

'Something of a pop title, I must admit,' she said with a chuckle.

'If it wouldn't be considered too sexist a way of putting it for the modern ear, I'd say it was masterly!'

She smiled and gave a little bow of her head in acknowledgement of the compliment. 'If you read between the lines, you'll find the Skang on every page,' she said.

She looked down at the paper in her hand, the note that Will had brought from the Doctor. '*If I should meet the Skang on the path, should I kill him?*' she read out. 'You are asking me whether the way of the Skang is a paradigm of the Buddha's way... Or even whether, in the last analysis, he can be essentially equated to the Buddhanature?' she said, looking up.

'Or Tillich's "Ground of Being". I am.'

Hilda's smile disappeared. The Doctor stroked his chin with the back of his forefinger. He must be careful. She was beginning to suspect that he wasn't just making conversation.

'Relatively speaking, it's more like the collective unconscious of Jung – or of Assagioli. In ultimate terms, I should have tended towards a comparison with the Beloved of the Sufis.'

The Doctor nodded. It was as he'd thought. 'But that would mean that you are equating the divinity of your Skang with God!'

Hilda looked at him over the top of her glasses. 'And would you have the intellectual arrogance to tell me that I am wrong?'

They were getting into very deep waters here. A change of course. 'What about the physical aspect?'

Dame Hilda frowned slightly. 'I don't follow you.'

'What is the significance of its... or should I say, *his* demonic appearance?'

Now Hilda was taking him very seriously. 'The word Skang is a shortening – a simplification – of his Indian name. And like many Indian Gods, he must first and foremost be a destroyer.'

The Doctor nodded. 'Shiva – and his wife Kali, with her necklace of skulls.'

'The Skang in the fierceness of his embrace pierces the very heart and mind – and the fire of his sublime love burns away the egotistical dross it finds there. And with that purification, the devotee vanishes forever in the ecstasy of divine union.'

The Doctor looked at her in amazement. Where had the severely rational philosopher, the supreme sceptic of her generation, disappeared to? The fervour in her voice, and the glow in her eyes made it abundantly clear. She actually believed it all to be true!

'Mm... And how is this unity made manifest to your devoted followers?' The Doctor was doing his best to sound no more than mildly interested; the implication being that this was nothing but the idle curiosity of an old academic acquaintance.

But the attempt was in vain. Hilda's expression changed from paradoxical absorbed openness to a stiff normality. 'We have our rituals, our ceremonies... Now, Doctor, I'm sure you'll understand...'

Had he given away too much?

'Of course, of course,' he said, getting to his feet.

Mother Hilda watched as the bearer showed him out, platitudes of empty politeness hanging in the air. Her social smile faded, leaving a slight frown. A moment later, a decision made, she rose and hurried inside the bungalow.

'Will!' she called. 'Where are you?'

He appeared at the door of his office.

'Good,' she said. 'Now listen carefully. There's been a change of plan.'

Were the crew all members of the cult? It might make a difference, thought Sarah, as she watched them swarming about the quayside, loading crates and boxes of all sorts and sizes onto wooden pallets, which were then hoisted aboard by crane-things; derricks weren't they called? The crew were all wearing white, certainly, but then so did sailors the world over when they were in the sunnier climes. White uniforms, like the Navy, or one of the posh cruise lines. This was no tramp steamer.

So far, so good. At least she'd managed to get into the dock area. Sarah's experience in an earlier trip to the East (tracking down the Brewster boy to Bangkok, after he'd staged an unconvincing suicide) had taught her the universal way of getting what you wanted. A hundred rupee note, judiciously folded and surreptitiously slipped into the hand of the security guard on the gate, had done the trick, just as she'd expected.

But now what? She wanted to find out two things – when the *Skang* was sailing, and where to. She took a deep breath and marched out of the shadow of the customs shed to the gangway, and straight up it, as confidently as she could manage.

Nobody seemed to be on guard; and the few people she could see on this deck, down nearer the bow, were far too busy to notice her. Now then... she needed to find the central hub of all this activity – the purser's office, perhaps? There'd bound to be all the info she needed there.

Where would it be? For'd, probably, in the area underneath

the bridge... or might it be amidships, where the passengers would congregate? Feeling a little smug about her nautical expertise, she turned into the first doorway she came to, which was in fact about halfway down the deck.

'And where do you think you're going?'

She swung round, her heart thumping. The speaker, a large female with close-cropped hair and a clipboard, who looked as if she'd be more at home in a prison than a luxury yacht, stood behind the open door at a table covered with papers.

'How did you get on board?'

'I... I just walked up the gangway. I've... I've come from the ashram.'

'Is that so? What's the password then?'

Oh, thank you, Jeremy! 'Open your heart!'

A grunt. She didn't seem to be taking the advice.

'Very well. What is it you want?'

Sarah's mind was working so fast that she could almost feel the wheels going round. 'Oh... I've got a message.'

'Give it to me, then.'

'No, I mean, Brother Alex said I was to talk to the Mate...'

Did she believe it? Didn't look like it, judging by the tight lips.

'So if you'd just tell me where I can find him...' Sarah went on desperately.

'The First Officer?' She looked over Sarah's shoulder and a gleam of spite appeared in her cold eyes. 'You're in luck... Mr Gorridge!' she called out. 'There's someone here who wants to speak to you. A message from... Brother Alex, was it?'

Oh Lor'!

Mr Gorridge came in from the upper deck. 'What is it?' His face twitched. 'Please be quick. We're behind schedule already. Who is Brother Alex?'

A wild hope. This could be the chance she'd been looking for. 'Oh... Mother Hilda has put Brother Alex in charge of getting everybody on board...' What was the word? Oh, yes.

'Embarkation. You know? And he would like you to give him an idea of... well... when he can get going.'

A snort of disgust from the prison warder; and the First Officer wasn't any more pleased.

'You'd never believe it!' he said. 'I've made it perfectly clear from the start. I cannot accept any passengers earlier than two hours before we slip. And that means 1500, and not a second before. Okay?' He screwed up his face and pulled at his nose as if he was trying to stop himself sneezing. 'Now, what was I doing? Oh yes...' He looked at his watch. 'Oh, God!' he said and turned to go.

Well, that wasn't much use.

'At this rate,' said Mr Gorridge as he disappeared, 'we'll be lucky to be ready by a *week* tomorrow!'

Thank you, Mr Gorridge! Thank you very much!

'Don't you see? It must mean that they're going to sail away tomorrow afternoon. The whole batch. At five o'clock!'

'Very good, Sarah. Very good indeed,' said the Brigadier. 'And *that* means, Doctor, that your softly, softly, catch monkey approach is kaput.'

The Doctor took another mouthful of chicken curry. 'Curious flavour,' he said. 'I haven't tasted anything like it since a sneg stew I had in a little bistro on Sirius Two.'

'What's a sneg?' asked Sarah, despite herself, her mouth full of buffburger.

'A type of hairy newt,' said the Doctor.

'Do you like the taste?' said Ron (who doubled as chef and waiter), as he passed by with a tray of dirty dishes from another table. He turned back at the kitchen door. 'If you promise not to tell anybody... A large dollop of chocolate powder, that's my secret ingredient. Takes the edge off the heat of the curry.

'Of course, some like it hot!' he added, and with a cheeky toss of his head and a giggle, he disappeared into the kitchen.

'Hmm. So that's what's wrong with it,' said the Brigadier,

sprinkling his curry with a generous spoonful of chopped green chillies from the dish in the centre of the table. 'You're changing the subject again, Doctor,' he went on. 'You'll no doubt be delighted to know that, thanks to the intervention of the British High Commissioner, Major Chatterjee and I will be paying this Mother Hilda a visit first thing tomorrow morning. She has some serious questions to answer.'

'Indeed? You have no more direct evidence to link the deaths with the Skang cult now than you had in London.'

'I don't need it. There's sufficient circumstantial evidence for a proper investigation. And that would be impossible if they were to take to the high seas. Until this whole thing is cleared up, they won't be going anywhere.'

'And how do you think you're going to stop them?' asked the Doctor.

'Not by having a bit of a chit-chat about philosophy,' replied the Brigadier, who had received the Doctor's report with some impatience. 'I have here...' he produced from his inside pocket an official-looking envelope, '...something which will stop them in their tracks!'

'Bully for you. It must be a very powerful bit of paper.'

'It is indeed. An injunction from a High Court judge.'

'And if they defy you?'

'They'll be arrested. All the organisers. I gather from Chatterjee that those in charge come from some twenty different countries. We'll bag the lot of them.'

'I'll believe that when I see it,' said the Doctor.

Here they go again, thought Sarah, and then she was struck by an appalling notion. What was so special about London? If there was a Skang creature hidden away in South Hill Park Square, why not in every country where the cult had a base? They could be looking at twenty of them, not just the one! 'Hang on!' she said urgently, interrupting an irritable exchange concerning the efficiency of the Indian police – indeed of any police, anywhere.

She told them her thought.

'Well of course,' said the Doctor. 'I'd taken it for granted that we'd all understood that. Why do you think I've been treading so carefully? As far as Earth is concerned, these are alien beings, and clearly inimical. The leaders of the cult are either in league with them or being controlled by them. With so much at stake, these people will stop at nothing.'

It was apparently as new a thought to the Brigadier as it had been to Sarah.

'In that case,' he said, 'it makes it all the more imperative that we take the strongest action possible. The Major is picking me up at nine o'clock. This has got to be settled once and for all!

'Sorry Sarah,' he went on, 'on an occasion like this, three's a crowd. Er... that is to say...' He'd caught the lift of the Doctor's eyebrow.

So they were going off without her. Right. She hadn't told them the whole of her idea. She'd remembered the gut-clenching thought she'd had when she first saw the *Skang*. If there were twenty of the things, where were they hidden? There could be only one answer.

She'd got onto the ship once. What was to stop her getting on board again?

CHAPTER NINE

Major Chatterjee arrived to pick the Doctor and the Brigadier up in a battered old Land Rover – not with a squad of policemen in tow, but with a large army sergeant with a fierce Kitchener moustache and a UNIT flash on his shoulder.

So the UNIT presence in Bombay wasn't confined to one individual after all, thought the Brigadier. Including the driver, there were at least two more members. Hardly enough to take twenty people in charge. Twenty at least.

For a moment, he felt a pang of nostalgia for the UNIT team back home; for the most part ex-SAS professionals, who had helped him solve so many problems in the past. He stole a glance at the sergeant. That moustache would put the fear of God into anyone. At least his presence would show they meant business.

Not that you would have known it, from the Major's conversation.

'From what city are you coming, Doctor?' said the Major, as they bumped over the potholes. 'I have had a training secondment in your beautiful country some years ago, and went swanning the length and breadth of it.'

'Oh, I've lived in so many different places,' replied the Doctor, 'I've lost count.'

'Indeed? I gather that Brigadier-General Lethbridge-Stewart is Scotch born – oh, pardon me, Scottish!'

The man was just showing off his English! the Brigadier thought. 'Just plain Brigadier, Chatterjee. Not a general…

'Yet…' he added under his breath.

Swerving to avoid a skinny cow, they swung round the corner and arrived outside the main entrance to the ashram.

'Gracious me!' said the Major.

The gate was wide open, and nobody was there to greet them or, for that matter, to hinder them. They drove straight in.

Not a soul.

They pulled up in the square outside the main block, which housed the offices, the canteen and so on. There was no sign of life save the sound of a bird that sounded like a half-hearted curlew. Even the fountain in the middle of the square was silenced.

'This is absurd,' said the Brigadier, climbing out.

'I should have foreseen this,' said the Doctor behind him. 'Maybe you were right, Lethbridge-Stewart. I would appear to have frightened them off myself.'

Major Chatterjee joined them. 'We must make all haste to the docks. These naughty people must not be evading our grasp.'

'One moment,' said the Brigadier, walking over to the open door. 'Is anybody there?' he called into the building.

No response.

'Let's go,' he said with abrupt decision, striding over to the Land Rover.

'Wait!' The Doctor held up his hand. 'What's that?'

They all froze.

No wonder they'd missed it, thought Lethbridge-Stewart. The faintest possible knocking – somebody hammering on a distant door, perhaps – and, yes, the ghost of a voice...

'He-e-elp! Help me! Let me out...!'

Sarah couldn't make up her mind. As she rode through the racket of the city centre and out to the comparative peace of the dockside (in a three-wheeler this time, like a motor bike inside a mini-taxi), she was contemplating her possible future with the adrenalin rush she always felt when she was about to dive into the deep end.

These people would stop at nothing, the Doctor had said; so if she were caught searching for the Skang creatures... And the alternative possibility, to stow away and get the entire story as it unfolded, was even more dicey. Let's face it, she needed the Doctor. Together they made a great team, whereas on her own...

'Come off it, Sarah Jane Smith,' she said to herself. 'Why not be honest? You're just plain scared!'

She soon forgot her dilemma when they arrived at the docks. Having paid off the driver, she was riffling through a bundle of notes from her bag in search of one hundred rupees – her unofficial ticket into the dockyard – when she became aware that she could see through the gate right across the harbour to the Royal Navy ship and the others at anchor. The *Skang* wasn't alongside the quay where she'd been yesterday.

Of course! If she were sailing this afternoon, she'd have to refuel, and get water and all that stuff.

She hurried across to the gate. Good. It was the same security man as the day before. His grinning face was alight with anticipation of favours yet to come, and his hand was hovering ready to receive his bribe.

'Where can I find her? The *Skang*?'

His face and his hand both fell. 'Go to the Harbour Master's office. They will be telling you to where she travels.'

'Yes, but where is she now? I need to go on board.'

He shrugged. She was no longer his friend. 'You have missed the boat, miss.'

'What? What do you mean? You mean she's gone?'

He gave the little sideways wobble of his head that signifies assent in India, together with a little smirk of pleasure at the bad news. 'They did not tell you? Your friends all came on board just after the middle of the night. She left Bombay at two o'clock this morning!'

'My name? Whitbread, Alex Whitbread. What does that matter? Have they gone? Have they sailed yet?'

Whitbread! The man they were after in London! Now they might get some answers, thought the Brigadier.

Brother Alex could hardly stand. His usual, carefully tanned complexion was now a jaundiced yellow–white, and his eyes were sunken in deep pits of shadow.

The man was obviously on his last legs. The questions would have to wait. 'You're ill, man. We must get you to a doctor,' the Brigadier said. 'Sorry,' he grunted to the Doctor, who, with a look, took hold of Alex's wrist to feel his pulse.

'Who was it that has locked you in the office, sir?' asked Major Chatterjee. 'That in itself, you know, is a criminal offence, no doubt.'

'For God's sake!' Alex was almost screaming. 'It can't go without me! I must be on that ship!'

'I'm sorry, sir. That's out of the question. Until you've answered our...'

But Alex wasn't listening. Wrenching himself free from the Doctor, he pushed violently past the others, in a rush to escape.

'Stop him!' barked the Brigadier.

'Sah!' barked back the enormous sergeant, who was standing by the broken door.

But Alex wasn't giving up easily. With an animal howl of desperation, struggling with a fanatical strength that was quite at odds with his apparent state of near-collapse, he beat at the sergeant's chest with his free hand as he fought to get away from the great hand clamped around his arm. For a moment, it almost looked as if he might manage it.

But the Doctor was beside them in an instant. He touched the frantic man at the base of his skull, finding some esoteric pressure point. The Brigadier had seen him do the same in the past, and was now equally taken aback at the result. For Alex Whitbread, with joints suddenly resembling those of a rag-doll, sank to the floor and lay still. His arm fell lifelessly as the sergeant let it go.

'Well!' said Major Chatterjee. 'You could knock me down with a feather, you know!'

The Brigadier pulled himself together. 'We'd better get him to the hospital.'

'That's the last thing we must do, Lethbridge-Stewart,' said the Doctor. 'Once in the grip of officialdom, he'll be lost to us.'

The Brigadier grunted. The Doctor was right, for once. If the rest of the cult had given them the slip, Whitbread was their only contact. And as for the others...

The telephone in the office was still connected. A quick call to the Harbour Master's office confirmed their fears. The *Skang* had sailed. But at least they now knew where she was going. She'd filed her sailing plans, as the regulations demanded.

The *Skang* was going to Sri Lanka.

Ron had been only too pleased to let them have another room, his normal business being passing trade, with more emphasis on the passing than the trade.

Habeas corpus: you may have the body... thought the Brigadier gloomily, as he watched the sergeant tenderly laying the limp figure on the bed. We've got the body – and much good may it do us. 'When shall we be able to interrogate him?' he said aloud.

'He'll be out for an hour or so,' the Doctor said. 'It's difficult to say precisely. You have to be careful, you see. It's a useful technique to sedate any vertebrate, but a few micrograms too much pressure, and the central nervous system would come to a dead stop.'

Having dispatched the sergeant to wait in the car, the two UNIT officers and the Doctor repaired to the hotel hallway, which doubled as a lounge, to have a council of war.

All the delays of the last two days churned through the Brigadier's mind. If only they had flown out straight away, instead of wasting so much time with the TARDIS! They'd missed their chance; and now they were in an impossible position, as he pointed out to the Doctor with scarcely concealed fury. To chase after the *Skang* in a helicopter, for instance, would certainly be counter-productive. What were they to do once they'd landed on the deck?

Their only hope of stopping the ship on the high seas would be to enlist the help of the Indian Navy. A destroyer, or even a frigate, could metaphorically (or even literally) fire a shot across the bows of the runaway vessel. But the chances of persuading those with the power to grant permission, purely on the strength of the Doctor's surmises...

'Surmises?' said the Doctor indignantly. 'These are the conclusions I have reached after due consideration of all the evidence. These alien beings could pose a threat to the very survival of *Homo sapiens*. They must be destroyed! Surmises indeed! When have you ever known me to be wrong?'

The Brigadier made a noble effort and managed to stop himself from pointing out the many times they'd run into trouble on the basis of the Doctor's assumptions. 'You agree that the evidence is circumstantial,' he said, tight-lipped. 'We'd have no hope of convincing them.'

'No, indeed,' said Major Chatterjee. 'It is maybe hoping for a miracle to persuade even the police to be taking the matter seriously.'

'The Yanks have a word for it,' said the Brigadier. 'Snafu. Situation normal, all –'

'So you've noticed. Situation normal indeed,' said the Doctor. 'Things aren't going the way we want? When has life ever been different?

'We have no option. It is vital that we intercept them in Sri Lanka. If we catch a plane...'

He was interrupted by a tumult and a shouting in the street.

'What the devil...?' said the Brigadier, rising to his feet. A moment later, the burly sergeant appeared at the main door, with Brother Alex held firmly in his grasp, as if he'd caught a naughty schoolboy.

'Absconding through the window, the miscreant was,' he said, his moustache twitching. 'I am seeing him, so I am taking initiative to apprehend him. Sah!'

'Quite right, Sergeant,' said the Major.

'Must get to the ship...' gasped Alex, with a sort of sob.

'You're too late, Mr Whitbread,' said the Doctor. 'The *Skang* will be over a hundred miles away by now.'

The effect on Alex was almost as dramatic as that resulting from the Doctor's earlier intervention. He sagged in the sergeant's massive hands. All the strength had gone from his legs, and his head drooped. Only the moan coming from his bloodless lips with every breath, like a child exhausted by too much weeping, told them that he was still conscious.

The sergeant picked him up and carried him like a baby over to the Victorian chaise longue near the reception desk. He laid him on its faded velvet.

'Thank you, Sergeant,' said the Brigadier. 'You've done well.'

'Sah!' said the sergeant. With a parade-ground salute, he turned smartly about and marched outside.

The Brigadier sighed with frustration. It was clear that he would get no information from Whitbread for some considerable time. 'So. We fly to Sri Lanka and wait for them. And what then? Are we going to arrest the entire ship?'

As he finished speaking, he realised that the noise from the chaise longue had changed. Alex was struggling to sit up, and taking deep shuddering breaths, trying to speak.

'What is it, man?'

'Sri Lanka...? You think they're... they're going to Sri Lanka? No, no, no!'

The words were scarcely audible. His face was like a drawing of a ghost in a children's horror story. He swayed, and his mouth opened and closed silently, as he tried to go on speaking.

The Doctor strode across to him, and seized him by the shoulders, fixing him with his eyes. 'You know where they're going?'

Alex's voice came from far away. 'Of course I do. They're going to...' A cunning expression came over the skeletal face. 'Are you... Are you going after them?'

'We are, if it's the last thing we do.'

A ghost of a sardonic smile. 'You'll never find them. Unless...' The feeble voice faded away completely.

'Unless? Unless what?'

The urgency in the Doctor's voice got through to him.

'Unless... unless you take me with you...' The effort was too much. His head dropped; and, as his body gave way, the Doctor gently let him fall back onto the braided cushions behind him.

CHAPTER TEN

'Sammy!'

The young Naval officer with red-gold hair and two rings on the epaulettes of his white shirt swung round to face her.

'Oh... sorry,' said Sarah, disappointed. 'I thought you were somebody I used to know.'

He grinned. 'Afraid not. More's the pity! You must be Sarah Jane Smith. Welcome aboard. Is that all your luggage? It's okay, Matthews, I'll take it.'

'Aye aye, sir.'

The sailor who'd greeted her with a salute at the top of the gangway handed over the backpack and returned to his post.

'Come on, I'll show you where your cabin is. And the wardroom and all that jazz.'

And away he went down the deck.

With a skip and a little run, Sarah caught up with him, and found herself almost scuttling along to keep up with his long legs. Of course it wasn't Sammy! Even if Sammy had grown a beard. Same colour hair, that was all. This chap was much taller, more solid and more... sort of grown up. But then, of course, Sammy would be by now.

It would be too much of a coincidence. Just as well. She'd had her fill of coincidences in the last year or so!

'I'm Peter Andrews. The Number One. That's –'

'The First Lieutenant. Yes, I know. Sammy told me.'

He came to a doorway and paused. 'That wouldn't be Sammy Brooks, by any chance?'

Oh no! 'Do you know him?'

'Left him behind in Hong Kong. Lucky blighter. When the flotilla was rejigged, he was given command of the *Cuffley*. We got flogged to the Irish Navy. Much to the disgust of the Old Man.'

'Who?'

'The Skipper. Lieutenant-Commander Gene Hogben. Let's hope this little jaunt of yours will cheer him up.'

He disappeared inside, followed by Sarah, who was trying to work out why she had an odd feeling of coming home.

'What are you?' she said as she followed him up a steep flight of stairs. 'A frigate? Or what?'

His laughter echoed down the corridor at the top of the ladder.

HMS *Hallaton*, Village Class Offshore Patrol Vessel, en route from the China Seas to Chatham Dockyard for her pre-sale refit, with a skeleton crew, was hardly the best craft to go chasing the sleek, streamlined *Skang* across the Indian Ocean. Built in Aberdeen, and based on the commercial design of a deep-sea trawler, she was about half the length of a frigate, but very nearly as broad in the beam.

Her armament was sparse. Her 40mm Bofors could certainly do some damage, and her assorted machine guns had often proved their worth. But the four surface-to-surface missiles mounted on the foredeck, though fully operational, were there simply as a deterrent to the curiosity of the Chinese navy. They certainly weren't meant to be used.

But since Alex had insisted that it was too far to fly, the *Hallaton* was the best the Brigadier could come up with. Moreover, as if to prove Major Chatterjee's point that the British had invented bureaucracy, it had taken the Brigadier's boss at UNIT HQ in Geneva – apparently fearing a diplomatic incident with India – nearly three days to persuade the Foreign Office to consider lending her to them, and the Ministry of Defence another two days to say yes.

'I am dumbfounded at the swiftness of New Delhi's agreement,' the Major had said. 'Skang sailing under the Indian flag, I would be making the assumption that you would have to wait for weeks. Even so, you have a long haul to pull. I am calculating that errant vessel will already have travelled at least twelve hundred miles, and more likely a couple of thousand or more, you know. I would be hazarding a large bet that they have already arrived there. Wherever they are going.'

And that was the trouble. There was no way they could make Brother Alex reveal their destination.

'South. Sail to the south. And when you have been at sea for two full days, with me on board, I shall tell you.'

And nothing they could do would persuade him otherwise.

With Major Chatterjee having been left behind to hold the fort, the UNIT team was reduced to its original size: the Brigadier, in a state of sustained frustration eased only slightly by their setting off at last; the Doctor, in one of his infuriating moods of equanimity ('There's nothing we can do, Lethbridge-Stewart, but wait...!'); and Sarah Jane Smith, determined to make the best of their enforced cruise.

She intended to use it as the basis of one of the articles that she would eventually be writing about the whole adventure, comprehensively illustrated by shots of the ship and its crew. 'If the Brigadier doesn't stop me again,' she thought ruefully, as she snapped him on the port wing of the bridge, staring glumly at the empty horizon.

'Ah. There you are,' he said, turning at the sound of the shutter of her little Olympus. 'We need to have a council of war, if that's the right thing to call it, to decide how much we tell them about the Doctor's suspicions.'

So far, as Sarah knew, the true aim of the expedition (and what was it exactly? What were they going to do when they caught up with the Skang?) had been concealed under a smoke screen of Intelligence. On a need-to-know basis as the Brig put it.

'If we can drag him away from his wretched fish,' the Brigadier continued, looking back towards the bow.

The day after they had left Bombay, they had been joined by a school of jolly grinning dolphins, who took it in turns to play in the white bow wave as the *Hallaton* cut through the deep blue of the Indian Ocean. Since then, the Doctor had spent most of his time in the stem of the ship, leaning over to watch them, and singing a wordless song.

'They're not fish, they're mammals,' said Sarah.

'Same meat, different gravy,' replied the Brigadier.

Was that a joke? He wasn't given to joking. But no, his face was as serious as ever as he returned to his grim contemplation of the empty sea ahead.

A plump face stuck itself out of the bridge door. 'Excuse me, sir.'

Chris Watts was a midshipman who seemed to be the general dogsbody of the officers, doing all the odd jobs not allocated to the others.

'The Captain asked me to tell you that Mr Whitbread has woken up and would like to have a word.'

The Brigadier's face lit up. 'Aha! Now we're getting somewhere,' he said.

Although the cabins of the Village Class Patrol Vessels were far more luxurious than those of the average Naval ship – there were even single cabins for the crew – they were hardly big enough to contain a smallish journalist and four large men. So Sarah had to hover hopefully in the open doorway, peeping through the gaps as the Doctor and the Brig, together with the Commanding Officer, Lieutenant-Commander Hogben (who seemed to be about thirty, in spite of his exalted position), and his navigating officer, the lanky Bob Simkins, crowded round the bunk where Alex Whitbread lay.

Unfortunately, she found that the gap between the two officers varied considerably in size, as the Captain seemed to be swaying gently from side to side, in a way that owed nothing to the motion of the ship. Peering past the Doctor she got a much better view of Brother Alex.

The sight of him when he'd been carried on board on a stretcher, unconscious, two days before, had taken her completely aback. The transformation of the matinée idol Alex Whitbread to such an insubstantial ghost of a man, in such a short time, seemed unbelievable – no, impossible. Yet it had plainly been the same person.

But at least he looked a bit better now. He had more colour in his cheeks, and his eyes, though still sunken into his face, were alight with a savage intensity.

It must be the thought that he was on his way back to his chums, thought Sarah.

'Well?' said the Doctor.

Alex waited a moment before he replied, his eyes flicking suspiciously across the faces of the four men. 'How far are we away from India?' he said.

They all looked at Simkins.

'India? We're about three hundred miles off the Keralan coast. If you mean Bombay, it's getting on for six hundred miles away.'

Alex grunted. 'Have I your word that you won't abandon me?'

'I've already given it, man,' said the Doctor. 'Are you going to tell us where we're heading, or aren't you?'

Alex sank back on his pillows, frowning. 'I suppose I've got to trust you...' He sighed heavily. 'We're going to Stella Island,' he said at last.

They all looked at Bob Simkins.

'Search me,' he said.

'It's the largest of the Fleming group.'

Simkins shrugged and shook his head.

Whitbread gave a little laugh. 'Nobody has heard of it,' he said. 'That's the point. Don't worry. The latitude and longitude are written on my heart. Twenty-four degrees fifteen minutes south; seventy-six degrees thirty-four minutes east. And you won't know whether I'm telling you the truth until you get there, will you?'

'This is a bloody farce,' said Lieutenant-Commander Hogben in a slightly blurred voice. 'Pilot, let me know when you've sorted yourselves out.'

'Aye aye, sir,' said Simkins.

The Captain turned and almost pushed his way out. Sarah just managed to dodge him. And when she turned back, she found herself looking straight into the eyes of Alex Whitbread. His mouth fell open, and he clutched at his throat as if he was choking. He fell back on the pillows, his eyes turned up.

'Good God!' said the Brigadier. 'What the devil's the matter with the man? I say, he's not dead, is he?'

'No, not dead,' said the Doctor, who had a finger on the artery in Alex's throat. 'He's just fainted, that's all. Maybe betraying the secret was simply too much for him.'

But Sarah knew better. For she had seen the recognition in those burning eyes.

Brigadier Lethbridge-Stewart, from his earliest experiences in the Army, had always found himself profoundly irritated by the casual assumption of the Royal Navy that, apart from being the senior service, they were also the most efficient. So he found a certain satisfaction, to offset his impatience, in watching Bob Simkins trying to find the islands on his chart.

'Well, that's the position,' he said, pointing to the lightly pencilled cross. 'But they must be so tiny that they just don't show up on such a small scale.'

The chart he had produced from the big shallow drawer under the chart table very nearly covered the entire Indian Ocean between Africa and Australia, with the tip of Sri Lanka peeping in at the top.

In the middle of nowhere, thought the Brigadier. For once it was just about accurate.

Now that they were back on the bridge, their number had been augmented by the First Lieutenant, who was Officer of the Watch, and Chris, the midshipman, who was hovering around the edges of the group trying to see through the gaps, just as Sarah had been – and was doing again.

'Bang in the middle of nowhere,' she said, echoing the Brigadier's thoughts.

'More to the point,' said the Doctor, 'it's bang in the middle of the Indian Ocean. I shouldn't think it gets many visitors.'

'Right away from the shipping lanes,' agreed Bob Simkins, who was busy with his dividers checking distances. 'About... eighteen hundred miles – nautical miles, that is – from Madagascar to the west, and... yes, near as dammit the same to Australia in the east.'

'I say! Why don't we... Sorry, sir,' said the midshipman, realising that the Brigadier was trying to say something.

'What about those islands up there?' said the Brigadier, pointing at some little circles up towards Sumatra in the north-east.

'Excuse me, sir...' It was the midshipman again, wanting to get past him. What was the matter with the wretched boy? Wanting to go to the loo, probably. 'The Cocos Islands, does it say?' he went on, moving aside.

'Getting on for a thousand miles,' said Bob, after a moment. 'I'd reckon the nearest outpost of proper civilisation would be Mauritius, and that would be a journey of something like thirteen hundred miles.'

The Doctor had been peering at the chart. 'How long will it take us to get there?'

'Mauritius?' said the Brigadier. 'Why should we want...'

'No, no. This Stella Island. How long before we catch up with the *Skang*?'

The Navigating Officer applied himself to the chart again, first drawing a line from their current position to the cross in the middle of the empty sea. Then, taking the scale from the side of the chart, he walked the dividers along the route.

'Bingo!'

The cry of delight made every head turn.

'What is it, Chris?' asked Pete Andrews.

'It's the Indian Ocean Pilot book,' he said, holding up a book a bit bigger than a paperback, identical to a shelf of others on the bulkhead behind him. 'No, I mean, listen to this,' he continued, scrabbling through the pages to find his place again. '"Stella Island. Volcanic rock, with coral-reef lagoon. Three miles long by half a mile wide – approx. Discovered in 1773 by Captain Harcourt Fleming, who named it after his wife. Still a British Territory. Uninhabited." And they've got a drawing of it – what it looks like as you approach it from the east...'

Bob Simkins looked up at the First Lieutenant with a rueful grin. 'Out of the mouths of babes...' he said.

'Well done, Chris,' said Pete.

There! Not so bloody efficient, thought Lethbridge-Stewart.

The Doctor had taken the book from Chris, and was scanning the text. 'Mm. Maybe our friend Whitbread has sent us chasing your wild goose after all, Lethbridge-Stewart.'

'What do you mean?'

The Doctor looked back at the book. '"Last visited January 1923 by a Norwegian whaler on passage to the Southern Ocean..." There's a translation of their report. "Good spring water... access via beach through eastern lagoon at high spring tide... Alternative landing place on northern shore..."' He looked up. 'So far, so good. But listen to this... "There is little sign of life. Apart from a few palm-trees, and some bamboo, the sparse vegetation consists of low-lying spikey shrubs resembling gorse. In spite of there being relatively few seabirds, very nearly the entire island is thick with ancient guano..."'

Chris looked enquiringly at Sarah.

'Fishy bird-crap,' she whispered.

'"...the stench of which catches the throat. It is quite clear why Stella Island is uninhabited..."'

There was quite a long silence after the Doctor stopped reading.

'I wonder what sort of marriage Captain Fleming had,' he said. 'Poor Stella.'

CHAPTER ELEVEN

Whyever should Mother Hilda take her flock to such an unwelcoming spot? Alex Whitbread must have given them the wrong information, either unknowingly, or deliberately to lead them astray.

The Brigadier, with grim face, led the way to Alex's cabin, determined to find the truth. But they couldn't tackle him. He'd been so frantic that Bob Simkins, in his capacity as surrogate medical officer, had raided the medicine chest to find one of the little ampoules of morphine, supplied with its own needle, which were available in case a member of the crew was severely wounded.

The young Alistair Lethbridge-Stewart, only thirteen years old, had crept into his grandmother's bedroom just after she died, despite having been forbidden to go anywhere near her. She'd been lying on her back, her face collapsed and sallow, her toothless mouth gaping wide. No way was she the dearly loved Granny McDougal who'd kissed him goodnight only the day before.

If it wasn't for his stertorous breathing, like the snoring of some sort of animal, the Brigadier would have said Brother Alex was as clearly dead as she had been. Nothing was going to stir him for some time, if ever.

The Skipper's reaction to his midshipman's discovery of the description of their destination was categorical.

'That's it, then,' he'd said when Pete Andrews had taken the bad news to his cabin. 'I've no intention of sailing nearly two and a half thousand miles in the wrong direction, just to turn round and sail back again, on the say-so of some sort of phoney sw... swami in a white nightie. The sooner we're back in Blighty and rid of this old tub the better, as far as I'm concerned. 'S time we all rejoined the real Navy. Back to Bombay!'

And he personally turned back to the gin bottle.

'Heaven preserve me from arrogant fools!' said the Doctor in an undertone to the Brigadier, when Pete arrived back on the bridge with the news. 'Doesn't he realise that this is the only lead we've got? Wasn't he listening when I told him that the very survival of the human race was at stake?'

'Starboard ten...'

'Starboard ten, sir... Ten of starboard wheel on, sir.'

The Brigadier gave a worried glance over at the First Lieutenant, who had just given the order to the quartermaster to turn the ship. The Commanding Officer was the only one of the crew who had been told the whole story.

'Not to worry, Doctor,' he said quietly. 'Leave it to me. I'll soon settle the the young clot's hash!'

'May I remind you, Lieutenant-Commander Hogben, that as a brigadier I outrank you by a considerable margin. Even a four-ring captain would only be the equivalent of a colonel. Or am I wrong?'

'And may I remind you, Brigadier, that as... as Commanding Officer of this ship, I have abso... absolute authority over it and everybody on board. And that includes you, sir.'

Only the occasional hesitation served to confirm the Brigadier's diagnosis that Hogben would have been neck and neck in a drinking competition with an alcoholic newt.

He tried again. 'What were your orders from London?'

'To put myself at the dis... disposal of the United Nations Intelligence Taskforce in all respects.'

'That's what I understood. You are proposing to disobey those orders?' The anger in the Brigadier's voice hung in the air.

There was a long pause.

'This is getting out of hand,' said Hogben. 'Sit down, Brigadier. Have a drink...'

For a moment, the Brigadier was tempted to give the young fool the benefit of his long experience in taming cocky young subalterns who felt they could get away with anything short of murder. But then... there was more than one way to skin a hare, as his dad used to say. And he could do with a dram.

'A wee one, I said,' he protested as Hogben poured out nearly half a tumbler of Scotch.

Hogben took a sip of his equally full tumbler of gin. He had seemed to be sobering up, thought the Brigadier. It wouldn't last long if he drank that lot.

The CO took another sip before he spoke. 'I don't think you quite realise how much power the skipper of any vessel has – let alone a Royal Navy ship.'

'I certainly...'

The CO held up his hand to stop the Brigadier. 'There's a story we were told in our last year at Dartmouth on this very point. The evacuation of Crete during the war...'

Now the Brigadier started to listen. He'd been amongst the first troops ashore when Crete was later retaken.

'There was a midshipman who'd been given the job of ferrying troops – in a small landing craft. Taking them to Egypt. He had on board as many as he thought he could safely manage – as you can imagine, they were queuing up like Saturday night at the Odeon, but the sea was getting nasty. And as he was about to slip, a major-general arrived and demanded to be taken too.'

You could see what was coming.

'Yes, the midshipman refused. Even when the general ordered him, he still wouldn't let him aboard. The day after he got to Egypt, he had a signal to report to the commander-in-chief's cabin. When he got there, there was the general.

'The admiral asked him if the story was true. And he said it was. And do you know what the admiral said? "Well done." That's what he said. He said, "I'm glad to know that my officers know how to do their duty..."'

There was another long pause.

'I take your point,' said the Brigadier, quietly. 'So you think the ship is in danger.'

'Well...'

'And you'll be willing to defend your action? For make no mistake, I shall see that you face a court martial.' He picked up his whisky. 'Cheers,' he said.

The Doctor and Bob Simkins were discussing the effect the deep ocean ridges near the island might have on tidal currents, with Sarah a rather bemused listener. Every head turned as the door burst open and in came Lieutenant-Commander Eugene Hogben, followed by the Brigadier.

The Doctor raised his eyebrows in a mute question. The Brigadier gave a little nod and a satisfied twitch of a smile.

The Commanding Officer of HMS *Hallaton* looked at the steering compass to check the course. He gave the First Lieutenant a furtive glance. He turned to the helmsman.

'Port ten,' he said.

Just after 3.30 in the afternoon, Whitbread came to his senses. A seaman who doubled as the Captain's steward – 'Blackie' Blackmore by name – had been put on Alex watch, and promptly fetched the Brigadier.

But when he was confronted with the description in the pilot book, Alex insisted that the book was wrong.

'Why the devil should I get you to take me to a place like that?' he said. 'Use the little intelligence the Almighty blessed you with. Just you wait and see. I tell you, you're going to find a paradise.' And he gave a feeble parody of a laugh. Then his face changed. 'Are you going to give me some food? Or would it be more convenient if I were to starve to death?'

They had just over two thousand nautical miles to go. That was just about two thousand three hundred common-or-garden land miles, Sarah worked out. If they went at the *Hallaton*'s maximum speed, which Pete Andrews had told her was seventeen knots, they would be there in five days.

'Sorry, love,' he said, when she produced this magnificently nautical calculation at the dinner table in the wardroom that night. 'The Old Man has insisted on our going at the normal cruising speed.'

At the moment the CO was on the bridge as Officer of the Watch, with Chris as his sidekick.

'And what is the normal cruising speed?' asked the Brigadier. He pushed aside, unfinished, his plate of sausage and mash (with a thick onion gravy that had an odd but familiar taste that Sarah couldn't place).

'Pretty slow, I'm afraid. Twelve knots. He's right in a way. It's only a couple of days more, when all's said and done. No point in thrashing the engines if we're not in any hurry.'

Sarah glanced across the table. Surely it was time for the Number One to be told the whole story? But the Doctor seemed more interested in his food.

'You have a Chinese cook, I take it,' he said.

Of course! Sarah recognised the flavour now. She had a quick flash of her favourite Chinese restaurant in Shaftesbury Avenue.

'Why yes,' said a surprised Bob, who had polished off his own bangers already. 'I signed him up in Hong Kong, just for the voyage home. I'm victualling officer, you see. We'd have ended up with one of the stokers otherwise.'

Pete turned back to the Brigadier. 'In any case, in the long run, it saves us time to travel more slowly. Gene wanted to stop off at Diego Garcia to refuel. But I pointed out that if we're going at the engines' economical speed, we'll have plenty. They put in extra tanks when she was building, you see, because of the OPEC oil crisis. He was obviously quite chocker about it. Looking forward to a run ashore, I suppose.'

Chocker. Sarah knew that one. Sailor talk for fed-up.

The Brigadier gave one of his grunts. 'Wanted to top up his supply of gin, I expect,' he said.

The Doctor raised an eyebrow, and the two officers turned their eyes firmly to their plates.

But had Sarah caught a tiny glance from Pete Andrews, and an even tinier wink?

Sarah decided to make the most of it. Her little cabin was quite luxurious, with a wide and comfortable bunk. The millpond sea and the sky were both a deep and heavenly blue. There was a shelf-full of thrillers in the wardroom, there was a well-stocked drinks cupboard (they'd agreed to pay their way, but it was duty-free after all), and she'd remembered to bring her costume and a bottle of sun-lotion for tanning purposes. Apart from a swimming pool and an on-board casino, there were all the ingredients of a luxury cruise. And she could justify her self-indulgence by writing up her notes and taking some shots of the ship.

The next morning, bikini-clad, she found herself accepting a hand-up from Able-Seaman 'Ginger' Gorleston from Norwich (who couldn't believe his luck) onto the top of a locker on the quarterdeck. From this vantage point, she could get a smashing shot of the Brigadier standing in the stern, staring moodily at the wake streaming out in a straight line to the northern horizon.

Never mind the flipping Skang lot. She was going to enjoy herself. She'd got a whole week.

But the weather had other ideas.

The first sign of trouble ahead came at breakfast-time the

next day. When she walked down the corridor (which the sailors strangely called a 'flat') towards the wardroom to get her breakfast, Sarah felt the odd sensation of being off-balance on a floor that, to the eye, was perfectly stable and horizontal, and a queasiness behind her eyes.

The wardroom was empty except for the plump figure of Chris.

'Morning, morning,' said he cheerfully but indistinctly, his mouth being somewhat full. 'Blowing up a bit, isn't it?'

Following a forced diagonal course to the table, she grabbed a chair and just managed to sit down before she fell over.

'Yeah,' said Chris, watching her, 'she's a right bitch in any sort of sea. You'll get used to it. Remember, one hand for the ship and one for yourself.'

Now that Sarah could see out, it was clear that the ship was rolling quite noticeably. The horizon was invisible, being masked by considerable waves that swooped out of sight to be replaced by an ominous sky, only to reappear a moment later.

'It's a real gale, isn't it?' she said, as the steward – a young seaman by the name of Miller, who'd volunteered for the job (so Sarah had gathered) largely to get out of weather like today's – appeared in the doorway and ducked out of sight when he saw her.

'Half a gale, perhaps,' said Chris.

She averted her eyes as he wiped the remains of his fried egg onto a large piece of fatty bacon.

'About a force seven, I reckon. You wait till it gets to nine!'

No, thanks. Seven would do very nicely, thank you.

With some difficulty, she poured herself three-quarters of a cup of coffee – all she could manage, the way it sloshed around – and kept her eyes down as Chris plastered a large dollop of marmalade on his last bit of fried bread.

'There you are, miss,' said Miller, plonking a full plate in front of her. 'You'll soon feel better once you get that down you.'

What was he talking about? She was an experienced sailor, wasn't she? Though the choppy lurches of a small sailing dinghy were vastly different from this. To start with, they never left your stomach behind, halfway to the ceiling... correction, halfway to the deck-head. It might not have been so bad if it had been a regular motion, but there seemed to be all sorts of extras superimposed on the main swinging roll.

She looked at the greasy fry-up, picked up her knife and fork, put them down again and said carefully, 'I think...'

What she thought Chris was never to know, for she stood up suddenly, saying 'Excuse me...' and lurched out of the room with her hand clapped over her mouth.

CHAPTER TWELVE

'Isn't this magnificent?'

The Doctor was jammed into the corner of the port wing of the bridge, his usually impeccable hair streaming in the wind, and his cloak flapping behind him like a giant wing, as if he was about to take off.

The Brigadier let the door slam behind him, and grabbed a safe hold. 'I'm glad you think so,' he shouted. 'I'm just thankful that my father was a colonel, not an admiral.'

His words were blown away like the spume from the crest of a breaking wave.

The Doctor had long since abandoned his post at the stem of the ship. Not only had his friends the dolphins vanished at the first sign of a rising sea, but also the *Hallaton* kept burying her nose and most of her foredeck in the oncoming waves, as she pitched and yawed with the eighty-knot squalls that were bringing what was by now a force ten gale that much nearer to a real storm.

'Listen,' shouted the Brigadier. 'It's the CO...'

'What's up? Is he in liquor again?' Although he hardly seemed to raise it, the Doctor's precise voice could be clearly heard above the howling of the wind.

'Didn't seem to be. Probably why he's been in such a filthy mood. I could hear him from my cabin. Bawling out Pete Andrews, as far as I could gather. No, it's not that. He's turned back. I checked the compass. And when I tried to tackle him about it, the wretched man just ignored me. He's sailing 020 degrees, not far off due north.'

The Doctor gave the Brigadier an exasperated glance. 'Well, of course he is, with a wind of this strength coming from the nor'nor'east and getting worse all the time. Much too dangerous to go with the wind. Even a ship this size could easily broach to, and founder...'

'Broach to? What are you talking about?'

But the Doctor wasn't listening. 'Look! Look!' he was crying, and pointing up into the scudding clouds.

What was he on about now? Nothing up there. Oh yes... some bird or other.

'It's an albatross! A big 'un too. That wingspan must be twelve feet if it's an inch. What's he doing in these latitudes?'

Not for the first time, the Brigadier was baffled by the Doctor. Having said that humanity was in the gravest danger, he seemed to have given up.

'Stop worrying, Lethbridge-Stewart!' The Doctor suddenly turned, almost as if he'd read his mind. 'We'll get there in the end – or we shan't. We'll save your extraordinary species – or they'll be wiped out. There's nothing we can do about it at the moment, is there?'

He just didn't react like any normal human being – but then again that's just what he wasn't, was he?

Sarah had managed to get to her cabin, where she sat down heavily on the bunk. But that made her feel worse. With each roll of the ship, she could feel her bum rising in the air as if she was becoming as weightless as she would in a spaceship; and then, before she actually took off, she was thrust back down, with her guts following a few seconds later. The result was inevitable.

With frequent visits to the washbasin, which was nearer than the loo, she eventually came to the point where she was heaving and retching, with no result.

When this subsided, she delicately hoisted herself onto the bunk and lay back. If she'd been on a normal Royal Navy ship, she'd have been fine. But the luxury of a bunk very nearly as wide as her divan in Hampstead meant that she kept rolling from side to side with the motion of the ship. It was worse than trying to stay upright.

What was she doing there? Investigative journalist? That was a laugh. At this precise moment she'd have swapped all her hopes of fame and fortune for the comfortable stability of a supermarket checkout, or a nice gentle job sweeping the roads.

There was a knock at the door.

Bob Simkins appeared. 'Chris told me that you weren't feeling quite the thing. You okay?'

She grabbed the edge of the bunk and lifted her head. 'Just bring me a slug of arsenic and I'll be fine,' she said. 'Oh, sugar!' she cried, as the *Hallaton* took a violent swing to starboard and she cracked her head on the wall as she went with it. She struggled to sit up. But now that felt even worse.

'Hang on,' said Bob, 'I'll soon sort you out.'

He disappeared, and within a couple of minutes was back with a largish green suitcase.

'Here you are,' he said. 'Move over in the bed.' And he jammed her into the pit of the bunk with the case, so that she couldn't roll even if she wanted to.

And at last she was able to relax.

In spite of the fact that all he'd been offered was a large bowl of noodle soup, Alex Whitbread was beginning to feel better. Of course, he couldn't expect complete recovery until the group had accepted him back. But he felt sure that, with a little bit of luck, he'd be able to convince Mother Hilda of his repentance. She was clever enough to see through most of his ploys, yes, but she was stupidly trusting, seeing the best in everybody and everything. And if he could just con *her*, the rest of them would follow like a flock of sheep through a hole in the fence.

There was just one thing...

He put a tentative foot out of bed and hauled himself to his feet, swayed, and abruptly sat down. Not only was the floor itself all a-tilt, his legs were still pretty weak.

Not ready yet then.

That was his first job, then: to get enough strength back to be able to deal with the kid from the magazine. He'd felt sure that she couldn't have seen anything she shouldn't have; as he'd told Hilda, when he'd got in through the window of her room in Hampstead, it had seemed that he'd found absolute proof of that just waiting for him on the table.

But, if that was the case, what was she doing here? Why had she come all the way to Bombay, and brought these two snoops with her? Who were they? Were they police? What was this ship he was on?

And what if she were to realise the true meaning of what she had seen? If she did, and if Mother Hilda were to talk to her, it would be the end for him.

He must make sure that she never reached the island...

Sarah found that, unaccountably, the very fact that she was tightly wedged into a position that made her one with the movement of the ship took away the ghastly nausea that came from the conflicting messages of her body. As long as she kept her eyes shut, held in the cradle of the bunk and Bob's suitcase she was able to sink into a comatose semi-trance, and eventually into a deep dreamless sleep.

And, miracle of miracles, when she woke up – it was mid-afternoon, just after 3.30 – she not only felt quite better, but ravenously hungry, and eager to experience for herself what a real full gale felt like. She wasn't likely to get another chance. Food could wait.

She was beginning to get her sealegs too. Though the motion of the ship was just as extreme, it seemed to her to have lost its violence, and was more regular, more predictable.

After all, she thought as she clambered up the ladder on her way to the upper deck, even Nelson used to be seasick when he went back to sea after a spell at home. Sammy would have been proud of her. She was a real sailor after all.

When she poked her nose out of the door onto the deck, she realised why it felt so different. The howling gale had gone. There was now no more than a strong breeze; and the waves had settled into a deep rolling swell, which the *Hallaton* was punching through almost as if she was enjoying herself in the fitful sunlight. True, when she was in the trough, the tops were as high as the bridge, or even higher; and her bow was still alternately plunging into the water and pointing at the still turbulent sky. But at least she wasn't rolling from side to side and staggering like a comedy drunk any more.

But the waves! As you rose to the top you could see them stretched in regular ranks far out to the horizon, and every one different and constantly changing, like a mobile work of art sculpted by a giant hand.

This was something like it! Clorinda would give her a double-page spread for shots like this.

Off she went to get her camera.

'Take over, Number One. And try to keep the bloody ship steady, will you? Can you manage that, do you think? I'm going to get my head down. Give me a shake if there's any change.'

Well, that's got rid of him for a bit, thought the Brigadier as the door closed behind Eugene Hogben. For this relief, much thanks... Granny McDougal was always quoting Shakespeare. *Macbeth*, wasn't it? Or *Hamlet*. One of those.

He looked doubtfully over at Pete Andrews. He was standing by the helmsman (who was still the grizzled Petty Officer Hardy, the veteran cox'n who had piloted them through the storm). He was staring grimly ahead, and showed no signs of turning the ship back onto the southbound course that would take them to Stella Island. Should he say something?

He glanced at the door to the port wing of the bridge. The Doctor was still out there – hadn't come in for hours. Perhaps he could persuade him to come and have a go.

On the other hand, he'd got short shrift from him when he'd suggested it earlier.

'Er... Is there any chance of our getting back on course?' he asked.

Andrews turned and looked at him, angry and preoccupied. 'I'm sorry?'

'I was just asking about the way we're heading. I mean, now that the gale is over...'

Andrews' face cleared, and he became, again, the amiable teddy-bear of a man they'd all come to respect. 'Forgive me, sir. The last few hours have been a little stressful, to say the least. No, I'm afraid we'll have to wait a while. It's not just the wind, you see. With a swell like this, it still wouldn't be safe.'

Ah! 'You mean we might... er... broach to?'

The First Lieutenant looked surprised. 'Precisely,' he said.

'Yes, well... What does that mean exactly?' It was hardly the sort of thing they taught at Sandhurst, for God's sake!

Petty Officer Hardy took his eyes off the gyro-repeater compass for a moment, and started to speak, 'Well, it's like this... Oh sorry, sir.'

But the First Lieutenant didn't seem to mind his interruption. 'No, no, Cox'n. You've had far more experience of this sort of thing than I have. I've spent most of my short career pootling round Hong Kong.'

The Brigadier was still irritated with himself for his lack of knowledge. 'Heard the expression, of course. But I've never quite...' He heard himself clearing his throat in a sort of '*Harrumph*!' Good God! He was turning into a real Colonel Blimp!

'Yeah, right,' said the Cox'n, keeping his eye on the compass, and automatically turning the wheel to keep them on course. 'Well now, as you know, to keep the rudder working you've got to be moving through the water. Have to have *way on*. But the trouble is, if you're going in the same direction as waves of any size, you lose way.

'If you try to go at the same speed, like surfing, then the rudder has no grip at all – and if you try to go faster or slower, you're on a sort of moving switchback. You're either slipping down the front of the wave, and speeding up, or sliding down the back, and slowing down.'

So you lose control. Of course.

'So you lose control?' the Brigadier said aloud.

'You got it, sir. There's always a time when the helm doesn't answer at all – and the ship can swing round broadside on to the waves. And when that happens, if she happens to be rolling in the same direction as the waves...'

'She can roll right over!'

'Right. And it's too late to say your prayers then.'

So that was 'broaching to'. Fair enough. As long as they knew what they were doing. But they were never going to get to the blasted island at this rate!

Brother Alex woke up feeling even better. One advantage of a high metabolic rate, he thought. He'd been well known for his drive even before, when he was in public life; like Winnie, he could get by on four hours' sleep a night. And since he'd left politics, he'd benefited from the extraordinary access of energy, of sheer vigour, that went with becoming one of the Skang 'teachers'.

He had no intention of losing that permanently. If he couldn't get it back, along with all the rest of it, life had no meaning, no savour, no worth.

So what to do?

After all, he was there officially, albeit on sufferance. If he got to know these people, he might be able find out what their game was. But his most important job was dealing with the Smith girl. ASAP. Get to know the layout of the vessel. That was the thing to do. And the movements of the girl. Sooner or later, he'd get her alone.

And his immediate problem would be solved.

CHAPTER THIRTEEN

Over all the years of the Doctor's jaunts through time and space, seeking the ultimate experience that he knew in his heart could never be found, it had become a joke, saying to those around him, '...there's nothing we can do – but wait'.

He'd taught himself the art of waiting: the wide-open acceptance of every perception, which took him to a timeless place of satisfaction where he vanished into the ever-changing immediacy and sharp reality of a totally experienced world.

The hours of the storm could have lasted a day or a minute. There was nobody keeping an eye on the clock.

Yet the very alertness that informed his awareness could, if necessary, instantly bring him back to the inexorable flow of one damn thing after another (as he put it when trying to describe it later to a bemused Brigadier). And the sight of Sarah Jane Smith, hanging on with one hand to the lines of one of the ship's boats in its davits, while she leaned out over the boiling sea, was enough to snap him back in an instant.

'Sarah! For Pete's sake! What do you think you're doing?'

'It's all right, Doctor!' she called, waving her little camera in the air. 'Look, one hand for me and one for the ship!'

There was nothing he could do but watch as she clambered into ever more precarious positions, reaching out for the perfect shot.

At last she was satisfied, and carefully manoeuvred herself back onto the deck. With a cheery wave, she vanished round the corner.

She was an adult, after all; and she seemed to know what she was doing. With a mental shrug, the Doctor settled back into his corner, noticing that, in spite of his cloak, he was very nearly as wet as if he had been swimming fully dressed; and he examined with interest the clammy touch of his shirt on the skin of his back.

Sarah on the lifeboat no longer existed, at that moment; not even as a memory.

It was pure luck that the girl was going down the corridor just when Alex had made the – surprisingly small – effort to get into his clothes and set off on his first recce. He heard the footsteps coming round the corner and was just in time to pull himself back through the door, leaving a crack to peep through.

At the sight of her, camera in hand, stepping out in that cocky, superior way she had, his guts convulsed with hate. It was her fault, her and her bloody camera, that he was in this mess; her fault that Hilda had turned against him; her fault that he'd lost everything that had made his life worth living, after he'd had to abandon any hope of reaching the top in politics.

This might be his chance. He looked round the cabin. There seemed to be nothing that he could use as a weapon.

But then he saw it: the simple, heavy wooden chair by the dressing table. In a moment, it was upended, his grip tightened around the base of one of the legs, and with a twist to break the brittle glue, and a wrench to free it from the joints, he was supplied with a club as deadly as any baseball bat.

Thank God he'd recovered his strength.

Hefting it in his hand, he cautiously followed the girl out onto the deck, being careful to keep out of sight.

Maybe he'd lost her. No! There she was, on the lifeboat.

At first it seemed that she was determined to keep within sight of the figure on the bridge, the one they called the Doctor.

But at last she climbed back onto the deck, and came towards him. He drew back into the shadow of a large ventilator and froze into the rapt stillness of a cat waiting for the moment to pounce, pressing himself against the ventilator to keep himself stationary as the ship swung up and down with the waves.

He watched, only his eyes moving, as she crossed the deck, pausing every so often to take a shot. If only...

Yes... she was coming closer, working her way down the guard rail, leaning out to find the shot she wanted.

And then she stopped not ten feet away, just out of sight of the bridge, with her back to him, snapping away as if she'd found the ideal position at last.

He took a step forward and froze again, as the ship sank into the trough of a wave.

There was no sign that she'd noticed him.

One more step... Wait for the pause at the top of the rise... Now!

He should have crept nearer to her. As he rushed forward, his makeshift club aloft, she heard the movement and turned.

And screamed.

The scream was cut short as the chair-leg marginally connected with the side of her skull. All in a moment, before she could slip to the deck, he grabbed her by the legs and tipped her over the guard rail.

He turned to flee, but there on the deck was the cursed camera. Picking it up, he hurled it viciously after her.

The job was done.

Alistair Lethbridge-Stewart had always been impatient. Being an only child, with a hefty pair of lungs, and a mother (and later a substitute mother in the shape of Granny McDougal) who couldn't deny him a thing, he'd soon learnt that his widower father, with the bark of a rottweiler, had the bite of a miniature poodle. It was school, and Sandhurst (public school writ large), that taught him that instant gratification was the privilege of the spoilt toddler.

But that didn't make him feel any better inside. Tucked out

of the way in a corner of the bridge house, peering through one of the spinning discs of glass that did duty in lieu of wind-screen wipers, he felt that the entire world was conspiring to thwart him.

The waves looked as big as ever, which seemed not only illogical but unfair – as the wind had by now dropped almost completely.

'We'll give it another hour or so,' said Pete Andrews. 'The swell's easing quite fast.'

You could have fooled him. It still felt more like a scenic rail-way than the bridge of one of Her Britannic Majesty's ships.

Bob Simkins was busy at his chart table as he tried to get some idea of how much they'd been swept off course, keeping a weather eye on the radar, to make sure there was nothing to collide with. Only half listening to himself, he'd explained that the waves were now 'a heavy swell', rather than 'a sea'.

But that was just playing with words, for God's sake. What difference did it make? It was the feeling of utter helplessness, that there was nothing he could do that...

The door of the port wing slammed open.

'Man overboard! It's Sarah!'

What!

'Where away?' sang out the Cox'n.

'Port side,' came the Doctor's voice.

Even before the First Lieutenant could give an order, the Cox'n was spinning the wheel to port, to swing the stern with its murderous screws away to starboard.

But by now the Brigadier was through the door, to find that the Doctor had flung off his cloak, and pulled off his boots, and was climbing up as if to dive into the water.

'What the devil?' cried the Brigadier, clinging onto the door jamb as the ship came broadside onto the swell, and rolled alarmingly to starboard.

'Look!'

As the ship came to the crest of the wave and started to recover, Sarah's body could be seen briefly on the next wave to the south.

She was face down in the water.

The Doctor didn't dive in. As the ship rolled to port, on the downhill side of the wave, he held his nose like a seven-year-old jumping off the side of the swimming bath and plunged feet first some thirty feet into the sea.

'Bob! Get a scrambling net rigged.'

'Aye aye sir. Which side?'

'Port. No, better make it both sides.'

The Navigating Officer shot off to see to it.

A scrambling net. The meaning of the term was self evident. But couldn't they lower a boat? It had been quite obvious that there was no point in hurling a life buoy after the pair in the water, but surely... 'What about a boat?' the Brigadier asked.

'Negative. No visibility so low in the water. At least we've a chance of spotting them from up here.'

Pete grabbed a pair of binoculars and vanished onto the wing of the bridge. The Brigadier tried to follow him, but the roll of the ship was so extreme that he lost his footing completely and landed on the deck.

When he regained his feet, he clung onto the ledge at the front and tried to see through the glass. He'd soon lost sight of the Doctor, swimming away from the ship with the confident strong strokes of an Olympic gold medallist. How old had he said he was? Four hundred years? Seven hundred? But how could anybody survive in these conditions?

The Cox'n's careful explanation of the danger of travelling with the waves had become fearsomely real. When the *Hallaton* was going precisely in the same direction as the swell, the rudder had no effect at all. But then, as her bow swung, it began to bite, and the Petty Officer spun the wheel hard over in the opposite direction, in an attempt to bring her back on course before she reached the critical point of utmost danger; and then he had to spin it back again, so that he wouldn't bring her round too far and let her roll over the other way.

The sum total was a series of near-fatal swoops and rolls, saved at the last moment, it seemed, by the hard-won skill of the man at the wheel.

'Okay, Cox'n?' Pete Andrews had reappeared, and was scanning ahead through his glasses.

'All right so far, sir, as the man said when he fell off the Blackpool tower.'

At least the Royal Navy lot seemed to know what they were doing, thought the Brigadier grudgingly.

'The trouble is that with our turning circle they'll have been swept quite a way off by now. Can't twizzle round like Margot Fonteyn. It takes time,' said Pete, who seemed as calm and in control as the Petty Officer. 'Haven't had a sight of them yet,' he went on. 'But it's early days. The theory is that if we keep on the reciprocal course, two hundred degrees – sou'sou'west near as dammit – we're bound to come across them. But in this weather...'

As if to confirm his thought, the *Hallaton* heeled over so violently that even he staggered and had to catch hold to save himself.

'Cox'n...'

'Sir?'

'I'm going up top. Get a better view from there.'

'Aye aye sir.'

Pete made his way towards the door in the corner. The Brigadier knew that this led to the deck above, which was a de facto additional bridge, open to the sky.

'Who give... who was't give th'order to change course?'

Lieutenant-Commander Eugene Hogben, whose eyes seemed to be as out-of-focus as his words, stood in the doorway, clinging onto the handle for a precarious swaying support.

Pete Andrews turned at the bottom of the ladder. 'I did sir. You see...'

'And why have you dis... dis'beyed a direct order, may I ask? Only asking.'

'Man overboard, sir. Or rather, two of them...'

'Who?'

'The Doctor and Miss Smith.'

'And you think you can pick 'em up? In a sea like this? You must be bloody joking, mate.'

'I thought...'

'Yes, well, stop thinking and start... start doing what you're told. Start 'beying bloody orders, right? Try this one for size. Resume...'

Before he could finish speaking another particularly severe lurch brought the Commanding Officer to his knees. Pete hurried over and helped him to his feet.

'Sir, don't you think it would be a good idea if...'

This brought out the CO's latent rage, which had been simmering below the surface, the blind anger of the alcoholic, disappointed and frustrated by the unjustness of life.

'Take your hands off me!' he said harshly. 'Or I'll have you for 'ssaulting a superi... sup... your commanding officer!'

Pete Andrews released his arm, and stood back, his face white with fury.

Hogben gave him a vicious look. 'I'll 'tend to you later,' he said. 'Cox'n!'

'Yessir?'

'Port ten!'

'Port ten, sir... Ten of port wheel on.'

'Very good. Bring her round and steer 020.' He turned back to his First Lieutenant. 'Is't my fault if they're fool enough to fall in?' he said.

CHAPTER FOURTEEN

Much later, Sarah would look back and wonder why she didn't actually say, 'Where am I?' when she came round. Perhaps it was the journalist in her – the years of trying to avoid clichés – that stopped her voicing what would have been an absolutely accurate expression of her feelings.

To wake up, lying back luxuriating in a moving bath, with a hand behind her head supporting her (with one finger pressing hard on the top of her spine), became doubly mysterious when she realised that the hand belonged to the Doctor. Then to be held firmly as the dreamy contentment gave way to a spluttering, choking, vomiting that sent salt water up her nose and, it seemed, into her very brain was no way to discover that she'd fallen into something like two hundred fathoms of Indian Ocean.

For a moment, she panicked, and clung to her rescuer with a grip the Doctor could hardly free himself from.

'Gently, gently,' said the Doctor, as he loosened her fingers.

'I'm sorry,' she gasped, 'but I can't swim. I mean, only a bit.'

'You're quite safe. I have positive buoyancy, you see. Think of me as one of those big blow-up spotted horses you see at the seaside.'

The image was so ludicrous that, even though she couldn't summon up a giggle, she was able to relax a little, and hang onto his shirt. It was then, as the sea carried them up towards the sky, that she saw the ship way off in the distance, and nearly freaked out again.

'They're miles away!' she said. 'How will they ever find us? What are we going to do?'

'There's nothing we can do, but wait,' said the Doctor, with a little smile; and this time she did giggle.

'What happened? Did you slip? I heard you scream and saw you falling.'

Yes, what had happened? She remembered waving to the Doctor... and then...'I don't know. It's just a blank.'

'I thought as much. Concussion. You must have hit your head as you fell.'

What did she remember? Oh yes. She remembered clinging onto the falls of the lifeboat, and - yes, leaning right out over the sea! She must have been bonkers!

'Oh, Doctor, I'm so sorry,' she said. 'It's my fault we're in this mess. I was all hyped up with... with the look of the waves, and...' Her voice trailed away.

'I know. I'd spent several hours just watching them myself. Immersed in them, you might say. But I didn't expect to be immersed quite so literally.'

He could always find a joke, even at the worst of times.

Down they went into the trough, and up again, twenty feet or more - and this time, the ship was nearer, much nearer!

'I told you. Don't worry, they'll find us. All we have to do is...'

'I know, wait!'

The water was fairly warm, in spite of the storm. It was lucky they were in the tropics, the Doctor said. If they'd been off Murmansk, they'd have been dead long ago.

He kept talking, taking her mind off the terrible situation they were in. He told her of his days at the Academy on Gallifrey, and the pet flubble he'd kept hidden under the bed in his first year, just so he'd have something to talk to - 'A flubble? It's a bit like a koala, I suppose, only with a smaller nose - and six legs' - and how he was nearly caught when his pet came on heat and started singing her mating song.

He told her about his friends, and the time they put their teacher (who deserved it) into a time loop, so that he relived the same lesson over and over for a whole day, while they whooped it up in the city.

He explained how it was that he was able to stand in for an inflatable beach toy. 'Two hearts wouldn't be much use without the respiratory system to go with them, now would they? And there wouldn't be room for a second set of lungs. So we have an ancillary pulmonary system which can open up as necessary – channels parallel to the lymphatic circulation. And that's what makes us buoyant. You might say that we're full of wind and... Well, perhaps not.'

Her burst of laughter suddenly stopped at the top of a wave as she caught a glimpse of the ship. 'Doctor! It's going away! They're leaving us!'

'Never!'

But they were. On the next rise they saw it clearly. The *Hallaton* was half the size she had been when they'd last looked.

That was when it started to get dark.

The Brigadier's mind was seething with anger – and with indecision. It had always seemed to him that as a defence 'But I was only obeying orders' was pretty dicey – not only when used by somebody guilty of horrendous war-crimes, but even when it was an excuse for not facing up to a difficult choice, like the one that faced Pete Andrews now. Equally well, it had to be admitted that he was in an impossible position.

On the one hand, the Skipper was as drunk as a skunk. There was no question of that. He really wasn't fit to take such a decision, a decision that would mean two lives being lost.

On the other hand, he had the law on his side – not only Admiralty regulations but the immemorial law of the sea, which made the Captain of a ship an absolute monarch. There was now no question, to turn back would endanger the ship.

Hogben had earlier been threatened with court martial; and he'd crumbled. If Pete Andrews were to take command, he would inevitably face one himself, and that could mean the end of his career.

The Brigadier looked again at the CO, perched on the high stool that took the weight off the legs, but enabled the Officer of the Watch to see out. He was swaying with the ship, and his eyes were closing as his head nodded forward. If he passed out completely, then presumably the choice would be out of Andrews' hands. He'd have to take command.

The First Lieutenant was standing alone at the far end of the bridge, lost in his own thoughts. What about the other officers? Bob and Chris were huddled over the chart, whispering together. It wouldn't be fair to involve them in this.

Right. There was only one thing to do. And the sooner the better. No way was he going to let his friends be drowned on the whim of an arrogant fool sodden with gin. He crossed behind the Cox'n, near enough to the Captain to be heard without the rest of the bridge hearing.

'Excuse me...' he said.

Hogben half woke up, and looked at him as if he'd never been introduced. 'Wha'?'

A glance round. Nobody could hear him. He went really close. 'Now, listen to me. I wouldn't want you to misunderstand me. If you don't turn back... if you don't do your damnedest to rescue those two, you'll regret it until the day they bury you. Never mind a court martial, I'll make sure that the story is headlined in every newspaper in the land. You'll be finished. For good. Do you understand?'

Hogben blinked at him blearily.

'Do you understand?!'

Hogben smiled and licked his lips. 'Get knotted,' he said.

The Brigadier nodded. He'd expected some such reaction. Right! In for a penny... Though of course he'd lay odds that the man wouldn't remember a thing in the morning.

'Sorry about this,' he said, with a glance round. Good. Nobody was looking his way.

Taking hold of the CO's collar, he hoisted him to his feet, and delivered the short jab uppercut that had won him the Public Schools Middleweight Cup in his last year at Fettes.

'Dear me,' he said loudly as Hogben's legs gave way, and the Cox'n hastily averted his gaze. 'He seems to have passed out.'

'Are we going to die?'

The Doctor didn't answer straight away. 'It's possible,' he said.

Sarah thought she'd long since come to terms with the knowledge that one day her life would inevitably come to an end. Like others who have had a near-death experience, she knew that there was nothing to fear. But she had taken it for granted that she'd have something like another fifty or sixty years before she had to take the idea seriously.

Was she really going to end her life here, in the middle of the ocean?

As night fell, the waves had taken the hint and settled down. It was over an hour now since sunset. There was still a considerable swell, but at least they were cradled in a relatively gentle rhythm that was very different from being hurtled up and down twenty feet at a time.

At first, the darkness made their predicament seem all the more frightening. But then the moon, enormous on the horizon, showed her familiar face. It was impossible not to feel comforted.

'I didn't know there were so many stars!'

The sky was now quite clear, the velvet depths of its blackness studded with a myriad of jewels.

The Doctor looked up. 'Yes, it's quite a sight, isn't it. But you know, you can only see a few thousand. You see the Milky Way?'

Yes, there it was, the splash of light across the sky behind the stars. You could never see it properly in London, because of all the street lights.

'We're looking into the heart of our galaxy. Billions of stars, too far away to make out. And there are billions of galaxies in the universe. And for all we know billions of universes.'

He paused for a moment.

'I wonder why we all think we're so important,' he said.

'Do you hear there? Do you hear there? Able Seaman Blackmore to the bridge. Able Seaman Blackmore. At the double.'

Bob Simkins' voice echoed throughout the decks, the flats and the cabins.

By the time the Captain's steward had arrived and – with the signalman, Bert Rogers, to help – had carted the Commanding Officer back to his cabin, the First Lieutenant had given the order, and HMS *Hallaton* was back doing her uncertain dance towards the south-south-west.

By now it was almost completely dark.

'We have three searchlights,' said Pete to the Brigadier. 'We'll rig all three on the upper bridge, and have every spare man on lookout up there. You may care to join them. I shall have to stay with the ship. But I must be honest, sir. The likelihood of our finding them now is just about nil. The current and the waves have been carrying them away from us, so that we have to catch them up. There's no hope of accurately retracing our steps. And even if we did, we could pass them within twenty yards and not see them.'

This was the last thing the Brigadier wanted to hear. Had he risked court martial for himself and Andrews for nothing?

No! If they weren't to try, the thought that Sarah and the Doctor were somewhere out there, and that this was their only hope, would be unbearable.

* * *

It was starting to get colder. Sarah's feet seemed to have disappeared, and the lack of feeling in her fingers made her grip on the Doctor's shirt more and more difficult to keep up.

'Doctor,' she said quietly, 'I'm scared. Really scared. I don't think I can hold on much longer, and I think I nearly fell asleep just now.'

It was quite a while since he'd stopped trying to jolly her along. He put his arm around her. To comfort her or to hold her up? Was she shivering or was she shaking with fear?

'I know. We're in grave danger. It would be foolish to pretend that we're not. But you know the old saying, "Never say die until you're dead"? That's saved my life many times. You never can tell what the future might bring. I promise I...' He stopped in mid-sentence. 'Fool!' he cried. 'Fool, fool, fool! Double-dyed unadulterated fool!'

He opened his mouth wide, and howled; a long, long howl.

'Doctor! Are you all right?'

That was all she needed – for the Doctor to go doolally. He didn't answer, but howled again in the same way.

Sarah's Aunt Norah used to have a poodle, Fudge, who would join in whenever anybody started singing, with a plaintive 'Woo-oo-oooo...' It was the polite Wirral equivalent of an Alaskan wolf baying at the moon. The Doctor's howl sounded very like Fudge's, only more musical, and more on one note, and it went on and on. When he stopped at last, he was panting, just as Fudge used to.

He shook his head in disbelief. 'Here was I desperately trying to think of an answer, and it's staring me in the face!' Again he howled, but with a slightly different tune. And again, but with even more variation.

She couldn't bear it any more. 'Doctor! What *are* you doing?'

He laughed a manic laugh. 'I'm calling for a taxi!'

Once more... But this time, it sounded almost like a strange wordless song, which subtly changed in pitch, with variations almost too fine to make out.

Of course! When the Doctor had been peering over the bow of the *Hallaton*... Like that picture on a Greek vase in the British Museum – a boy riding on the back of a dolphin.

'You're singing the dolphin song!'

The Doctor took a deep breath. 'There don't seem to be any around,' he said. 'So I'm trying to find out if any of their cousins are nearby. Inter-species communication. I knew it would come in useful.'

Even as he spoke, there came a distant reply, eerily echoing the Doctor's last call.

'Aha!' he said, 'Orcas. Just what we need.'

Answering them, with slight variations that even Sarah could recognise, he went on for quite a long time, and then listened for a response.

When it came, it was nearly as long as the Doctor's song, and more to the point, it was much closer.

This time when the Doctor laughed, it was a laugh of pure joy. 'They're on their way. I told them what a pickle we're in. And they're going to help us!'

It felt as if the sun had come out. As the relief swept through Sarah's body, she felt the strength flooding back into her muscles.

'Orcas? I've never heard of them.'

'Orcas? Killer whales.'

'Killer whales!'

'Yes. A pod – that's a family – on a trip up from the Southern Ocean. Having a bit of a holiday. Transients, I shouldn't wonder.'

As if it mattered! 'Transients?'

'Mm. An adventurous lot. Their stay-at-home cousins like to be near to where the fish congregate. The transients don't particularly like fish. They'd rather eat mammals.'

There was quite a long pause before Sarah spoke again, in a very small voice.

'I'm a mammal,' she said.

CHAPTER FIFTEEN

The difficulty, of course, was controlling the sweep of the three hastily rigged searchlights, one facing for'd and the others on each side, so that in theory the whole arc was covered from the port beam, via straight ahead, right through to the starboard beam. But since the ship was now travelling with the waves once more, the Cox'n was again forced to weave a looping course, and the lights swung erratically to and fro, and up and down, despite the struggles of the seamen in charge of them.

Hour after hour the *Hallaton* risked taking one roll too far; hour after hour, Petty Officer Hardy caught her just in time.

The Brigadier felt sure that he could have managed the lights better himself. But when he asked Bob Simkins, who was in charge of the whole operation, if he could have a go with one he found that his land-learned reflexes were even less effective than those of the sailors.

They'd been searching now for nearly five and a half hours. They hadn't a chance of finding them, he thought grimly, as he gladly relinquished the thing.

But then, a shout. 'There they are! Green four five!'

It was the signalman, Rogers, who was at the starboard light. Immediately, the other two lights swung around to focus as best they could on the same area. The Brigadier and the two officers crowded round Rogers, straining to see as the ship yawed and rolled, and the waves appeared and disappeared in the uncertain beams.

'It's not them,' the Brigadier said heavily, as they caught a glimpse.

'Sorry, sir,' said the signalman. 'You're right. It's them dolphins back again.'

'Not dolphins, Rogers,' said Bob, who was doing his best to check on the sighting through his binoculars. 'It's a school of whales... and... good God!'

'What is it, man?'

'Have a look for yourself!' He was laughing in sheer pleasure and relief.

'We were waving like mad and shouting as loud as we could, and it looked as if you were going to sail straight past us!' said Sarah, who was wrapped in a woolly blanket, and clutching a glass of hot rum toddy. Her voice was still somewhat shaky.

The three of them were sitting in the wardroom. It was well past midnight, but nobody felt like going to bed yet. The rolling of the ship was by now comparatively gentle, and it was good just to sit and luxuriate in a cocoon of comfort and relief.

The Doctor, looking far from his usual dapper self in Chris's heavy schoolboy-checked dressing gown, lifted his glass to the Brigadier, as if in a toast. 'Thanks,' he said.

The Brigadier harrumphed and took a sip of his dram. He wouldn't have told them about his decisive intervention, but, thanks to the Cox'n, the story of his knockout blow was now known throughout the *Hallaton* (to the glee of the entire ship's company), and Bob had, off the record, passed it onto the Doctor and Sarah.

He took another sip of whisky. No wonder she was still shaking, he thought. Bad enough to have nearly been drowned. But those great things – twenty feet long if they were an inch – were killers. The Doctor had said so. And the way they tossed their passengers onto the scrambling nets with their noses must have been the last straw.

He said as much.

'Natural to them,' said the Doctor. 'It's the way they play with the small seals, tossing them in the air and catching them.'

'Before they eat them?' said Sarah, wide-eyed with horror.

'Of course.'

'But that's horrible!'

'No different from the way your pussy cat plays with a mouse.'

'I haven't got a cat,' said Sarah, still unhappy.

The Doctor put down his glass. He sat down next to her.

'You're bound to be upset,' he said. 'But they're only being themselves. We must just thank the quirk of evolution that seems to make them friendly to humans. But, yes, they're carnivorous animals. They eat seals, and penguins – even porpoises – and fish of course.' He paused a moment and then went on, 'I seem to remember someone who thoroughly enjoyed eating a lump of minced buffalo.'

Sarah grinned ruefully. 'Take no notice of me. I'm a silly ungrateful mare. I'm just being childish.'

'And what's wrong with that?' said the Doctor.

'How much longer will it take us, do you reckon,' asked Sarah.

Like the Doctor and the Brigadier, Sarah had been officially invited to come onto the bridge whenever she cared to. But in practice this meant only about half the time – whenever the CO was off duty. He never told her to leave, but his manner to her was always so cold – and she found it so embarrassing when he shouted and swore at the crew – that she confined her visits to those times when either Pete Andrews or Bob Simkins was Officer of the Watch and in charge of the ship.

'How much longer? That's difficult to say exactly,' answered Bob, who'd just put their noon position on the chart. 'We lost about two hundred miles yesterday, what with one thing and another. Bit more. If we don't hit anything else like that, it should be about five days. We've a pretty good idea of the way the tidal currents go, but it's not like driving down to Brighton for a day out.'

Five days. Okay, forget the photography. Let's face it, after yesterday she needed a holiday. Her head was still sore, and there was an impressive lump just above her left ear. And the whole thing had left her feeling sort of wobbly inside.

Concentrate on the pleasure-cruise bit, that was the thing. Lounging on a deck chair, being brought beef tea by white jacketed stewards, like in the old thirties films. Huh! That'd be the day. Or what about a ship-board romance? Who with, though? She ran her mind's eye over the possible candidates: the nice but impossibly furry Pete; lanky Bob, who'd always be rushing off to his beloved charts; or the plump Chris. Not a lot of choice. Where was Sammy when she needed him?

She suddenly giggled. Out loud. How snobby could you get? Only the officers had been asked to audition for the part! Miller, the steward – Dusty Miller didn't they call him? – he was just about the yummiest male on board, so why hadn't she even considered him? Briefly, she did just that; and recoiled from the hideous social complications that might ensue.

Forget it.

One thing, she must get some exercise. She was really missing her morning jog. She could hardly go for a three-mile run, but in all the books she'd read with cruises in them, it was traditional every morning to have a brisk walk round and round the deck – thirty or forty laps, or whatever. It would have to do.

Dusty Miller picked up the tray of food from the table. He looked across at the unmoving figure on the bunk, its back to him and to the door. 'You okay, Mr Whitbread?'

Brother Alex kept quite still. He wouldn't have an alibi for the attack (if it was needed), but if people took it for granted that he'd been out of action, that could be just as good. As soon as he'd got back to the cabin, he'd got rid of the remains of the chair over the side – making quite sure he wasn't seen – and then retired to bed again.

'You haven't hardly eaten a thing – and you didn't touch your breakfast neither.'

The answer came as a groan, and a muffled feeble voice. 'What day is it?'

'Day? It's Wednesday. No, I tell a lie. It's Thursday. And a lovely day and all. Sun scorching your bleeding eyes out.'

Another groan.

Miller turned back at the door. 'You want me to get somebody, sir?'

Whitbread heaved himself round. 'No, no. I'll be all right. I must have slept all day yesterday...'

'Yeah. Ask me, you were well out of it. What with Miss Smith and the Doctor and all.'

His heart leapt. The Doctor as well? 'What about them?' he asked.

'Only went overboard, didn't they?'

Praise be to Skang! The Doctor as well!

'Still, all's well that ends well...' The door slammed behind him.

What? What did he mean by that? He sat up in bed, meaning to call the steward back – and just managed to stop himself. It could mean only one thing. She'd been rescued.

He had to do the job all over again.

Sarah got up early the next morning, feeling almost back to normal, put on her trainers and set off on her first constitutional.

She'd done a recce as soon as she'd had the idea. There was no way it would be possible to establish a high-speed walking track around the main deck. There was far too much equipment – and for that matter, at that time of the morning, there'd be too many men indulging in the Royal Navy's obsession for spotless cleanliness.

But the boat deck, she realised, where the ship's boats hung from their davits, was a different matter. Open to the sky, it ran along each side and aft of the officers' living quarters. The wardroom was at the back, and a corridor ran down the middle, with the cabins each side. The Captain's suite – a grand name for his sleeping cabin and his day cabin – ran across the for'd end.

The only snag was that the open deck didn't continue round the front of the bridge structure. Instead, there was a door at the front end of each side into the control part of the ship: the sonar; the sparks's cabin; the main gyro-compass room with its auxiliary wheel for steering if the bridge above was damaged; and so on. So you couldn't get round to the other side.

However, there was also a door each side into the cabin area that opened into a short corridor going from one side to the other. So, by going indoors – not very nautical sounding that, thought Sarah, but she could hardly say (or even think) 'going below' when it was all on the same level – by going indoors for a moment or two, she'd be able to complete the circuit.

Hang on. It must be the CO's private entrance to his cabins. It didn't go anywhere else. That was a bummer.

She'd just have to be ultra quiet.

So here she was, bright and early on Friday morning, striding out at a speed she reckoned to be four miles an hour; or even five. Power-walking they called it, didn't they? So if she kept up the same speed for half an hour, she would have gone at least two miles. If she really pushed it she might get as big a buzz as she did from her run on Hampstead Heath – if it wasn't for the silly hiatus when she had to slow down and creep through the short corridor past Hogben's cabin. But she hadn't any choice, had she?

It was a bore. He was a bore. She could even hear him snoring as she tiptoed by.

Horrible man.

Having spent Thursday establishing to the world that he was barely convalescent, Whitbread rose very early on Friday and presented himself in the wardroom (once he'd found it) for breakfast.

There must be no more mistakes. From the way they'd behaved so far it seemed that the Doctor and the Brigadier had nothing to go on but suspicions of the cult. But if the Smith girl started putting two and two together...

'Good morning, Mr Whitbread. Glad to see you up. Feeling better?' Pete Andrews was the only one in the wardroom. The welcome was so obviously sincere that he was instantly reassured. If the truth had been discovered, he would have had a very different welcome.

He settled down to eating a frugal poached egg on toast, and concentrated on listening to the First Lieutenant, asking disingenuous questions, so that he could learn all about the *Hallaton* and its people.

If everybody got used to seeing him around the ship, he'd be able to keep an eye open and establish the pattern of the girl's day, and spot any regularities, so that he would be able to predict when she'd be alone and vulnerable.

But then, as he was sipping his second cup of coffee, he saw her, whipping past the open windows of the wardroom as if she was in a race. Round she went, past the after door and round to the other side, disappearing up the deck outside; and then, a few minutes later, there she was again. And again. And again.

Pete Andrews finished his breakfast and disappeared, but the girl kept on passing by. He didn't count the number of times, but it must have been twenty-five minutes or more before she stopped appearing. Did she do this every morning? Was this what he'd been looking for?

His mind gave a little lurch. Now, what was that all about?

He examined his twisted complex of emotions, and began to untangle them. Pleasure that the girl hadn't been drowned? Surely not. A sort of guilt? He'd been pretty ruthless in the hidden back alleys of his public life, but he'd never been responsible for anyone's death. Then again, it had never been necessary before.

As the pieces fell into place, the picture revealed itself. It wasn't guilt or remorse, just a fear that he might get caught – and a fierce determination not to let it happen. And as for the other emotion...

Yes, it was true that he was pleased that Sarah Jane Smith (stupid name) had been saved, but only because it meant that he could experience once more the rush of simple pleasure that he'd felt as the chair leg smashed into her skull.

He was really looking forward to killing her.

CHAPTER SIXTEEN

'Sarah!' The Doctor's voice came from his open door as she passed it on her way back to her cabin.

Hastily hiding her book under the blanket she was carrying – she wouldn't want the Doctor to know she was an addict of such rubbish! – she turned back. 'Yes?'

'Are you busy?'

Busy! For the first time in her life since she'd left kindergarten, there was nothing, nothing at all, that she really ought to be doing. She'd still be lying on the deserted upper bridge if it hadn't turned so hot as the sun climbed up towards noon.

'Nothing that can't wait.'

Like getting a tan, or finding out whether Lady Amelia would really fall for the manipulative charms of Sir Percival.

'Good. If you can spare a moment or two...'

She entered the Doctor's cabin and he gestured towards an empty chair with the object in his hand. It looked a bit like a long version of one of those things you use to test the pressure in a car tyre. Of course! The sonic screwdiver!

He aimed it at an open silver box on the table. Now she recognised that as well; she'd seen it before, the Doctor was always fiddling with it. As she heard the strange sound of the screwdriver, the box's contents gave a sort of wobble, rather like a mirage she'd seen in the Moroccan desert three holidays ago.

'That's better,' said the Doctor, closing it.

'That's the bit from the TARDIS, isn't it?' she said, sitting opposite him.

'The relativity circuit of the temporal balancing governor. That's right,' he replied, minutely adjusting one of the many small knobs on the side of the box. Then he pressed the largest button. The box responded by making its tinkly music-box noise. 'I thought I'd improve the shining hour by having another go at it,' he went on. 'Improve the shining hour! Ridiculous expression. Like polishing a diamond. Like polishing a diamond. Like polishing a diamond.'

What *was* he on about!

'Did you notice anything?' he asked.

'Like what?'

'Anything at all. Anything odd.'

Well... 'Not really. Only you saying "like polishing a diamond" over and over again.'

'Ah! How many times?'

'Three.'

'Mm.'

It was like when he had started howling in the sea. Just Doctorish. It was no good trying to keep up with him.

'That should do it,' he said, as he gave a couple of the knobs another tiny tweak. 'Mark you,' he continued as he pressed the main button again, 'an unpolished diamond looks like something you'd pick up on the beach and toss into the sea. So perhaps it's not so ridiculous. Well?'

'Well what?'

'Notice anything this time?'

What on earth was he talking about? 'What am I supposed to notice?' she asked.

'Nothing. Nothing at all.'

She laughed. 'Well, good on you, Doctor. You're in luck! That's exactly what I did notice. Nothing! Come on, what's this all about?'

The Doctor was laughing too. 'Well you see...'

Footsteps. The Brigadier appeared in the doorway.

The Doctor lifted his little silver case and pressed the button again.

'Ah, there you are, Doctor...' said the Brigadier.

And vanished.

'Blimey!' said Sarah.

Footsteps. The Brigadier appeared in the doorway.

'Ah, there you are, Doctor...' he said, and vanished once more.

'I've got it!' said Sarah. 'It's a time loop!'

The Brigadier appeared again. This time the Doctor didn't press the button.

'Ah, there you are, Doctor,' he said.

'Why, so I am,' said the Doctor, putting away the sonic screwdriver. 'Except that I would have called it a temporal recursion,' he went onto Sarah, 'but you're quite right. A time loop. And you never noticed a thing when I aimed it at you?'

'Not a sausage.'

'The temporal recursion algorithm is the basic default setting for the relativity circuit. If you get that right, everything else falls into place.'

The Brigadier was waiting patiently. 'It's just been pointed out to me that the sun is over the yard arm,' he said. 'Our hosts have invited us for a snifter before lunch. You too, Sarah.'

'Great! I'll be right along.'

Sarah returned to her cabin. Having dumped the blanket and book on her bunk, she pulled a pair of – less provocative – shorts over her bikini, and found a clean shirt (beautifully ironed by Wong Chang, who happily moonlighted as dhobi-man).

Funny that, she thought, the Brigadier calling her Sarah. He didn't often address her by her first name. Depended on the circs. When formality was appropriate it was 'Miss Smith'. Like the junior officers saying 'sir' to the Number One on the bridge, and calling him 'Pete' in the wardroom.

With the Doctor, anything could happen at any time. Time loops, for example. That's what made him so exciting. On the

other hand, you knew where you were with the Brigadier. It made you feel sort of safe.

Alex was pretty certain that the Smith girl would start her walkabout just after seven o'clock, as usual. Certainly she seemed to have established a routine for herself that hadn't varied for the past three days. It had been tricky, keeping an eye on her without it being noticed. But, bit by bit, Alex had managed to build up a picture of her activities – or lack of them; she seemed to spend a lot of her time lying in the sun, or reading in the shade.

The trouble was, she was hardly ever out of sight of somebody or other. It was supposed to be a skeleton crew, but the number of seamen on board was surely excessive, far more than you'd get on a merchant ship. Even when she was sunbathing on the upper bridge, all by herself, there was no way up there that wasn't in view of somebody most of the time.

On the other hand, before breakfast, people were either in their cabins or else had very specific jobs to do. And the upper bridge area was always deserted at that time of the morning, as it was most of the day. It must be used only when they were going into action, or entering harbour or something. If he got up there early enough on the fourth morning, nobody would know. He'd be able to slip up there – and down again – quite safely. This would be his last chance. According to the Navigating Officer, they would probably arrive at Stella Island the next day.

So, on the fourth morning, he slipped out just when it started to get light, and established himself in the after corner of the open bridge, where the starboard searchlight was rigged. He peeped over the edge. Just as he'd estimated from his quick recce the previous day, the overhang was immediately above where she came out of the door in her clockwise perambulation.

Keeping well down, just in case, he loosened even further the large butterfly fastening of the bracket that supported the heavy searchlight, unscrewing it until it was hanging by a thread.

This time he had to be certain.

Everybody on board knew better than to wake up the Skipper unless it was really necessary. If he didn't turn up for his watch, it would be quietly covered by either Pete or Bob, who, although he was only a sub-lieutenant, already had his Watch-keeping Certificate and was fully qualified to be in charge.

It wasn't that he woke with a hangover. His body was long habituated to a bloodstream that could have been used to make a passable cocktail without the addition of further alcohol. But until he'd knocked back the half-tumbler of gin that always stood by his bedside, he had such a filthy temper that whoever had woken him would be lucky to live to regret it.

Sarah's first invasion of his territory had made no impression on him. His snoring didn't falter for a second. Nor did he stir on the second day.

On the third day, however, she was becoming rather care-less. As there'd been no reaction from the cabin, her passage through the little corridor was getting faster and faster, and the click of the doors as they closed was becoming a small thump as she let them swing to. On each circuit he half woke up, blearily saw her going by with a sort of obscure irritation that subsided as soon as she disappeared, and fell back into the heavy torpor that now passed for sleep.

But on the fourth morning...

The footsteps were unmistakable. Quicker than ever, and much faster than anybody would normally walk on board, they alerted Alex Whitbread at once; and the sound of the door below, which had become almost a slam by now, told him when she'd passed beneath the corner of the bridge.

It was essential to get the timing right. He was in no hurry. He would be able to hear the sound of the first door when she came into the corridor, and by watching a couple of times he would be able to judge exactly when she would be coming out the other side.

Here she came, on her second lap. Through the first door, one, two, three... and, yes, out of the second door. About three and a half seconds then, and as the door swung to, she was a couple of paces from where the searchlight would land. Couldn't be better.

Another check. Just the same. The only snag was that if he was peering over, he wasn't in the right position to heave the thing over the edge.

Ah! He could go by the sound of the door. If he gave the thing the lift and the shove it needed as soon as he heard the second slam...

Right. Next time...

This particular morning, the CO was so far gone into his accustomed abyss (nearly two bottles deep), that the first couple of bangs hardly registered. It was the second pair that roused him, and when he caught a glimpse of Sarah – and what was happening filtered through – the fury started to boil up inside him.

By her third time round, he was heaving himself out of bed. He had to stand for a while to get his bearings, and once he'd got to the door, she was back again. He staggered into the corridor, but he was too late – she was already at the second door. He was just in time to catch it as it swung behind her.

Out he went, incandescent with rage, and as the door slammed behind him, he stopped and shouted after her retreating back. 'Hey! You!'

They were the last words that Lieutenant-Commander Hogben ever spoke.

* * *

'...dwell in the house of the Lord forever.'

The First Lieutenant closed the Bible that he'd borrowed (surprisingly) from Petty Officer Hardy. Queen's Regs would certainly say that they should have had a Prayer Book with the right form of words for a burial at sea, but no doubt a reading of the Twenty-third Psalm would do just as well. If the Lord was a shepherd, his flock must surely include a blackish sheep like Hogben.

He nodded to the Cox'n, and at a murmured order the door of the galley, which had been pressed into service as a stretcher, was tilted up, and the weighted body slid from under the White Ensign that hid it from view. A small splash, and it disappeared into the depths of the Indian Ocean.

'Make and mend this afternoon for everybody who's not on watch, Cox'n.'

'Aye aye, sir.'

The least he could do for the poor sod they'd just sent down to Davey Jones was to give the crew the afternoon off. Maybe they'd treat it as a celebration, but it would perhaps make them remember him a bit more kindly.

As the crew dispersed, and Bob Simkins went back to the bridge to get the *Hallaton* under way again, he turned to the Brigadier. 'Sir. I would be obliged if you and your party would have a word with me in the wardroom. In ten minutes?'

He didn't wait for an answer. Although the sun was sinking towards the horizon, this was no invitation for a pre-dinner noggin. The authority in his voice made that quite clear.

Ever since Hogben's death Sarah had been struggling with the irrational thought that it was her fault. The searchlight must have been loosened by the rolling of the ship. And she could have been underneath it when it fell. If she hadn't kept going through the CO's corridor, if she hadn't disturbed him by letting the doors bang, he'd still be alive.

Pete Andrews didn't ask them to sit down. He stood waiting for them in the traditional pose of the Royal Navy officer on semi-official duty, with his hands clasped behind his back, like Prince Philip. There had been some discussion as to whether Alex Whitbread should be counted as one of their party. The First Lieutenant didn't seem to be bothered by his absence.

He got straight to the point, without any preamble. 'I would trust Rogers with my life. In fact, there have been a couple of occasions... Well, never mind that. If he says that he'd made that searchlight secure, I believe him. This was no accident.'

'I quite agree with you,' said the Doctor.

The Brigadier looked doubtful. 'I know that the Commanding Officer was hardly the most popular man on the ship, but how could anybody have known that he would be there?

'Ah. See what you mean,' he went on after a moment, with a glance at Sarah.

Sarah suddenly got the point as well. If it wasn't an accident at all, then...

'Oh God!' she said, and sat down. There was only one person on board who could want her dead.

'I can't conceive of any motive that would make any member of my crew wish to harm Sarah,' went on Andrews. 'So one of you must be responsible. The question is, which one? And why?'

The Doctor started to speak, but the First Lieutenant held up a hand to stop him and went straight on, in a grim, official way that made his anger very apparent. 'I have of course made a signal to London, and they've confirmed my position as acting Commanding Officer. I reported my view of the matter, and I fully expected to be ordered to return forthwith for a full investigation. Instead, I was informed that the original orders would stand, and that we were to place the ship, and the ship's company, entirely at your disposal, Brigadier.

'This is a warship. We have been on active service in the South China Seas. We have a full complement of gunnery, and

four surface-to-surface missiles, which, thank God, we have never had to use. We're ready for anything you can ask of us.

'But I have to tell you that I have no intention of putting my people at risk without knowing exactly what's going on –'

The Brigadier started to speak, but Andrews held up his hand to stop him. He hadn't finished.

'And I wish to make it perfectly clear that I consider it not only discourteous but dangerous in the extreme that I have been kept in the dark up to this point.'

Sarah could hardly blame him for feeling cross. In spite of the fact that he'd been second-in-command, he'd had the responsibility of running the ship. From what she'd gathered, nobody else had been told because the Captain had insisted. Typical of the sort of man he'd been. Basically incompetent, and frightened of giving away his authority in case he was found out.

Even after Pete had had a look at the photograph that started the whole thing, he took a lot of convincing. And why not? Even though Sarah knew the whole story already, she found it difficult to believe that it was not only the two hundred cult members who were in danger but the entire population of the world.

Even the Brigadier, it seemed, shared their doubts. 'The bodies on Hampstead Heath are evidence that we're dealing with something quite alien, certainly,' he said to the Doctor, 'and the photograph bears out your hypothesis that this Skang creature is probably responsible, and I suppose there must be a number of them, but...'

The Doctor, obviously irritated, interrupted him. 'If this were a simple incursion onto this planet of a bunch of predatory aliens, using humans as food, the pattern of events would be quite different. To start with, there would be reports of many many more similar deaths.

'Even if they had managed to get control of a group of humans to protect them, as it seems this lot has, they would

use them merely as a cover. Ask yourselves this question? Given what we know, why should they go to all the trouble of transporting so many of their potential victims thousands of miles away from the prying eyes of the world?

'It would seem that there is going to be a mass slaughter of the cult members. And what then? The creatures will have no further food. Isn't that right?'

What on earth was he getting at? thought Sarah.

'I am convinced that what we are seeing is merely an advance guard – a scouting party. If we are concerned for the lives of a hundred and eighty-eight poor deluded fools...'

Trust the Doctor to know the exact number!

'...because of a mere twenty or so Skangs, what would we be looking at if there were thousands or even millions of them on the planet?'

It made sense, what he was saying. There was no logical reason for the trip to Stella Island. He must be right. Unless they could stop it happening, the Earth would be taken over by these nightmare creatures.

And the human race would become nothing more than their cattle.

CHAPTER SEVENTEEN

Alex Whitbread lay on his bunk in a state of utter despair. Even on an everyday level he was in deep trouble. Although he hadn't been seen that morning, he had been placed under arrest, pending further investigation.

Nobody, it seemed, thought that the searchlight had fallen by accident. The target was obviously Sarah Jane Smith – and it would be ludicrous to believe that any member of the ship's crew had suddenly turned into a homicidal maniac. So that left only the Brigadier, the Doctor and himself; and the other two had a perfect alibi, as they were being served their bacon and eggs at the very moment when Sarah screamed.

Every so often his whole bunk was shaken by his violent shivering as he recalled yet again that his last chance of getting rid of the journalist kid had gone.

How was it that she hadn't worked it out already? Or had she? The very fact that the Brigadier and the Doctor were going to all this trouble seemed to indicate that they knew that they were dealing with something far more serious than just a cult. If they confronted Mother Hilda with their suspicions, or perhaps their certain knowledge...

The rigor of desperation shook him once more.

...if Mother Hilda knew for sure that it was through him that their secret had been betrayed, he would be condemned forever to this state of half-existence, terminally cut off from his brothers and sisters of the Skang community, never again to be absorbed into the collective bliss.

He turned his face to the wall, to shut out the sight of the armed guard outside, and gave himself up to his misery.

'But why are you heading to the west instead of the south, Bob? Have you missed it?' Sarah stared down at the chart with its pencil line that showed their course making a right-angle, some way off to the east of the supposed position of Stella Island.

Chris, who was perched on the stool near the man at the wheel, apparently practising being the Officer of the Watch, laughed. 'That's right. He's missed it. Can't get the staff these days.'

'Take no notice of the lower orders,' said Bob. 'I've missed it on purpose.'

'Eh?'

'The island's position we've been given may be way out. As far as we know, it's only been visited twice. If we aimed straight there and there was no sign of it, we'd have no idea whether to turn to port or to starboard, to the east or to the west. Doing it like this, we'll know which area is the most likely for a box search.'

It all sounded a bit hit or miss. 'What about the radar?' she asked.

'Steam-driven. They wouldn't waste state-of-the-art on the likes of us. The poor old *Hallaton* can't see over the horizon any more than you can!

'Don't worry,' he went on. 'According to the pilot book, we can get in on a high spring tide. Well, my love, you can't have anything higher than the equinoctial spring tides. Tomorrow is September the twentieth, the day before the equinox, when the day is as long as the night. With any luck, we'll be anchoring in the lagoon well before lunch.'

'Are you suggesting that some sort of UFO full of these creatures has landed without anybody noticing? Don't you think we might have heard about it?'

That had been Pete Andrews' first question, the evening before, once they got down to the nitty-gritty of planning their next step, and the atmosphere had become markedly more friendly.

'If the Skang make a habit of finding inhabited planets to colonise,' answered the Doctor, 'they'll have long ago perfected a way of arriving without getting a headline in the *Daily Mail*.'

'Such as?' said the Brigadier.

'I have my own ideas on the subject, but I'd hesitate to put them forward without more evidence. Just ask yourself this question: Why were the bodies that have been found those of young humans, rather than your local farmer's prize beef cattle?'

This was greeted by a baffled silence.

'Well, why?' asked the Brigadier at last.

'Maybe we'll find that out tomorrow,' said the Doctor.

But what else would they find out, thought Sarah, as she left Bob checking, yet again, the effect that the tidal currents (which were apparently rather vaguely charted) might have on their new course.

She wandered across the bridge to look at the radar repeater screen, with its cursor endlessly going round and round. Would the *Hallaton* herself be the first to spot the island, or would they hear a hail from the lookout who'd been stationed on the upper bridge? Belt and braces, Pete had said with a grin.

Once he'd taken on board the idea of the Skang, he'd turned back into the amiable, slightly furry, friend-to-the-world they'd got to know. After dinner, he'd entered with enthusiasm into a discussion with the Brigadier about how to go about arresting the leaders of the cult, as had originally been intended, or how to hold off an armed attack if it should arise.

It was agreed almost at once that it would be foolish for the landing party not to be fully armed and ready for anything.

But what were they going to do with the stranded devotees? They'd have to bring them back on the *Skang*, obviously, but that was taking for granted the co-operation of its crew. They might have to arrest them as well.

Not for the first time, the Brigadier had bemoaned out loud his serious lack of UNIT back-up.

Sarah had gone to bed, leaving them to it, noticing that the Doctor, with his second glass of what Pete called 'cooking port' in his hand, was quietly listening with an ironic smile.

She could understand why. In their professional enthusiasm for their contingency plans, covering the logistics of every eventuality, they seemed to have quite forgotten who the actual enemy was.

Watching the radar screen was almost hypnotic; and as the line of light went round it had something of the flavour of a roulette wheel. Would this time be the winner? Would this be the time that a little blip would show up near the top of the screen that...

There it was! A spot of light on the very edge of the display, a little bit to the left.

As she turned in excitement to tell Bob, she heard a buzzer, and a disembodied voice. 'Radar, bridge. I have a trace, sir. Bearing two six seven degrees.'

By this time, Bob was by her side, looking at the screen. And suddenly she had a doubt. 'Maybe it's the *Skang*,' she said.

'There was never a chance of catching her up,' he said. 'No, she'll be waiting for us when we get there. In any case, that's far too big a blip to be a ship. That's the island all right! Fifty quid to a penny bun, that's it. It's just where it ought to be. Chris! Give Pete a shout, will you?'

You could practically hear his grin of satisfaction.

Chris disappeared at a run, giving Bob a thumbs-up as he passed.

'Red one zero! Something on the horizon...' Another voice,

hollow through the voice-pipe coming down from the upper bridge: the lookout. 'Fine on the port bow... Looks like land, sir.'

Belt and braces.

The Brigadier, in the cotton slacks and open-necked shirt that had become his preferred 'dress-of-the-day' while on board, hardly looked the part of a senior Army officer in charge of a vital operation.

He was more like a little boy getting ready for a game of cowboys and Indians, thought the Doctor, as he watched him restlessly pacing up and down the upper bridge, from where Pete Andrews, with the Cox'n at the wheel, was conning the ship through the narrow gap in the reef that made an entrance into Stella Island's large and peaceful lagoon.

Sarah seemed calmer than the Brigadier. The Doctor watched her as she leaned over the side of the bridge, trying to make out what awaited them. She was obviously excited. Nevertheless, her face betrayed her underlying uneasiness at what might lie ahead. Of all the many companions he'd had on his travels through space and time, she was one of the most remarkable – on the face of it, an intrepid adventurer, with all the intense curiosity of an eager child, yet with much of a child's anxiety as well.

'I can't see a flipping thing,' she said.

As there was a band of mist in the way, through which the shape of the island could just be made out (very like the drawing they had seen in the Pilot book), it still wasn't possible to get a good look at the shore.

Just before they reached the mist, Chris's voice sang out through the voice-pipe from the bridge below, where he was watching the sonar echo-sounder. 'Seven fathoms!'

'Stop both engines.'

The *tring-tring* of the engine-room telegraphs answered Pete Andrews' order.

'Five and a half fathoms. Shelving rapidly, sir.'

As the *Hallaton* ghosted forward, the new CO picked up the microphone of the Tannoy. 'Stand by!'

Bob Simkins, in charge of the party on the foredeck, raised a hand in acknowledgement of the order.

'Four fathoms.'

Another engine order. 'Slow astern together.'

The twin screws took hold, the ship came to a stop, and as she gathered way astern, the order came.

'Drop anchor!'

They had arrived at Stella Island. But where was the *Skang*?

'Maybe they've anchored on the western side,' said Pete Andrews.

'Why on earth should they? No, this Whitbread creature has deliberately misled us. Let's get him up here and get the truth out of him! One way or another!'

'No, no, Lethbridge-Stewart,' said the Doctor. 'He wasn't lying. You could see that he was desperate. If that was acting it was the finest I've seen since Garrick's Lear.'

Pete Andrews, ignoring what must have been a joke, thought it time to bring a little sense into the discussion, which was becoming a touch heated. 'I'd say we have a choice.' He nodded towards the island, still shrouded in fog. 'We can either wait for it to clear, so that we can get a good look, or we can do a recce.'

The Doctor nodded. 'Absolutely. If you'll give me a boat, I'll go and have a look. If I can get a chance to talk to Dame Hilda again, we'll be in a position to assess the situation more accurately.'

The Brigadier was listening with a frown. 'I'm sorry, Doctor. I couldn't allow it. The situation is very different from the one in Bombay. Now they are out of the public eye, there's nothing to stop the aliens showing their hand. The last thing we want to do is to give them a hostage.

'And to wait would be to sacrifice the advantage of surprise,'

he went on. 'There's no reason to suppose that they could have been expecting us.'

At least he was facing the facts, thought Andrews. 'In that case, sir, I'd suggest that there's only one thing we can do. We go and have a look, but we make sure that we're ready for anything. Don't forget that my people have spent the last few years coping with some very dodgy characters. They won't run away from a bunch of lizards from outer space.'

The Brigadier glanced at the Doctor, who gave a little shrug. He nodded to Pete. 'Good man,' he said. 'Thank you.'

After much discussion, it was decided that the landing party would consist of two motor launches, each with a group of well-tried veterans, fully armed and ready for anything.

Pete Andrews suggested that, as non-combatants who might get in the way, the Doctor and Sarah should be left out of the first foray.

'For your own safety, you understand,' the Brigadier said.

'You're not leaving me behind,' said Sarah. 'Not after what I've been through to get here.'

The Doctor soon put them right. He spoke quite gently, but even the First Lieutenant, well-used throughout his career in the Royal Navy to being blasted by his seniors, was taken aback.

Brigadier Alistair Lethbridge-Stewart DSO MC always looked forward to a scrap.

As he stood on the upper bridge with his two companions, waiting for the word from the Commanding Officer to embark in the launch, his mind went back to his most memorable experiences in the last year of the war – in particular the engagements that had earned him his gongs.

From the frustrations of his job with UNIT – especially since he'd teamed up with the Doctor, and encountered an extraordinary variety of unpleasant alien creatures, most of whom seemed to be impervious to bullets – he'd learnt not

to expect clean-cut military operations like those he'd experienced in World War Two. No matter how horrible those experiences had been, he still found himself gripped by the same excitement, the same keen awareness that he was ready for anything that fate might throw at him. It felt like... like the moment before the start of an unknown ski-run off piste.

He was using a pair of the powerful binoculars provided for the lookouts, vainly trying to see through the mist, which still hadn't shown any sign of clearing. What was waiting for them on the other side of it? The wretched followers of the cult herded together in this horrible place to await the pleasure of their alien masters?

That would be the good news. At the worst, they could be looking at a pile of bodies reduced to skin and bone – including that poor foolish lad who was a friend of Sarah's – what was his name? Oh yes, Jeremy. Jeremy Fitzoliver.

Whatever. He was going to make damn sure that those responsible – human or non-human – paid the price. In blood if necessary.

There was an air of suppressed excitement on board now that the other two officers and the Cox'n had been given the whole story, which the petty officer greeted with a sceptical raised eyebrow. They had been told that the standing orders for action stations, which had fallen into abeyance as soon as they left the South China Sea with its smugglers and pirates, were to be reinstated.

'Landing party... As you were! Rogers! Wipe that grin off your face! Landing party... HOWNG!' Long years of Petty-Officer Hardy's bellowing of the word 'Shun' had mangled it past recognition.

The Brigadier peered over at the boat deck below. The port launch was already in the water, and the dozen men who were to be transported in it were on the deck by the davits, dressed in full battle gear, helmets and all, with rifles by their sides, bar the two who had machine guns instead. They were standing

at an easy attention (very different from the rigid smartness he was accustomed to from the men of his erstwhile regiment), as the Petty Officer reported their readiness to Bob Simkins, who was to lead them. Like the Brigadier, they both had pistol holsters at their belts, and, in addition, the Cox'n was sporting an old-fashioned naval cutlass in its scabbard.

The sight of them made him all the more certain that they had made the right decision about Alex Whitbread, leaving him on board under guard. Not exactly cricket, of course. After all, they had agreed to bring him to the island in return for his information. But then, the fellow was obviously not to be trusted, even if he hadn't tried to murder Sarah – and that was almost impossible to prove, one way or the other.

'Right Brigadier, Doctor, when you're ready.' Pete Andrews had climbed the ladder and gave an inclusive nod towards Sarah as he spoke. The three were to accompany him in the smaller launch, which would also carry another six seamen, armed to the teeth like their fellows.

But Sarah wasn't looking at him. 'That's funny...' she said.

They all turned to see what she was looking at. The band of mist that had seemed to cover the entire island had shrunk to a patch about two hundred feet across, which nevertheless still hid from them the landing place described in the Pilot book.

Blown by an offshore breeze, it was approaching the *Hallaton* at a brisk walking pace, and in a few moments it had enveloped the ship from stem to stern. There the haze remained, sitting on the ship, a slight blue dampness pervading the atmosphere with a subtle smell, a smell of... of what, exactly?

'What a lovely scent,' said Sarah. 'What is it?'

The Brigadier knew exactly what it was. It took him straight back to the English garden his mother had so lovingly tended at their summer home in Simla, so many years ago. He'd left India at the age of eight to go to prep school, never to see his mother again. But that particular perfume would always bring her back.

'Roses,' he said. 'It smells of roses.'

They all looked at him in surprise.

'Not roses,' said the Doctor. 'It's a flower, certainly, but not from Earth. It's very similar to the scent of the schlenk blossom – and you only get that on Gallifrey. When you walk through the fields, it's almost overpowering.'

'Not violets?' said Sarah, uncertainly.

Pete Andrews suddenly burst out laughing. 'You're round the bend, the lot of you. It's unmistakable. That's the smell of bacon frying in the open air!'

CHAPTER EIGHTEEN

It was the Doctor who noticed first.

Still chuckling over Pete's ludicrous interpretation of the flower-like scent – yet pigeon-holing the oddity of their different reactions as something to be considered later – he turned to look at the island.

Now that they were no longer trying to see through the thick mist, the landing place was quite visible, between cliffs of ancient volcanic rock that were white with nesting seabirds, some of which were circling overhead. At a glance, the island didn't look much like the description in the whaler's report.

'They were right about the seagulls, anyway,' said the Brigadier.

'They're gannets, aren't they?' said Sarah.

'Boobies!' said the Doctor, picking up the glasses that the Brigadier had discarded.

'I beg your pardon?' said the Brigadier, indignantly.

'The birds. They're boobies. More specifically, masked boobies. You get them all over the world in the tropics.'

'They look like gannets,' said Sarah.

'I thought you did Biology at school,' replied Doctor, looking through the glasses at the beach. 'Gannets don't have black tails.' He paused. 'Well, well, well,' he went on, 'the developers have been busy.'

He was surprised to feel the glow of pleasure that surged up inside him at the sight of a beach of golden sand framed by lush greenery covered with flowers. A number of figures clad in white were gathered near the shore, gazing out towards

the ship. Behind the beach was what could only be thought of as a street: a double row of little pavilions or stone chalets of shining white (of course!) separated by a wide avenue of elegant palms, curving away into the interior, the causeway of golden sand looking for all the world like the yellow-brick road in Oz.

'Here, Lethbridge-Stewart, take a look,' he said, handing him the glasses.

'Good grief!' said the Brigadier, after a moment. 'There you are you see, Doctor,' he went on. 'I never did buy your doom-and-gloom scenario. We're going to look a proper lot of onions if we charge in all dressed up ready for World War Three. Like a police raid on the vicarage tea party. I've always believed we were dealing with nothing more sinister than a few New Age Utopia merchants. Harmless nuts.'

'I'm not sure about the nutty bit,' said Sarah. 'I jolly nearly joined, myself. I wish I had now.'

Pete Andrews lowered his own binoculars. 'Stand 'em down, shall I? Bit hot in all that gear.'

'Of course, of course,' replied the Brigadier, as if it went without saying.

Down below on both sides of the boat deck there was a rising tide of chatter from the two landing parties. The Petty Officer's voice could be heard gently admonishing his charges. 'Now, now. This is no way to behave on parade. Let's have a bit of hush, shall we? There's good boys.'

He was utterly ignored.

'Can the boat trip stand, sir?' he called up, when Pete told him to belay action stations. 'I'm sure the lads would appreciate a run ashore.'

Pete's instant agreement was drowned in a cheer, and a chorus of 'For he's a jolly good fellow...'

The Doctor stood watching and listening, and experiencing something he'd felt only once before in his entire life (at infant school, when trying to come to grips with the spookiness

of quantum mechanics). It was a very nearly total cognitive dissonance – a split between two areas of his understanding, both of which seemed self evident. On the one hand, he could remember quite well the reasons why they were there, and they seemed as valid as ever; but on the other hand, he found himself agreeing with everything that the Brigadier was saying, and sharing the party feeling that seemed to be taking over.

What on earth was going on?

As he filed this puzzle away, too, for later analysis, his thoughts were interrupted by Sarah, turning back from inspecting the island through the communal glasses.

'I say... What about Alex, shut up down there all by himself? Shouldn't we let him out, and take him ashore with us? He deserves a bit of fun. And we did promise, after all. Poor old blighter.'

This was a step too far. For a moment, the Doctor's world view shattered into ten thousand shards of broken concepts. But then it settled, as the pieces of glass in a kaleidoscope settle, to make a new picture. If you came down to it, the world didn't make sense. Any proposition, taken to its ultimate extent, could dissolve into contradiction. Why else did no philosopher ever reach an unarguable conclusion? And what about Zen?

It was supposed to be a sign of a mature intelligence, to be able to hold as true two totally contradictory views. The main thing was to hang onto them both, and not let either take over. And if he wasn't mature after all these years...

Even though he could still see the evident danger, he found himself nodding in agreement as the Brigadier took up Sarah's suggestion with enthusiasm, and gave the order for the release of Brother Alex.

As the first launch came alongside the large flat rock that almost seemed to have been designed as a landing stage, and

the Captain's party climbed out, Alex kept down low, letting himself be obscured by the burly figures of the half-dozen seamen as they hung back not quite sure of what to do.

He couldn't help feeling a vast sense of relief – in spite of his contempt for the methods Hilda Hutchens always chose to use. Everything that the Skang community could do had been done to ensure that the suspicions of the investigators were completely allayed. Even if the Smith girl had been thinking of betraying him, she'd be quite disarmed by their reception.

He should have anticipated it. If he had still been part of the group, he'd have taken it for granted that this was the way she'd play it. His paranoid behaviour must have been a regression to the old pre-Skang Whitbread, quite understandable in the circumstances.

Hilda herself, a motherly figure in her long white robe, with Will Cabot in close attendance, stood with both arms outstretched as if she were greeting her long-lost children. 'Welcome!' she said. 'Welcome to Skang Island!'

Behind her, led by the teachers and organisers in their long robes, the white-clad crowd of smiling followers burst into spontaneous applause.

'Doctor! How good of you to come all this way to see us. Won't you introduce me to your friends?'

As Alex, still doing his best to stay hidden, watched the little party exchanging courtesies, he was swept once more with a wave of bitterness at the way he'd been treated. It had nothing to do with his behaviour in London, of that he was sure. It was a political ploy by Hilda to get rid of a rival who looked at their project in a very different way.

Never mind. This very softness of heart, this craven use of the Skang secret to engender good will, had turned out on this occasion to be to his advantage – and if he played the game correctly, he could use it to get his position back, and then...

When he'd fallen from grace and been dismissed from the government, the bitterest thing to face was the inevitable loss

of his long-standing ambition to become prime minister – but now, with the help of his friends in the group, a much bigger prize could be his.

'Where's the beer, then?' Dusty Miller's voice rang out, followed by a cheer from his mates, now divested of their armoury and determined to live up to their reputation as jolly Jack Tars.

The second boat had now come alongside the first, and Hilda turned with a smile and nodded to the assembled Skang faithful.

Laughing and chattering, they swarmed forward towards the remaining occupants of the two boats as they piled ashore. Taking them by their hands, they led them towards the tables, laden with platefuls of luscious fruits and other delicacies, and the goblets of sparkling drink, which had been set out at the top of the beach.

Alex Whitbread allowed himself to be swept up with the rest. Now was not the moment.

Sarah still had, at the back of her mind, the image of the Skang in her photograph, with the proboscis that had apparently been responsible for the fearsome deaths on Hampstead Heath, but somehow it didn't seem to matter any more. This place was a sort of paradise; and its young inhabitants were the most beautiful people she'd ever seen. She could feel happiness as a physical sensation throughout her body, almost oozing out of her skin. As the Brig had implied, the Doctor's prediction of planetary disaster seemed ludicrous. One had to humour the poor old codger, of course, but that was as far as it went.

While her seniors were exchanging polite platitudes with Mother Hilda, she was scanning the knots of people behind her, on the lookout for Jeremy. After all, that's why she was here, wasn't it? On behalf of Mama, to make sure that he was safe.

There he was, up at the back, waving like mad!

As a smile of sisterly affection spread across her face, she noticed something with a small but very real shock, like briefly touching the terminals of a naked lamp socket. What? She couldn't stand him! Snobbish, rich and dim – a combination that meant he took for granted the idea that he belonged to a superior species of mankind – he was very difficult to like. And yet, as soon as the general melee of welcoming Skangites swept forward, she found herself eagerly pushing her way through to him.

'Jeremy! I can't tell you how glad I am to see you,' she cried, and gave him a big hug. It was the truth. But somewhere, deep down inside, there was the other Sarah, a very small one, watching what she was doing with utter incredulity.

As she drew back, she became aware of a tall young woman, standing behind Jeremy, with a look of surprised disdain on her face.

'Won't you introduce me to your friend, Jeremy?' she said.

'Oh, yes. Sorry. This is Sarah. She's at *Metropolitan* too. She's worked with me on a couple of stories.'

One way of putting it, thought Sarah.

'I'm sure you had great fun together,' said the girl.

Miaow!

'This is Emma, Sarah. Turns out her flat is in Sloane Street too, only a couple of doors down from mine! Extraordinary! Isn't that right, Emma?'

'Yah,' said Emma. 'Must be fate. See you around, Jeremy. *Ciao*.'

She nodded to Sarah, turned and walked away with a greyhound grace that she must have learnt at one of the posh modelling schools. Lucy Clayton? Did they teach her how to be such a cow too?

'Is she your girlfriend?' said Sarah, seeing Jeremy unhappily gazing at her retreating back (with its unfairly small bum).

'Sort of. Well, I'm sort of her boyfriend. One of them. Sort of. You know?'

'Poor old Jeremy.' She really did feel sympathetic!

'It's like that with us, you know. Sharing and all. I mean...' He stopped. He was blushing.

Well, well, well!

'Mother Hilda told us that you were on your way,' he said, brightly.

'How did she know?'

'Don't ask me. Come on, the food's out of this world – and there's lashings of it.'

Sarah looked round. Mother Hilda was leading the Doctor and the rest of the little group, which had now been joined by Bob Simkins, towards the tables. Great. She'd rather been off her food since the Captain had been killed. She'd only had a small slice of toast for breakfast, and now she was ravenous.

But where to begin? She picked up a plate, and surveyed the choice. It was all vegetarian. You'd expect that from a cult that was derived from the Hindu faith, as Mother Hilda's book had said. But it didn't seem to matter. There was every sort of salad, artfully designed to be a feast of colour as well as taste; there were cooked vegetable dishes – green, red, yellow and purple with white and brown rice; if there was a pasta shape that had been invented, it was there, in its own particular sauce. And the fruit! Red-black and golden grapes the size of plums; actual plums so ripe that the skin was bursting with their juice; oranges like miniature suns; apples and pears and quinces and kumquats and...

'Here,' said Jeremy, pouring out a sparkling juice from a crystal flask. 'Have a drink. Non-alcoholic of course, but that doesn't matter. It really gives you a lift.'

'There's all sorts,' he went on, gesturing to a line of casks with taps, from which jugs were being filled with different-coloured juices. 'Or plain water, of course. That's the one at the end.'

Funny. The diamond-clear spring running through the rocks behind the table must be the one mentioned by the whaler.

'Why should they bother to put it in a barrel?' Sarah asked.

'Filter it or something I suppose. I never bother with it, anyway. This purple thingy juice is my tipple. Honestly, Sarah, it's the bee's knees!'

Sarah laughed affectionately. Jeremy's slang was always out of date. He probably got the expression from Mama. Funny how it used to irritate her. 'Not the cat's whiskers?' she said, taking the goblet.

'Probably that as well,' said Jeremy with a laugh. 'Have a taste and see for yourself!' He took a long swig from his own glass.

She lifted it to her lips, and was about to take a sip, when she happened to catch the eye of the Doctor, who was at the other end of the table. He was shaking his head at her. Vehemently shaking his head. What was he on about?

She lifted the glass again, and this time he not only shook his head, but was mouthing 'NO!'.

Oh. Yes, of course.

What was it he'd told them in London? Three per cent of some sort of drug in the fruit juice she'd nicked from the Skang place? Extremely powerful, he'd said.

Jeremy was busy filling up his own plate. She quietly put down the drink untasted.

'Mmmm! Dee-lish! The cat's whiskers, no question. In fact, I'd even go so far as to say it's the cat's pyjamas!'

'Hey! Is this mango?' she said, changing the subject. She reached over to scoop the orangey-gold cubes onto her plate.

'Mm,' he said with a mouth full of cherries and a nod.

The spoon was just about to go into her mouth when she thought to take another look at the Doctor. Maybe the food was off limits as well. But he seemed to have lost interest in her, once he'd stopped her drinking, and was talking intently to Mother Hilda.

Oh well, it couldn't kill her... A spoonful of sunshine! Oh, bliss!

'You know what, Jeremy? I'm seriously thinking of becoming a mangoholic!'

It wasn't as funny as all that, she thought, as he spluttered bits of raspberry, giggling at the idea.

Extraordinary that they had such an enormous variety of superb fruits and stuff, of all different seasons and from all the countries of the world. Better than any supermarket. A sort of Fortnum and Mason in the middle of the Indian Ocean.

She scooped up a dollop of the most colourful fruit salad and, as she munched, her eyes wandered over the scene. The sailors didn't seem to mind that their hoped-for pints had been replaced by draughts of 'thingy juice'. On the contrary, you'd have thought it was Pompey on a Saturday night. She even spotted the delicious Miller slipping off into the darkness of the greenery behind the palms, with his arm around a slim white waist.

She recognised two or three of the London Skangites, yacking away as if they were at a party in Hampstead. One had produced a guitar, and was belting out a Beatles number.

Another face... Yes, of course! It was Mr Gorridge, singing along like a teenager, happily swaying with the rhythm, hardly recognisable as the neurotically wound up First Officer of the *Skang*.

That's where all the food came from, of course. The *Skang*. It would be bound to have umpteen cold stores and galleys and stuff. After all, it was designed for a millionaire – and a millionaire's guests.

'By the way,' she said to Jeremy, who was concentrating on an ear of sweet corn, trying to stop the melted butter from running down his chin, 'we were wondering. Where's the *Skang*?'

He blinked.

'Sorry?' he said, his mouth full. 'Oh, fish hooks! It's all over my shirt!' He dived into his pocket for a handkerchief, and feebly dabbed at the greasy spots. 'Sorry. I wasn't listening. What did you say?'

'The *Skang*. What have they done with her?'

He looked puzzled. 'The Skang?' His face cleared. 'Oh, you mean the ship. They took it out into the deep water and sank it… Do you suppose this'll wash out?'

CHAPTER NINETEEN

The Brigadier had always had his doubts about bringing Sarah along with them, and now she was proving to be a real pain.

Dame Hilda was a charming woman – and, it had turned out, from a decent family. His grandmother had often talked about the fabled Olivia Hutchens, the first *Tatler* 'Debutante of the Year' after the end of the Great War. Hilda's aunt, apparently.

She and Brother Will (where had he seen him before?) were taking the Doctor and himself – with the two *Hallaton* officers trailing along behind – on a guided tour of the island, and as the official representative of the United Nations it was his duty to be polite and follow protocol. Whatever that might be in such odd circumstances, it surely didn't include rudeness such as Miss Smith's behaviour, tagging along just behind him trying to get his attention.

'Psst!' she said, for the third time.

Ignoring her yet again, he turned back to what Dame Hilda was saying.

'Of course, the number of the faithful is relatively small at the moment...'

The Brigadier uttered a non-committal grunt, noticing that the irritating child was now pestering the Doctor. Good. The Doctor was shaking his head at Sarah and whispering, 'Later!'

'But we are merely planting the seed. In years to come, the harvest will feed the hungry soul of humankind the world over. But it will take time.'

The road from the village (which had turned out to be, yes, made of golden-yellow bricks rather than the sand they'd

assumed) swept round the corner away from the rows of little villas to reveal a wall of stone, soaring upwards out of the lush jungle. It was the side of what could only be the extinct volcano mentioned in the Pilot book. An age-old rock slide had produced an almost vertical precipice some five hundred feet high.

'But then the spirit of the Skang is something quite new to us in the West,' Dame Hilda was saying. 'It can transform the world, as you'll see in just a moment.'

What was the woman talking about? Following her with the others as the road disappeared through a mini-canyon of volcanic rock, the Brigadier tried to concentrate on the matter in hand. Sightseeing, especially traipsing round buildings, ancient or modern, had never been his bag.

But... this was something else! For once the phrase was literally true. The yellow bricks ended in a largish clearing at the foot of a majestic staircase of white marble, which climbed in a perfect curve up the side of the steep hill. The top was crowned with a featherlight confection of intricately carved pillars, gleaming in the tropical sun whiter than any white he'd ever seen. It had a harmony that brought a yearning to the heart and tears to the eyes.

Nobody spoke. For a moment, nobody could have spoken.

'Our temple, dedicated to the great Skang,' said Hilda reverently.

It must have cost a bomb and a half, thought the Brigadier, coming down to earth as he followed them up the stairs. Bad form to say so, though.

As they neared the summit, all very much out of breath save Mother Hilda and Brother Will – and of course, the Doctor – the Brigadier noticed that, in spite of everything, Sarah was still up to her monkey tricks. She was now whispering intently to Pete Andrews, who was listening with a frown on his face. He seemed to be taking her seriously.

As they arrived outside the temple itself, they saw that the

pillars were the setting for two immense mahogany doors, twenty feet tall, with the deep sheen of a dining table that has been wax-polished daily for hundreds of years. At a lift of Mother Hilda's hand, the two tall guards who stood on either side swung them open as easily as if they were mounted on silken hinges.

She led the way inside. 'The island had a gift for us, as you can see.'

They were looking down into the crater of the extinct volcano, which had been turned into a circular amphitheatre, open to the sky, with concentric rows of seats. Behind the seats there were doors, each in its own alcove, which broke the curve with exactly the right sharp angle. As with the pillars outside, the total effect seemed so right that it couldn't have been otherwise.

Opposite the doors was a giant icon of the Skang, a painting of superlative quality, as striking in its way as the portrait of the Sutherland Christ in Coventry Cathedral – which even the Brigadier, dragged there by an enthusiastic girlfriend soon after its opening, had to admit caught the eye, much as he disliked it.

Again, there were no comments. Nobody, it seemed could think of adequate words. Mother Hilda and Will exchanged a smile.

'We'll leave you here,' she said. 'Our quarters – the rooms of the teachers and our organisers – are here in the temple. Please feel free to go anywhere. We have nothing to hide.'

So much for the Doctor's insane theory of an alien invasion.

'Thank you, Dame... ah... Mother Hilda,' said the Brigadier. 'You've been most helpful. You've completely set my mind at rest.'

'I'm very glad to hear it, Brigadier. I'm only sorry you had to come such a long way. If I'd known about your concerns before we left Bombay, we could have cleared this up in no time.'

'Yes, well... we'll have a bit of a look round and then we'll

be on our way. Nothing more to keep us here. We'll sail at once.'

The Doctor was frowning! Never mind, he could be dealt with later. This was a UNIT investigation, after all.

'We'll say goodbye now then,' she said with a smile. 'Tomorrow is the biggest festival of our year. I shall be very busy with the preparations for the ceremonies.'

Better be polite. 'Ah... can't we stay and watch?'

She laughed. 'Not unless you want to become a devotee of the Skang,' she said.

Heaven forbid!

'We've missed today's tide,' said Bob Simkins. 'We couldn't get over the reef at the moment. If we don't want to sail in the middle of the night, we'll have to wait until tomorrow.'

Did Dame Hilda look worried for a moment? No, no. He'd imagined it.

As the two figures in their white robes, who seemed to complement the scene so perfectly, turned to go, the Brigadier noticed that Sarah, now even more agitated than before, was about to speak. No! He wouldn't have it!

But instead, it was Pete Andrews who stepped forward. 'Excuse me, Mother Hilda. Before you go, I wonder if you'd satisfy a sailor's curiosity?'

'Of course.'

'Where is your ship, the *Skang*? Is there another anchorage apart from the part of the lagoon where we are?'

She looked surprised. 'No, no. She isn't here. The Captain had to go to Mauritius to refuel and so on. It's a long way, but it seems it's the nearest place.'

So that was what Sarah had been on about. Well, no harm done. But he'd have to have a word with the girl. Point out that she was only here on sufferance.

'I'm sorry, Brigadier, but I'm not daft!' Was he plain stupid? What was the matter with the man? She'd seen him dig his

heels in before, but this was beyond reason.

'Now look here, Miss Smith...'

'Of course he was speaking the truth. You should have seen how worried he was when he realised he'd let it out. They've scuttled it, I tell you!'

'But why on earth would they want to do a thing like that?' said Pete Andrews, mildly. 'One of the most beautiful craft I've ever set eyes on?'

Bob Simkins joined in. 'If you ask me, she *has* gone to Mauritius, just as Mother Hilda said.'

'Without the First Officer? Come off it!' Her earlier euphoria was fading fast. She turned in exasperation to the Doctor. 'You haven't said anything. What do you think?'

The Doctor tilted his head and stroked his chin with the back of his forefinger, which he often did when he wasn't quite sure. 'Mm. I must admit that I'd expected something of the sort. It bears out my conviction that these poor benighted youngsters aren't intended to return. On the other hand, it seems a crass thing to do if they knew we were going to turn up.'

The argument had broken out halfway down the marble staircase, when Sarah could contain herself no longer and blurted out what Jeremy had said, not giving a damn whether Mother Hilda and her satellite were still within earshot or not.

'Now, that's ridiculous. No way could they have known we were coming,' said the Brigadier.

'Oh, but they did. Jeremy told me that too.'

He looked at her with an infuriating smile. 'Of course he did, Miss Smith. And the place is swarming with your mysterious bug-eyed monsters from outer space. Good Lord! Look! There's half a dozen of them over there, swinging through the palm trees!' He set off down the stairs, laughing merrily, followed by the two officers, both trying not to grin.

Sarcasm always got under her skin. She opened her mouth,

looking for a withering retort – something to the effect that he'd better be careful not to trip – 'the thicker they come the harder they fall'– when she noticed that the Doctor had his fingers to his lips, and was shaking his head at her again. The message was different but just as plain:'Cool it!'

So she shut up. She felt that there was a fair chance that she might burst, but she took a deep breath and kept quiet; and followed the Doctor as he went after the others.

Hilda thoroughly disliked the term 'clairvoyance' because of its connotations of self-deceiving mediums giving dodgy demonstrations – 'Does the name Eric mean anything to you?' – or, even worse, private 'readings' at an exorbitant cost. 'Far-seeing' was much to be preferred, with its plain Anglo-Saxon etymology; and it certainly expressed with far more accuracy the faculty she and the others had developed since becoming Skang teachers – or perhaps the word should be 'adepts'? (Neither was entirely accurate. There was really no way of expressing a relationship that was unique in human experience.)

Hilda was sitting deep in concentration in her elegantly plain room off the temple, watching – in her mind's eye – Brother Alex climbing the long staircase. Was he coming to see her?

As she relinquished the image, she noticed again the regret, almost irritation, which she had so often felt before. If only far-hearing had developed along with far-seeing! Or even better, some form of simple telepathy. No matter how hard she tried, or what techniques she used, she'd found that they were limited to seeing – and even that was rudimentary, requiring total absorption for a very simple sighting.

When Will had first picked up the approach of the Royal Navy ship during a routine scan of the surrounding area, he had reported that Alex was on board, apparently ill, and most distressed. But had Alex betrayed them? There was no

question that the Doctor and the companion whom he addressed as 'Brigadier' were highly suspicious; why else should they have come? For that matter, the very fact that they had been prepared to mount an armed attack was evidence enough.

Being forewarned, she had managed to deal with the immediate situation. But she still had no idea whether she could now trust Alex. Whether or no, maybe it would be safer to allow him to rejoin, so that she could keep an eye on him during the next critical twenty-four hours.

It was too much for her to decide alone. She would have to refer the matter to the inner council.

'Mother Hilda...'

She opened her eyes. Alex was standing in the open doorway.

That was it, thought Sarah. They were all stoned out of their skulls on Jeremy's thingy juice, or one of its variants.

You'd have thought they were as squiffy as if they'd just been turned out of the pub and were on their way to the curry house, if it wasn't for the way they climbed into the boats for the trip back. It was starting to get dark, but nobody fell in; nobody even staggered or lost their balance. Nor was anybody looking for a quarrel. But their laughter, their shouting, their uninhibited behaviour would surely have earned them a reprimand at the very least if the Cox'n hadn't been in much the same state.

Even the Brigadier and the two officers had reverted to party mood, chatting volubly and guffawing like schoolboys. Telling dirty jokes, probably.

As they approached the mist surrounding the ship, which had thinned considerably by this time, she looked over at the Doctor, who was near the Brig at the other end of the launch. He was sitting as quietly and soberly as she was herself. She'd tried to get near him, so that they could talk and

compare notes, but he seemed to have deliberately kept away from her.

He was the only one who had believed her when she'd told them that the *Skang* was lying hundreds of feet under the sea. But after that, he'd ignored her. In the past he'd treated her like a trusted friend, so what was going on?

It wasn't until they were safely back on board, with the two launches secured alongside the ship, ready to act as ferries again if needed, that she cheered up a bit. As her feet touched the deck, she found herself taking a deep breath and relaxing as the tension went from her muscles. The smell of the mist... Violets? It felt like coming home.

A touch on her shoulder. It was the Doctor.

'You feel it too, don't you?' he murmured. 'Incredibly powerful stuff.'

What was he on about? The juice? But they hadn't had any.

'We can't talk now,' he went on in the same quiet voice, as the crew noisily thronged past them.

'Hey, Dusty!' came a voice from the crowd. The dishy steward turned.

'What?'

'As good as Kowloon Katie, was she?'

Dusty grinned and gave a two-fingered answer.

A cheerful shout: 'Doctor? Where've you gone?' It was the Brigadier, somewhere in the milling crowd.

The Doctor took her arm and drew her into the corner behind a ventilator. 'Just hang on tight. I'll see you in the morning.'

'Blighter's disappeared... Doctor! It's well gone six o'clock. Time for a burra peg!'

He took her hand and pressed something into it, and was gone.

'Ah, there you are, Doctor.'

'So I am,' came his voice, receding into the general hubbub.

A folded piece of paper.

'Be ready at 5am. Bring your camera - that Polaroid of yours. Don't let it take you over.'

It?

Again the faint whiff of violets...

Of course! It was after the mist had so strangely descended on the *Hallaton* that the others all began to behave so oddly. Come to think of it, she hadn't been exactly normal herself.

It must have been one of the effects of the stuff itself that had stopped her realising before. With every breath, they'd been absorbing a smaller dose of the very same drug that was in the drink.

She made her way to her cabin in a warm glow of relief. Everything was falling into place.

Now then, the camera...

Ah, there it was. Why didn't she think of taking it with her before? Why did he want the Polaroid?. Not that she had any choice. She'd lost her lovely little Olympus when she'd fallen into the drink.

Fancy her believing that the Doctor had turned against her! He must mean to go ashore at first light, and do a proper recce. And she'd be able to get some ace shots, and they'd be able to prove once and for all that the Brig was right, and that the Skang lot were just a bunch of harmless nuts. And all that nonsense about their sinking the ship! After all...

With a shock that almost made her jump, she seemed to come to, as if she was waking up from a dream. This was what he'd meant. It was taking her over.

Hang on tight, he'd said.

It was going to be a difficult night.

CHAPTER TWENTY

'I freely admit that I was wrong. I failed in my duty as the senior Skang representative in the region by allowing my own ideas to take precedence over the decisions that had been made, and by risking the security of the whole in allowing my emotions to be the motivation for my actions. I humbly beg that the inner council will recommend to my brothers and sisters...'

Drop the head, as though overcome. A little pause. Careful... Not too much...

'... recommend that my excision should be reversed, and that I should be allowed to enjoy once more... the fullness of the unity of the Skang.' Alex kept his eyes cast down. The little tremor in his voice on the last word might just swing it, he thought.

He knew quite well that his wretched appearance spoke for him. The sallow skin of his face, hollow on the cheeks, and sagging like that of an old man; the rawness of his eyes; the drooping of his shoulders – all bore witness to his desperation.

Hilda was sitting in a marble chair slightly to one side of the great icon of the Skang, like a bishop in a cathedral, with the massive Will Cabot at her shoulder. The remainder of the inner council were grouped around her on the raised platform, while Alex stood facing them, humbly alone.

He risked a quick glance. He knew three of them: Shunryu from Tokyo, who wouldn't catch his eye; Joseph Moskowicz from Warsaw, who had listened to him in Rome when he'd first mooted the possibility of a change of leadership; Sister Juanita from Brazil, who always sat on the fence. But the black man with one gold earring, and the woman with the mass of ginger hair who looked like a refugee from a Pre-Raphaelite painting were strangers to him.

It was difficult to tell what they were all thinking, as they murmured to each other. But then his heart leapt, as he saw Hilda's expression. She was a different matter. Hilda was sorry for him, no question.

Will Cabot caught his eye. 'Tell me, Whitbread...'

He didn't call him Brother. Or even Alex. Not a good sign.

'...why did you bring the Doctor and the Brigadier here? And the journalist girl? Why did you tell them where we had gone?'

Injured innocence, that was best. 'Me? How can you...? I would never have done such a thing! They already knew. I promise you. One of the crew of the *Skang* must have let it out. I expect the whole of Bombay knows.'

'Mm. You're probably right about the last bit,' said Cabot, who showed no sign of believing anything else he'd said.

Alex shook his head gently, as if saddened that one of his brothers could be so untrusting.

Joseph Moskowicz seemed to agree with him. He'd been frowning as Will spoke, and as he spoke to Alex, his face softened. 'Though I have to say that the way you behaved fully merited the punishment the council decreed, I consider that you have suffered enough.'

Will started to interrupt, but Brother Joseph put up his hand to stop him. 'In my opinion,' he went on, 'if a man of Brother Alex's standing is as willing to humble himself as he has shown himself to be, then it would be against all that we stand for, for us to deny him.'

But Will was not to be silenced. 'This man hasn't been caught smoking behind the bike sheds, for God's sake! We still can't be sure that he hasn't screwed up the entire project. If we trust him now, we could lose everything. I tell you, he is a bloody traitor!'

Alex could see the sympathy draining out of the other faces. It would do him no good to get angry with this fool.

'That's not only untrue, but illogical,' he said, letting his voice quaver a little. 'Why should I want to betray what has become the only reason for my existence? Can't you see that I'm pleading for my very life? If you refuse me, I tell you that I shall end it. There'd be no point in...'

Even as he let his voice trail away as if overcome with emotion, he realised, with a mental spasm that shook his whole body, that he was telling them nothing but the truth. No way could he go on as he was. His only hope must be that they would believe him.

But if Will felt any sympathy for his plight, like the Pharaoh in the Bible he hardened his heart. 'Right from the beginning, you've been sounding off about Mother Hilda's way of doing things. If we had listened to you...'

Hilda stopped him with a gesture. 'That is an entirely different matter, Brother Will.'

'But...'

'Enough!'

He was about to argue, but then turned away, his face set and grim.

For the first time, the tall black man spoke up. A Masai chief probably, thought Alex. Not one of the West Indians who were swamping the UK, thank the Lord. They were no friends of his.

'Nevertheless, Mother, the matter should be considered. For some it might speak in his favour.'

'It will be dealt with later, Brother Azeke. We've wasted enough time on what is essentially a trivial matter.'

With an almost regal nod, Azeke accepted the rebuke. But what had he meant exactly? Which side was he on? And what about the red-head? Was that a smile, before she looked away?

'However, Brother Alex needs to know where he stands...' Hilda continued.

Brother!

After a glance at the others, Hilda spoke directly to Alex. 'I can see that we are not likely to reach a consensus tonight. So, in accordance with our practice, the matter will be decided by a majority vote of a full meeting. Tomorrow morning. It may be that they will be as divided as we are. In which case, it may come to my having to use my casting vote. It's only fair to tell you that as I feel at the moment, I consider that you have recognised the culpable nature of your behaviour. If I am not persuaded otherwise tomorrow, I shall make it known that I think you deserve another chance.'

For a moment it looked as if Will Cabot was about to object, and object with some force. Instead, he took a deep breath and pushed his way through the group towards Alex.

Was he going to attack him physically?

But no. He came to a stop less than a yard in front of him, leaned forward, looked him straight in the eye, and spoke quite softly. 'Over my dead body, mate.'

Alex watched him as he stalked away towards the door in the marble wall that lead to his chamber.

'Okay,' he thought. 'If that's the way you want to play it.'

It was indeed a difficult night. Sarah thought it best to keep well away from everybody else, in case their artificial bonhomie infected her and she lost her grip on reality along with the rest. But sheer hunger drove her from her cabin, where she'd been keeping her feet precariously on the ground with the help of John Betjeman, her favourite modern poet, doing her best not to listen to the unmistakable sounds of a ship-wide booze-up.

'Sarah! Where've you been? We've missed your pretty face. Where's the delectable Miss Smith, the world's been asking. Come and join the party!'

Unbelievably, it was the Brig uttering these totally un-Briggish words. He was sitting in the wardroom with a half-empty bottle of Scotch at his hand and half shouting over the voice of Fats Waller, at full volume, telling the assembled company what his very good friend the milkman had said to him.

The Brig of all people! She knew he liked a dram or three, but he'd always known when to stop.

Two of the three officers gave her an even bigger welcome, pressing large gins and dry-roasted peanuts on her.

'Here's to Sarah, for she's true blue! She's a good 'un through and through...' sang Bob Simkins off-key, a slight bowdlerisation of the real words (which Sammy had taught her).

Chris, who was sitting on the floor, raised his glass and said vaguely, 'So drink, chug-a-lug, chug-a-lug...' and draining his glass he sank onto the carpet, gently snoring.

Pete Andrews lifted his own gin. 'To Sarah Jane Smith, the one and only,' he said, solemnly, with all the dignity of his recent elevation, spoilt only by a furriness of the voice to match his beard, and the Chinese coolie hat on his head, which had 'A Present from Hong Kong' printed on the side.

For a moment, the flattery of being treated as the only woman in the world nearly pulled her into the stream of inexorable jollity, to be swept away by the current. But then she caught sight of the Doctor, sitting quietly in the corner with an untouched glass of wine on the table in front of him. He didn't even have to raise an eyebrow.

Grabbing a handful of Wong Chang's best eggy sandwiches, she fled, with a quick 'See you later!'. Cries of protest followed her out onto the deck.

When she went to bed, she found it impossible to sleep. Although the sounds of the British seaman at play started to die down at about two o'clock, it was 3.25 when she looked at her alarm clock for the umpteenth time. In just over an hour the Doctor expected her to be ready... what was that expression the American astronauts used? Yeah. '...bright-eyed and bushy-tailed.' Huh! He'd be lucky.

Her exhausted brain gave up the struggle and she fell into the depths of sleep.

Brother Alex's night was no easier than Sarah's. His excision had not only had the most devastating effect on himself, it had also completely thrown the timetable for his takeover bid. It must succeed either before or soon after the ceremony. His erstwhile allies would have to be brought on board anew, and then the rest of them; and there would be no chance of that if he hadn't been re-admitted.

The thought of the bleakness of his future if he was turned away clamped his mind and cramped his guts. Instead of inheriting the lordship of the world, he'd be starving in a gutter.

He had to be sure that he would be accepted; and that meant neutralising Brother Will. But how? Plan after plan came into his mind, and each was discarded. One would take too long; the next was so complex that the slightest hitch could kill it; another meant involving too many people; and so on, and so on.

But by the time the stars were beginning to fade he'd made up his mind how to do it. There was only one snag. He'd have to find someone to help him.

Even with her camera case slung over her shoulder, it was very tricky getting down the rope ladder into the smaller of the two boats, especially as the Doctor had said they mustn't attract any attention.

Luckily, the sun wasn't up yet and there didn't seem to be anybody on watch. In fact, Sarah felt that if she really listened hard she might be able to hear the ship herself snoring. After last night, there was going to be one helluva hangover.

Once he'd got the boat far enough out not to be heard, the Doctor put away the paddle, started the engine and brought the bow round on a course for the island, though he didn't seem to be making for the beach.

'I'm beginning to get a pretty good idea of what's going on,' he said. 'You were quite right in guessing that there are many more than one of the aliens. I've thought for some time that the leaders of the Skang cult have been inveigled in some way into acting as herdsmen for them.'

'And Jeremy and all the others are their cattle?' She'd been struggling not to have that very thought.

'Exactly. I'm pretty certain that the Skang themselves aren't on the island. If they were, we would never have been given carte blanche to wander wherever we wanted.'

'So... where are they?'

'That's what we've got to find out. Maybe the ship wasn't sunk after all. But the first thing we have to do is stop the *Hallaton* from sailing on the tide.'

Good luck, mate!

He caught her doubtful expression. 'Exactly,' he said. 'I wouldn't have a hope of persuading Lethbridge-Stewart and the others not to leave. Even though the mist has nearly cleared, the effects of the juice are bound to last for quite a while. So it's up to you and me to get the evidence to convince them that it's not all hunky-dory on the island.'

Hunky-dory! The Doctor was even more out of date than Jeremy. But then, if anyone was, he was entitled to be.

'How are you feeling now?'

'Well, I could do with a cup of coffee,' said Sarah. 'I've only had a couple of hours' sleep. But I must admit, I feel a lot better than I thought I would.'

'Me too. We're still being affected by the mist.' He was steering towards the rocks south of the landing place. 'We must keep our voices down,' he said. 'I'm pretty sure they'll have some of those guard fellows keeping an eye open.'

He found a place where they could get ashore, a tiny inlet through the rocks with a few yards of sand and a convenient shrub to tie the painter to.

'What are we looking for?' said Sarah, in an undertone.

He put a finger to his lips. 'Ssh!' he said; and, with a last look round, he crouched down low and disappeared, snake-fashion, into the undergrowth.

Hitching the strap round her so that the camera case lay on her back, Sarah followed as best she could.

Aggravating man. Why couldn't he tell her what he was hoping to find out?

Alex took a deep breath. At all costs, he must hang onto the appearance of normality. This fool was proving more difficult to persuade than he'd expected. He would need all his old skills to do it.

'Once I am reinstated, the way forward will be clear,' he said. 'But Hilda's foolish habit of seeing both sides to every question means that she always listens to her precious Will.'

'But she said...'

'She goes the way the wind blows. Once he get to work on her...'

Dafydd was still frowning.

Alex had brought him here, outside the temple wall, ostensibly so that there could be no chance of their being overheard; but more to the point, the rim of the crater, on the side where the rock had fallen away, was the place to which he needed Dafydd to lure his victim.

'Dafydd, my old friend...' Just a light touch on the arm... mustn't frighten him off. 'I knew from that first meeting in Rome that you were the one. The incisive mind, the indomitable will...' – the susceptibility to flattery – 'Ultimately, to achieve the purpose of the Skang, this planet must be held in a grip of iron. I recognised at once that you are the one I need. You are the one who has the strength to make it happen. Would you let the mouse go free after it had eaten the cheese, and hope that you'd manage to catch it again? Mother Hilda's way is not only weak, it's inefficient. Don't you agree?'

'You know I do. But... but murder...'

Alex held up his hands in mock surrender. 'Okay, okay! You

win! My dear Dafydd, believe me when I tell you that I'm full of admiration for the integrity of your morals. I promise you, you won't be involved. Just bring him here. Bring him here – and then go and have your breakfast. That's all I'm asking of you!'

Dafydd opened his mouth to speak; and closed it again.

Got him! 'Good man! I knew I could count on you!'

Dafydd shook his head, still worried. 'What do you want me to tell him?' he said.

After he'd left, Alex found a good place to hide, and settled down to wait. He was back on course. Though he'd have to watch Dafydd afterwards. It might be a good idea to get rid of him too, before his squeamishness really screwed things up.

CHAPTER TWENTY-ONE

The journey through the jungle seemed interminable. Every few feet the Doctor would stop. For a moment or two he would be as still as if he were made of stone, listening. Nodding to Sarah, he'd set off again, with only a soft rustle, which merged into the background noise of the birds and the squeaks and grunts of unidentifiable animals.

Sarah found it difficult not to add a few squeaks of her own. Something very odd was going on. Although they were crawling over a soft carpet of leaves and powdery sand, her bare legs and arms were objecting strongly, as if they were being scratched. When she had an opportunity to take a quick look, she saw that her limbs were covered in a network of marks, and some of them were oozing blood. Yet, when they stopped again, and she snatched another glimpse, her skin was as clear as it ever was.

She tried to catch the Doctor's attention, but he didn't even notice.

At last, they arrived at the edge of the greenery, just beyond the tables with the remains of yesterday's feast, where the golden sand led up to the beginning of the two rows of little white villas each side of their shady avenue of flowers and palms. By now the sun had risen, and the red-gold light and the low defining shadows gave the scene before them a dimension of fairy-tale charm, and yet it was too aesthetically satisfying to be chocolate-box sentimental.

The Doctor held up his hand in warning. Down by the edge of the beach, next to the rock where they had landed the day before, stood one of the tall guards. As he shaded his eyes against the eastern sun, he was gazing across the still blue water of the lagoon at the anchored *Hallaton* and speaking into a walkie-talkie. He was too far away for them to make out his words, but he could have been doing nothing else than reporting on the few early birds who were now moving about the deck. Just as well that they'd set off in the near-darkness before the dawn.

The Doctor beckoned her over to him, and held a finger up to his lips.

She inched over, and saw that there was another guard, walking slowly down the yellow road, glancing from side to side as if checking that the inhabitants of the chalets were still abed, and scanning the edges of the beach.

'Got your camera?' the Doctor breathed into her ear.

In answer she hauled the case into view, opened it and took out the clunky great Polaroid. Oh, for her faithful old miniature!

'Get a shot of the street,' he went on.

What? Well, if that's what he wanted. Easier said than done, with that flipping guard keeping such a sharp eye on everything.

Moving very slowly, she pushed the camera out to the full extent of her arms, and lined it up as best she could without looking through the viewfinder.

As soon as he'd heard the click of the shutter, the Doctor backed silently into the shadow of the undergrowth behind them, indicating with a flick of his head that she should follow. Once they were safely out of sight, she sat up to find out what sort of shot she'd managed to take.

What was he on about?

As she tucked the pack under her arm to speed up the developing, she started to ask him in a whisper, but again he put his finger to his lips.

Oh well. All would become clear. Perhaps.

It was quite safe. Those men were much too far away to hear them. He really could be the most infuriating...

Hang on, she thought as she peeled away the top layer of the print and watched the image as it darkened. She must have put in a used cassette.

This wasn't the shot she'd just taken, the street of cottages, golden in the morning sun, with its double row of palm trees. She was looking at a street of buildings, yes, but they were nasty little huts, seemingly cobbled together out of old driftwood, patchy brown and sickly green with lichen and moss; and the road was a track of rutted mud and broken rocks, bordered with a few spiky bushes and the odd moth-eaten old palm.

She'd never seen this place in her life, so how could it have been in her camera? She looked up, and saw that the Doctor, with a very serious face, was holding out his hand for the print.

When he'd taken a look, he gave a nod, as if the image was no surprise to him; and then, seeing her puzzlement, he showed it to her again, and silently pointed to a figure standing in the middle of the rutted track.

It couldn't be!

But it was. It was quite plainly the second guard in his white robe. With a shock that seemed to blank out every other thought, she realised that there could be only one explanation.

It was nonsense to say that the camera never lied, but on this occasion it was telling her the simple honest truth. She was looking at a picture of the real Stella Island. The romantic view they'd seen only minutes before, the island paradise of yesterday, was nothing but an illusion, a hallucination, manufactured by her drug-fuelled brain.

'No, I'm not sure. It was only a glimpse,' said Dafydd.

Maybe Brother Will would mistake the shakiness of his voice for the anxiety he would naturally feel if the sailors were really gathering for an attack. As Dafydd had expected, Will was already out of bed and having his breakfast. He was dressed in his best white robe, ready for this important day. As the right hand of Mother Hilda, he would be largely responsible for the organisation of the ceremony.

'What were you doing out there anyway?' Will asked.

'Oh... I was out for a walk. And then I saw them. I can't be sure. But they certainly looked like the men from the ship.'

'Mm... I find it difficult to believe, Brother. Their brains must still be enfolded.'

Will was right, the whole ship's company would be under the influence of the juice for hours to come. This wasn't going to work! Alex had persuaded Dafydd against his will, and now he was going to be in trouble, real trouble.

'Yes, that's why I was so surprised,' he said. 'But I thought I'd better let you know.'

Will sighed and got up from the table. 'I suppose I'll have to come and have a look. Show me where you saw them. Are you suggesting that they might climb the cliff face?'

A reprieve!

'It seems unlikely, I know,' said Dafydd, as he led Will out of the door. 'But it wouldn't be the first time. Remember General Wolfe and the Heights of Abraham.'

That's what Alex had said.

Will, who was taking out his walkie-talkie, gave him an exasperated look. 'What the heck are you on about now?'

'Seventeen fifty-nine. The year of victories.'

Will gave a grunt. 'Oh, history. Load of shit.'

As they came out through the immense wooden doors of the temple, he spoke into the handset. 'Attention all units! Those near the foot of the mount, proceed to the cliff side. Intruders reported.'

Even more reason to get out of sight quick, thought Dafydd.

* * *

The next shot the Doctor wanted her to get was one of the temple. But that, too, was easier said than done.

To start with, it was nearly a mile away – and they could hardly dance like Dorothy and her friends up the yellow-brick road. In any case, thought Sarah, according to the Polaroid it was really more of a mule-track, like the one they'd come across in Anatolia, when Jenny took the wrong turning. For that matter, the guard showed no sign of moving off. And there'd bound to be some of his mates scattered along the way.

So they had to make their way through the jungle, which turned out to be more difficult than one might think. Clambering up and down the sandy slopes, and fighting through the thick vegetation in the dips between, was extraordinarily tiring.

But even worse, there would be moments, brief flashes, when the trees, the beautiful flowering bushes and the lush undergrowth seemed to vanish and in their stead she found herself struggling with thorny shrubs, and the scent of tropical flowers was transmuted into the stink of the guano that covered the rocks at their feet. At first, it lasted only a fleeting moment at a time, but as it happened more and more often, it lasted longer, and in the end took over completely.

The Doctor glanced round at her. 'It's wearing off,' he said, and ploughed on.

They must have been nearly there, when everything became too much. The effort of moving at all, together with the turmoil in her mind, brought Sarah to a halt.

'I'm sorry, Doctor,' she gasped, as he showed no signs of stopping for a rest, 'I'm knackered! You'd better go on without me. Here, take the camera.'

'Of course not,' he said, immediately turning back. 'How very thoughtless of me. We can't waste time, but a few minutes either way won't make a scrap of difference.

'Here, come and sit down,' he went on, indicating a convenient rock.

After a moment, she couldn't help blurting out what was uppermost in her thoughts. 'What *is* going on, Doctor? Is it a sort of hypnotism, or what?'

'Keep your voice down,' he said, with a glance in the direction of the road.

'Sorry,' she said in a half-whisper. 'But I'm thoroughly confused. We all saw the same things didn't we? I mean, everybody gets different trips on acid and stuff, don't they? So how can it be the effect of the juice, or the mist?'

'I'm not absolutely certain myself yet,' he said after a pause. 'A whole world has been constructed. As you say, we all experienced it. It's not the first time I've come across something of the sort. In fact, you've seen it yourself.'

'You mean the Experienced Reality thing on Parakon?'

'That's right.'

'A sort of telepathic computer, wasn't it?'

'More accurately, a radiated matrix of modulated psychomagnetic beams.'

Well, of course it was. How stupid of her not to know that!

'So this is the same sort of thing?' she asked.

The Doctor shook his head. 'It can't be. None of the requisite conditions are here. In any case, that was purely a visual and auditory illusion. Don't forget, you actually ate some of that food yesterday.'

'You mean... all the fruit and stuff wasn't real?'

'Oh, it was real, all right. It would have been something different, that's all.'

This didn't sound too good. 'Different? What do you mean? What, for example?'

'Oh, seaweed, old leaves, slugs, that sort of thing.' He laughed when he saw her face. 'Very nutritious,' he said. He stood up. 'Ready?'

She hauled herself to her feet.

As ready as she'd ever be.

* * *

'Funny place to come for a walk,' said Will, as they came out onto the clifftop.

'I just wanted a breath of fresh air,' replied Dafydd, leading the way along the edge.

'Mm. Bloody stupid if you ask me.'

Dafydd didn't answer. He'd be glad to see the back of Brother Will. He'd always been a bully.

'It's vanished!'

They had risked going through the gap in the rocks that, the day before, had taken them to the clearing at the foot of the great marble staircase.

'I mean to say! How could we have climbed it, if it wasn't there?' said Sarah in a half-whisper.

'All perception has a large input from the various structures of the brain,' the Doctor replied, equally quietly. 'The raw sense perceptions would never mean anything. They have to be recognised, and categorised. And a lot more than fifty per cent of that process is a matter of making new clay fit into the old mould.'

'But if there's nothing there to be recognised...?'

'There's a track, isn't there? And your brain was manipulated in some way by your Skang friends.'

'No friends of mine,' muttered Sarah.

The Doctor didn't reply, but silently pointed upwards.

Of course. The temple had disappeared as well. Instead of the graceful pillars that had so elegantly crowned the summit, there was nothing but a few piles of boulders.

Now, why should she feel so sad? Yesterday, the tears had sprung to her eyes at the very beauty of what they were seeing. But now she felt as if she'd lost something... no, somebody. It was like grieving for a dead friend.

She pulled out the Polaroid, and took a shot. Whether it would convince the Brig was doubtful. Everything looked so different it hardly seemed that they were in the same place.

* * *

'There. Where that bit sticks out. That's where I was standing when I saw them. Just below there, right at the bottom in the undergrowth.'

Would he take the bait?

With a sceptical look at Dafydd, Brother Will strode across to the very edge and peered over.

Now! Slip away into the bushes, and try not to notice him as he turns to comment; and try not to hear the sound of the running footsteps, and the gut-wrenching yell that follows, only to be abruptly chopped off.

In the awful silence afterwards, Dafydd scurried back the way they'd come, in a total panic, as if he were being chased.

'Oh, my God!'

The Doctor had turned back at the sound of the scream. 'What? What was it?'

'A man! I saw a man falling!'

'From the top?'

'Must have been. Come on!' Sarah took off along the track that had been cleared at the bottom of the cliff.

'Sarah, come back!'

But if she heard his hoarse shout, she took no notice.

Good grief! If the guards saw her, they'd be in real trouble. The Doctor gave a quick look round, and ran after her as she disappeared around the corner.

It was typical of Sarah. It wouldn't be the first time her impulsiveness had led them into real danger. Nobody could survive a fall like that. He'd be smashed into a bloody mess. She was going to be very shaken by what she found.

But even the Doctor was utterly taken aback by what he saw when he caught her up.

Her shoulders heaving as she tried to get her breath, she was looking incredulously at the body at her feet. It was dressed in the flowing white robe of a teacher. The legs and feet were hidden by the undergrowth, but the upper torso and the head had landed on the path, face down.

It wasn't a man at all. It was a Skang.

CHAPTER TWENTY-TWO

'I... I don't get it,' said Sarah. 'I'd swear this is where he fell.'

The Doctor was squatting down beside the alien corpse, turning it over to examine its features more closely. 'It's amazingly light in weight,' he murmured. He put out a hand to close the great staring eyes. He touched the proboscis and looked closely at its needle tip.

He looked up at Sarah. 'Are you sure that this wasn't what you saw?'

'Quite sure. It was a man. I only got a glimpse, but there's no way I could have made a mistake. I mean, look at the size of its head.'

It certainly didn't seem likely.

The Doctor stood up. His face was grave. 'You know what this means, don't you? You'd better get a shot of it.' But before she could even get the camera out, his head snapped round.

Voices. Somebody was coming.

As they crouched in the shadow of the nearest bush, hardly concealed, the words became clear. An Australian voice: '...round the entire perimeter. What about you?'

'*Niente*. Not a thing. I think Signor Cabot is maybe a little punch-drunk, eh?'

The voices were getting nearer. Sarah shrank back, as if to hide herself more. The Doctor pressed her arm to stop her moving.

Whoever they were, they were just around the corner. There was no hope of getting away. Their only hope was to keep as still as possible.

'The sooner the Limey ship gets going, the sooner I'll...'

Two guards had come round the corner and stopped dead.

'Holy cow!' said the Australian.

Not exactly an appropriate reaction from a devotee, thought the Doctor. And as for the other crossing himself...

'*Madonna mia*! It's... him...!' he breathed.

They both knelt down and the Aussie reverently touched the Skang as if to make sure that it was real.

'He is dead, isn't he?'

'You'd better believe it, Giovanni, me old cobber.' As he spoke, he was digging out his walkie-talkie. 'Brother Will, this is Brother Ed. Do you read me? Over?'

No reply.

'Brother Will, come in please. Over.'

Giovanni looked up, startled. 'Say that again!'

'What?'

'Say something, anything. Keep talking.'

'What you on about?'

'Do it.'

He shrugged and spoke into the handset. 'Mary had a little lamb. One two three four five...'

As he spoke, Giovanni was feeling through the robe of the dead Skang, and soon pulled out another handset, which announced its presence with the piercing shriek of howl-round.

The counting stopped. In the silence, the two guards looked at each other, nonplussed.

'We'd better get it up to the temple. Mother Hilda'll go spare. If the Skang is dead, that fouls up the reward ceremony completely.'

As he spoke, the Doctor felt an involuntary movement from Sarah. He tightened his grip on her arm, and as soon as the guards disappeared round the corner carrying the body, he slipped back into the jungle.

'What was it? What did they say?' he hissed to Sarah as soon as she caught him up.

'It was the word "reward"! The reward ceremony. That's what Jeremy said they were coming here for, to get their reward!'

That settled it. It was all falling into place. 'Right,' said the Doctor. 'One way or another, it's got to be stopped. The guard was wrong. It'll go ahead even if one of them is dead. There must be at least twenty other Skang to take part.'

She still looked bewildered.

'You still don't get it, do you? That was the significance of the walkie-talkie. They were calling Brother Will, weren't they?'

'You mean that the dead Skang...'

'...wasn't all that he seemed. Brother Will fell from the cliff, or was pushed maybe, and when he landed and was killed, he resumed his real shape.'

'Every one of those teachers, from Mother Hilda down, is a Skang!'

Bob Simkins, staring unseeingly at his cup of black coffee, removed his head from his hands, and said, 'Do you have to make such a bloody clatter with your knife and fork?'

'Sorree!' sang Chris, his mouth full of sausage and fried egg. Funny, he thought, he seemed to be the only one who was finding life as jolly as they all had yesterday. Never mind about last night's piss-up, they'd come back on board as happy as a crowd of soccer fans after they'd won the cup. And now – well, the blue mist had long gone, but it was as if the whole ship was sitting in a black fog of gloom. When they were about to go home! But then he'd never been able to understand why people fluctuated up and down the way they did.

The CO had sent a message to say that he wasn't to be disturbed until it was time to weigh anchor; the Brigadier, the Doctor and Sarah hadn't surfaced at all; and if Bob, as the acting Number One, hadn't had to get up to make the ship ready for sea, he'd still be crashed out, no question.

It had been a good party.

The Cox'n appeared in the doorway. Bob didn't even open his eyes. 'Excuse me, sir...'

Bob sat up with a jerk. 'Ah yes, Cox'n. Everything in hand?'

'I couldn't say that, sir. The Doctor and Miss Smith have gone ashore, it seems.'

'Oh no!'

'The small launch has gone, and both their cabins are empty. I checked. Shall I send someone across to chase them up?'

Bob groaned. 'The good Lord protect me from the clever clogs of this world. You'd think he'd know better... No. We'll leave it as late as possible. He's aware that we're sailing on the tide.'

'Aye, aye, sir.'

'Better tell the Brigadier, though.'

'Wake him up, sir?'

'If necessary.'

Rather you than me, thought Chris, mopping up his egg yolk with a bit of toast.

It made a sort of sense, thought Sarah, as she hastily wound her uncomfortable way back through the jungle. That would be why Alex Whitbread was so keen to get back. He was cut off from his own kind. He must have been left in Bombay by mistake.

And the way he'd reacted when she'd tried to take his photograph in London – presumably it would have shown him as he really was.

But of course! That's exactly what had happened! The Polaroid she'd managed to snatch through the curtain was a shot of Brother Alex without his disguise – if that's what you'd call it.

'You mean the Skang are shape-shifters?' she'd said, after she'd recovered from the initial shock of the Doctor's revelation.

In some of the tales with which the Doctor had whiled away their previous tedious trips through the Time Vortex, he had told her of his various encounters with those strange beings who could change their shape as readily as the chameleon its colour. For that matter, he'd told her, the TARDIS herself should have been an automated equivalent, if only one of her circuits hadn't given up the ghost – just as the relativity circuit had.

'Shape-shifters? Well... Like so many questions, the answer has to be yes and no.' He'd spoken impatiently, urgently. 'This is something different. But we haven't got time to go into it now. You must get back to the ship as fast as you can and tell the Brigadier that things are about to come to a head. It's time for action. He must remount his raiding party – but double it in size – treble it. Every available man! It may be hopeless. After all, we have no idea what powers these aliens have. But we can't wait to find out.

'Show him your photos and tell him what we've discovered. Everything. Tell him that I was right. The future of the human race does lie in our hands... and not at some time in the future. Now!'

'But... but I don't know everything. I mean, what do you think is going to happen?'

'It couldn't be more clear. There's going to be a mass ingurgitation.'

'A what?'

'The disciples are going to get their reward all right. By the end of today there'll be nothing left inside their skins but their bones.'

Jeremy! And all of those poor kids!

'But that's not the worst of it. I'm convinced that this is only an advance party. If the Skang manage this successfully, there won't be just twenty of them, there'll be thousands; and by then it'll be too late. They mustn't even start this "reward ceremony". You must make Lethbridge-Stewart understand that. He must do whatever is necessary to prevent it – whatever the cost. Now, go!'

'But what are you going to do?'

'Me? I'm going up to try to stop them myself.'

Of course he was.

Alex hadn't expected to find Brother Dafydd exulting in their success to the same extent that he was. But he was a little surprised to find Dafydd lying curled up on his bed, hugging himself to still the shaking in his body. If he turned up at the council hearing in that state, it wouldn't take long before the whole story came out.

'Dafydd,' he said quietly, so as not to startle him.

Nevertheless, he gave a convulsive jump, and a twist to see who'd come up on him so silently. 'Oh, it's you,' he said with a gulp.

Alex sat down on the end of the bed. 'I've come to say thank you. I felt in my bones that I could trust you, and you've proved me right.'

Brother Dafydd shuddered. 'I was okay until I heard that scream.'

Alex nodded. 'I was afraid it might catch somebody's attention too. Evidently not.'

Dafydd sat up. 'No, no, I mean that I...'

Alex's voice hardened. 'If you feel that you've soiled your lilywhite hands, then give them a scrub with carbolic soap. That's all in the past. We've other things to think about. I need your help. It's going to be a busy day for both of us.'

'No. No more. I should never have agreed to go along with your plan. I've always tried to keep the...' He couldn't go on. His face was working and twisting as his emotions took charge.

'I'd say you had no choice. Wouldn't you agree?' Alex let the threat in his voice be quite apparent.

Dafydd's head dropped. His shoulders were heaving.

Great Heavens! The man was crying!

Alex changed his tone. 'My dear fellow, you mustn't think that I don't know how you feel. I didn't sleep at all last night. To the end of my days I shall be grieving for dear Brother Will, who's been our anchor and our rock throughout these long months...' Was he going too far? No. The fool had stopped weeping. He was listening. 'For the rest of my life I shall have to carry the weight of guilt for what had to be done, for what was absolutely necessary for the success of the project. Be it on my head. You have nothing to reproach yourself for.'

Dafydd looked up. Alex leaned forward and took him by the shoulders. He looked deep into his eyes. He was enjoying himself. Like a concert violinist who'd practised until the music itself played the instrument, he relaxed into the skill he'd acquired in the Oxford Union and at the hustings, and perfected at Westminster.

'Oh, Dafydd, Dafydd. Haven't you understood? I must have you - and nobody but you - at my side. Who else can I trust? I shall be supreme on this planet, yes, but you... you will be the agent of my will. You will be my first minister, my chancellor, with total power over all, Skang and human alike. But nothing comes without a price. We must bear the pain together. We must learn to love the anguish. We can't escape our destiny.'

The old rule of three. It never failed. He could almost feel Conference rising to give him a standing ovation.

Don't let him look away.

'As I said, we have no choice. We must carry the burdens of leadership between us, you and I, for the greater good of the Skang.'

Now he must keep quiet; hold the eye and keep his trap shut.

Hold it...

Hold it...

Dafydd blinked. 'What do you want me to do?' he said.

* * *

Would he be in time?

The Doctor dismissed the thought, which kept popping up as an unspoken sub-text to his cogitations.

'No, not shape-shifters...' he was saying. 'They've shown no signs of taking on anything other than the human form. But it's not just that. In my conversation with Dame Hilda, there wasn't an iota to make me suspicious. I would have sworn in a court of law that I was talking to the same woman as the one I'd met before.'

He was talking to himself. Like the voluble wife who said to her mocking husband, 'How can I know what I think until I hear what I say?', the Doctor, when faced with an intractable problem, had a secret habit of discussing things with himself out loud – or rather, sotto voce. Though on this occasion it wouldn't have mattered if he had chattered away at full volume, as he was halfway up the five-hundred-foot cliff, clinging on by his fingertips and the toes of his boots.

The Gallifreyan duplication of physiological function was not confined to the heart, as the Doctor had told Sarah when they were precariously afloat together. One of its most useful aspects was the ability to separate the operation of the two hemispheres of the brain.

In the normal course of events, he would have tackled the mammoth task of scaling the very nearly vertical side of the volcano by letting the cack-handed rationality of the left brain be quiescent. The 'I' that was the Doctor would take a back seat and enjoy watching the expertise of the trained climber that resided in the spatial somatic genius of his right brain.

But if it was necessary, as now, he could leave his body–brain complex to its own devices and retreat into the logical common-sense processes of left brain thought.

He had decided that he had no hope of stopping the progress of the ingurgitation by tackling it head on. There were certainly as many Skang as there were national teachers and organisers.

Every one was a Skang, an alien with unguessable powers; and as he'd said to Sarah, there were at least twenty of them, possibly more.

His best bet was to get through to whatever remained of the humanity of Dame Hilda – the Hilda Hutchens who was, after all, a Fellow of All Souls as well as a Nobel Laureate – and persuade her to abort the reward ceremony before it started.

But would he be in time? The thought came bubbling up once more. Perhaps it was foolish to have started on a such a climb – a climb that would have merited an entry in the record books. But how else could he have got to her unseen?

'Stop your nattering,' he said aloud to his unruly mind. 'I'll either do it, or I won't, and that's all there is to it.'

He'd often said something of the sort to others. But somehow it seemed far less comforting now.

CHAPTER TWENTY-THREE

As Sarah neared the end of her arduous journey through the now doubly uncomfortable jungle back to the shore, she stopped and let herself drop down onto the ground. For a moment, she lay prone, letting the exhaustion seep out of her muscles, trying to ignore the smarting of the myriad scratches on her legs and arms.

It was bad enough the first time, but the second trip was just too much, especially towards the end when she was near the avenue of huts by the beach, where she had to be extra careful because of the Skangite followers she could see milling about.

She raised her head. Now that she was almost at the little inlet where they'd left the boat, there was the danger that she might be heard – or even worse, seen – by one of the watching guards. It was time to revert to the Doctor's snaking movements. It was slow, yes, but much safer.

It was a good thing she did. She spotted the boat through a gap in the bushes, and as far as she could see the mini-beach was empty, but as she moved cautiously forward she heard the murmur of a voice. She could just make out the words.

'Try Brother Will again.'

'What's the point? He must have the bloody thing turned off.'

She inched her way to a position where she could see the cove more plainly. Yes, there they were. A glimpse of white was showing through the dirty shrubs where they were hiding.

The boat was out of the question. How was she going to warn the Brig?

* * *

'And so you will vote for Brother Alex's reinstatement?'

Brother Bunnag from Thailand smiled. His twinkling eyes were smiling too. 'I think it would be the compassionate thing to do, yes. And skilful too, as you have indicated.'

With a word of thanks, Dafydd moved on, glancing round to make sure that his lobbying was as discreet as Alex had insisted it should be. If he could convince an ex-Buddhist monk, the rest should be easy.

Luckily, Dafydd found this first task given to him by Alex more than congenial. He was able to put himself heart and soul behind it. From the start, he'd thought that Hilda's softly-softly approach was not only unnecessary, but ultimately harmful to the cause. Yes, of course they should use the Skang bio-chemical method of gaining recruits to the cult and enfolding their minds until the moment of assimilation, but in purely human terms the organisation was so lax that, projected to a planetary level, it was guaranteed to collapse.

This planet was ripe, like a Victoria plum tree at the end of a hot summer, with its fruits so dripping with sweetness that the birds and the wasps vied with each other for the juice. The Skang could search for aeons and not find its like. It must not be lost.

Brother Alex was right. What had to be done, had to be done.

Curiously enough, it was only due to the influence of the late Brother Will that the whole thing hadn't fallen apart already. If only they'd been able to persuade him to join them! But his almost canine devotion to Mother Hilda had ruled that out.

But these others, whom he was working on one by one, had been unerringly picked out by the political acumen of Alex Whitbread. They were a far softer target. If Alex had had the time to do the same in Bombay he'd never have been excised.

Brother Alex had really understood how he felt about the death of Will; and he trusted him. Dafydd took a deep breath to still the sudden flutter of fear inside him as he thought of the other commission that had been assigned to him.

One thing at a time.

Who was that? Oh, yes... He glanced down at his list. Good. Another. He was doing well.

'Ah, Brother Gyogy, may I have a word?'

She'd have to swim.

But as she'd told the Doctor, she could hardly keep afloat. When Sammy had taught her to sail, she'd never stepped into the dinghy without a life jacket. How could she hope that her feeble breaststroke (that always degenerated into a frantic doggy-paddle) would take her all the way to the ship? She'd never managed more than a spluttering length, and the *Hallaton* must be at least a couple of hundred yards away.

It was no good trying to attract their attention. Even if she managed it, she had no way of signalling a message. Why hadn't they taught semaphore at St Margaret's Grammar? There was no way to warn them.

Oh yes there was! It was only a slim chance, but it was worth a go.

But first she had to get away from the two guards. She snaked her way down the coast until she was round the next headland, safely out of sight.

Yes, it really looked as if it might be possible. If she kept her nerve, she might be able to swim out to the reef that rimmed the lagoon – which at that point was much nearer than the ship – climb out onto it, and then make her way along its length until she was near enough to the *Hallaton* to have a chance of making it in the water.

But there was another thing... One of the snags of swimming – apart from the possibility that she mightn't be strong enough to make it, or might end up as a shark's lunch – would be how to keep the shots of the island dry. She had no idea what prolonged immersion in salt water might do to the Polaroid prints. And without them there wasn't a hope that they'd believe her.

She was still trying to think of a better idea than swimming when she pulled the strap of the camera case over her head, to hide it under a bush.

Aha! One problem solved, anyway. She unclipped the strap and experimented with changing its length. Yup! She could slip it under her chin, and fix the snaps onto the top of her head.

Shoes off. Keep the rest on, in the hope that it might afford a mite of protection from the coral. She waded into the sea, wincing as the salt bit into her scratched legs.

At least the water was warm.

He stood on the clifftop, taking deep breaths and letting his arms and legs recover from that last extra effort needed to get himself past the grassy overhang onto the clifftop. There seemed to be a slight ache and a trembling in his biceps – yes, and in his deltoids too.

Good grief! Was he feeling his age? Maybe the time for his next regeneration was just around the corner.

He dragged his thoughts back to the immediate problem. Now he was at the top, he had to get into the temple and find Dame Hilda. He could hardly walk in through the front door... but of course, there was no front door. Those spectacular gates of polished timber would have been a hallucination along with the rest. But the entrance would still be guarded.

If his perception of the temple had been still conditioned by the effects of the mist, there would have been no way that he could have climbed over the top of the sheer perimeter wall at the top of the cliff. But now it was a heap of boulders...

As he forced his limbs into action again, his mind wandered off under its own devices. Even to have built this makeshift barrier would have taken considerable effort. Did the Skang have super strength? The body of the dead one showed little sign of it.

Or had they employed contractors from Mauritius or some-where? It seemed somehow banal even to consider it. If so, what had happened to them? The Skang could never have let them go home.

He had a mental image of a scruffy tramp steamer leaving the island, with a load of brown-skinned workers asleep on the deck, and the captain in his cabin gloating over a box full of gold coins, like a pirates' treasure chest. Ridiculous. But maybe it came somewhere near the truth. Maybe their ship was sent to the bottom too; with all hands still on board.

He came out of his reverie to find that he was at the top of the fifteen-foot wall, and he could hear the murmur of voices on the other side.

He crawled forward until he could see down into the barren crater, half expecting to see an assembly of figures like the dead Skang.

But no. There was a small crowd of white-robed humans, settling in to the front rows of the seats, which now appeared as stool-sized rocks. A few of the teachers were coming into the natural arena from the caves in the sides of the crater. In the front row, he spotted Alex Whitbread, a pitiable figure, looking if anything even more haggard and ill than he had on the ship. The jigsaw was becoming clearer. This was why the man had been so desperate. As a Skang, he would have been hell-bent to rejoin the others.

The grand image of the Great Skang, which had dominated the temple, had disappeared entirely. Where it had been was nothing but the bare wall of the crater itself. In front of it, Hilda was already on the raised area, an expanse of roughly flattened pumice, talking to somebody the Doctor didn't recognise.

His mind went into high gear. This must be the beginning of the reward ceremony. The devotees must be getting ready to be brought in at this very moment. He was only just in time.

But how was he going to get to Hilda?

A change of plan. He would have to wait until the Skang had shown themselves in their true guise, and then intervene. After that... what?

Hilda held up her hand for silence. The subdued talking died down as the latecomers took their seats. The teacher who had been speaking to Hilda had left her to find his seat with the others, joining Alex Whitbread in the front row.

'Before we proceed to the proper business of the meeting, we have a sorrowful duty to perform,' said Mother Hilda. Again she lifted her hand, nodding, but this time it was directed towards the gap in the wall of rock that was the entrance to the temple.

All heads turned to look.

Through the gap in the boulders, down the roughly hewn steps, came four guards, bearing on their shoulders, like a dead prince, the body of a Skang.

Must be the same one we found, thought the Doctor.

As they progressed down the central aisle, there were murmurs of horror and shock.

The body was laid at the side of the platform, and at a nod from Hilda the four guards left the arena, back through the front entrance. The alarmed assembly grew silent as Hilda moved forwards to stand by the body, and started to speak, telling them that Brother Will seemed to have slipped at the top and fallen to his death.

'...and this is confirmed by one of our brothers. Dafydd? Would you be so good as to tell us what you know?'

The teacher who had been speaking to her earlier stood up. 'I was coming up from the village. It was less than an hour after sunrise – I'd been making sure that my people were ready for the ceremony – and I met Brother Will coming out of the temple. I walked with him along the clifftop for a short way. He told me that he'd had a report of intruders at the base of the rock wall. He said it was nonsense, but that he was going to have a look...' Dafydd, seemingly shaking with emotion, struggled to continue. 'If only I'd stayed with him! But I'd promised to be with my friend Brother Alex at this troubled time; and so I turned back to go to his room to try to comfort him.'

'There was nobody else on the clifftop path?'

'I could see the whole length of it quite clearly. There was no one.'

Hilda thanked him and he sat down. 'This is the first of our number on Earth to experience bodily termination,' Hilda went on. 'In the present exceptional circumstances, I think it would be inappropriate to continue at once. If Brother Alex is to be returned to the fold... and I do say, *if*... then it would be manifestly unfair to exclude him. I therefore suggest that we should briefly postpone the final Incandescence.'

Incandescence? Some sort of cremation?

It was very quiet. The cries of the gannet lookalikes seemed very thin and far away. The narrow strips of foam – like the lace at the hem of an old-world petticoat – which lapped at the edge of the multicoloured coral, made less noise than Sarah did herself as she splashed more and more inefficiently through the ripples.

She had found, to her relief, that the water near the reef was only about as deep as the shallow end of the pool where she'd been sent to learn to swim, going on the bus on Saturday mornings, clutching her shilling for the lesson (until her father lost his job and even a bob was too much).

So she was spared the ordeal of scrambling over the harsh coral of the reef, and she was able to stop and rest with her toes in the sand whenever it felt as though her muscles were about to give out.

She kept a weather eye on the *Hallaton*, so that the moment she felt it was near enough, she could change course, and make straight for it. It was when she was on her fourth break, as she was seriously beginning to think that she'd taken on more than she could manage, that she became aware of an extra sound on top of the natural ones. It was coming from the ship: voices calling out - and the distant throb of the engine starting up.

They were getting ready to sail.

CHAPTER TWENTY-FOUR

There seemed to be some sort of a trial going on. Dame Hilda had taken her place on the rough seat hacked out of a lump of pumice that was in the place of the regal throne of white marble the Doctor remembered from the day before.

In spite of his bowed shoulders, which spoke of the extreme weakness of his emaciated body, Alex Whitbread, who was standing to her left, had his chin arrogantly raised as he surveyed those about to judge him and pass sentence.

One by one, members of the group came up to stand on Hilda's right and speak either for or against reinstatement.

The Doctor was only half listening. Though, of course, the delay would give Sarah time to get to the Brigadier, the internal politics of the Skang surely couldn't have much to do with the business in hand?

After the first three or four speeches, which all seemed to be in Alex's favour, and the reaction from the rest of the teachers, the Doctor felt that the outcome was only too predictable. It almost seemed as if they were just going through a ritual.

Still listening with half an ear, his mind wandered off to consider the puzzles that still remained unsolved. How were the Skang able to disguise themselves as human beings with such uncanny accuracy? What had happened to the original humans? And how did the aliens land on the Earth in the first place?

He cast his mind back to the innumerable forms of life he'd encountered during his long years of wandering through space and time, and could think of none that matched the

Skang – though, of course, he still had to contend with the unpredictable gaps in his memory that resulted from the process of regeneration.

His thoughts returned to the present with a jolt. This was exactly the sort of distraction they'd been taught at the Academy to guard against. This was when one was most vulnerable.

As if he hadn't learnt the lesson for himself! There was the time, for instance, when he'd nearly lost a leg to a Sclaponian dragonfly, because he'd been daydreaming about the voluptuous wife of the Grand Vizier. Quite vainly, of course. Any sort of union with a Sclaponian, whether permanent or temporary, would have been a disaster. He'd have lost more than a leg...

A movement below caught his eye. Good grief, he'd let his mind wander off again! What was going on?

There'd been a show of hands. He'd registered that. Alex Whitbread had overwhelmingly won the vote. But what was happening now?

All the teachers were standing.

All, including Dame Hilda and Whitbread himself, had thrown their heads back, and had closed their eyes. A murmur floated up, a murmur that was not quite a chant, the guttural voices sounding profoundly non-human.

As the sound grew louder, the Doctor felt as if his brain was shaking in his skull – and he remembered something that had been hidden from him up to this moment. The only time he'd felt anything like it before was in the run-up to his last regeneration.

Desperate to stop his mind dissolving altogether, he covered his ears, and brought his awareness to a sharp point of concentration, hearing the sound as a mere unmeaningful noise.

Louder and louder, the off-key inharmonious tones echoed round the perfect acoustic of the crater, until, with a final shout, they abruptly stopped.

The Doctor blinked and took his hands from his ears. The atmosphere above the white-clad figures was shimmering like the air above a hot tarmac road in the height of summer. Or was it his mind that was losing its hold on the sight before his eyes?

A feeling of utter relaxation and peace swept over him as his sight cleared. It was as if he'd been looking at the group of Skang all along. The large heads, the staring eyes, the needle probosces, the shining bronze skin – all seemed utterly natural and right. These creatures, for all their gargoyle features, were not in the least threatening.

He was part of their family.

'Are you telling me that I can't believe the evidence of my own eyes, Miss Smith?'

The Alka-Seltzer had merely dulled the throbbing in the Brigadier's head. It had certainly done nothing to make him view the Doctor's latest escapade any more kindly. And now this preposterous tale!

The prints had been handed round the upper bridge for everybody to look at, including the Cox'n.

Even in the heat of the midday sun, Sarah was still dripping lagoon water all over the deck. When she'd arrived at the ship, it had been moving very very slowly ahead as they pulled in the anchor cable. Luckily, they'd left the rope ladder over the side, for when she and the Doctor came back with the launch.

Seeing how desperate she was, they aborted the weighing of the anchor, and were lying to the cable at half its proper length while they listened to her story.

'Please, Brigadier, you must believe me! The Doctor said that if we don't stop it, all the Skang followers are going to be ingurgitated, and...'

'What? What do you mean?' What the devil was the child babbling about?

'You know, like those people on Hampstead Heath. That's what the reward ceremony is all about.'

The Doctor was obsessed. Hadn't they had proof enough that it was all above board? 'Is that right? And how does he know that? Were they marching up and down with placards?'

'He... he worked it out.'

'You mean he guessed!'

Sarah almost stamped her foot in frustration. 'It wasn't like that at all! We saw a dead Skang!'

Mm. That might be a different matter. But the child was a journalist. She was quite capable of making it up.

Pete Andrews, as Commanding Officer, seemed as doubtful as the Brigadier. 'We have to catch the tide, you know, otherwise we'll be stuck here until tomorrow. I've no intention of trying that narrow entrance in the middle of the night. If the Doctor's not back soon, we may even have to sail without him. He'll just have to come back with the others.'

'But that's the whole point! They're not coming back! Why won't you listen to me!'

'Good God!' As she was speaking, Chris had picked up a pair of binoculars and was staring through them at the island.

Sarah turned to see what he was looking at. Her expression changed from despair to triumph. 'Look!' she cried, pointing at the beach.

The Brigadier had been wondering whether it would be okay to take another dose of Alka-Seltzer so soon after the first. But Sarah's change of tone brought him swiftly back to the matter in hand. 'What? What is it?'

'Have a look for yourself, sir,' said Chris, handing him the glasses.

As the *Hallaton* had moved forward half the length of the anchor cable, she had come into a position where they could see the beach quite clearly – and not just the beginning of the road and the huts, but in the distance, the top of the volcano in the middle of the island.

It was too far away to see at a glance with the naked eye, but as the image came into focus, he could see that the golden sand seemed to have turned black, and the avenue of neat white villas with its shapely palm trees had become something more like a mini-version of the shantytown on the outskirts of Bombay, in the middle of a bleak tangle of thorny shrubs.

'She's right, you know,' came Pete Andrews' voice. 'There's no temple, either.'

The Brigadier shifted his gaze.

As he registered the piles of rocks sitting at the top of the volcano where he had seen – and walked among – the pillars of marble, and the space where he'd seen the great doors, he felt his head swim; and it had nothing to do with the bottle he'd left nearly empty in the wardroom when he went to bed.

How could this be true?

He pulled himself together. Why hadn't he believed her? The Doctor usually turned out to be right in the end. They had been drugged, just as she'd said; and it must still have been having an effect.

'Miss Smith... Sarah. I owe you an apology. My behaviour has been inexcusable. Now tell me again exactly what the Doctor said. And this time I'll listen to you.'

The Doctor shook himself. These were the alien monsters who could easily become the agents of the end of the human race. Why should he feel such overwhelming warmth towards them?

All the Skang raised their heads and turned together to look at the one who had been Alex Whitbread, standing alone at the side of the makeshift stage. The creature he had become looked as sorry as the human he had been. Its white robe hung loosely on its thin frame, its cheeks were sunken, and its eyes, unlike the glistening orbs of its fellows, were half closed, dull and discoloured. Even the bronze skin had dulled to a blotchy mud colour.

The Skang on the other side of the platform, who used to be Hilda, lifted her hand and pointed to Alex. As if she were a puppet master pulling a string, all the rest, with one accord, raised their right arms to point at him as well; and at the same time their voices could be heard again.

But how very different! At first there was nothing but a soft hum, but gradually it grew into a changing chorus of chanted notes, with shifting harmonies strange to the human ear, which would meet each other – and then be lost – only to join again in ever sweeter concord.

The Doctor was fighting to keep a hold on the reality of the situation. This could be the siren song that lured him to an unknown doom.

He must be true to his purpose! These creatures must be forced to leave the planet, or pitilessly annihilated, utterly wiped out... but ah! How could his heart not melt? How could it not be entranced by such a heavenly sound? Surely this must be the very music of the spheres, the song sung by the stars themselves in the silence of space.

As the crescendo reached a climax that touched him more deeply than the most sublime of symphonies, it began to fade. The voices fell away, one by one, until there was nothing but one high, sweet note, purer than any flute, which lingered into a stillness that had the touch of silk.

Only then did the Doctor notice what had been happening to the forlorn figure of Alex. As if he had been absorbing the very essence of the sound itself, the bony figure had rounded into the muscular form of perfection; his bronze skin was shining as though polished by the sun; his eyes, now wide open and alert, were arrogantly defying the world; and he was standing tall, triumphantly restored to his former Skangness.

As the Skang that was Hilda dropped her hand and the rest followed suit, Alex, apparently to her surprise, walked firmly across the stage to where the corpse lay waiting. Raising his hand, he pointed. All the Skang bar Hilda followed suit, and after a moment she too complied with the unspoken command.

Naked politics, thought the Doctor, whose normal objectivity was fast returning. Maybe there was something there that he could use.

He became conscious of another sound coming from the assembled Skang. But this time it was a sustained hissing, an intense sibilation, a white noise that burnt into the brain and made it shrink away in self-defence.

Presently, as the sibilance became almost unbearable, he noticed a scintillation, a web of sparks, dancing over the skin of the dead Skang, which spread and expanded until it was one unbroken sheet of fire.

Soon the blaze of light was too bright to bear, illuminating the arena, shaming the sunlight itself. The Doctor had to close his eyes and look away.

A *whoosh* like the take-off of a Guy Fawkes rocket; and the light on his eyelids was gone. The sound of the Skang faded away.

The Doctor looked up. Alex and the others had dropped their hands; and where the burning corpse had been there was nothing but a little dust, and a wisp of smoke.

Incandescence.

CHAPTER TWENTY-FIVE

'Were you really going to go without us?'

'Well, it hadn't actually come to that, you know. We were keeping an eye out for the launch. We felt sure that you'd be back in time.'

Pete Andrews seemed a bit sheepish.

Quite right too, thought Sarah, glancing at the Brig, who for at least five minutes had been motionlessly standing and staring at the shoreline through his binoculars.

Surely he wouldn't have abandoned his old chum the Doctor, even if he was prepared to sacrifice her. But then, of course, they'd still thought everything was all gas and gaiters. Extraordinary cliché, that. What on earth could it mean?

She could hear the brisk sounds of the crew, as they pre-pared themselves for a resumption of the original plan for an armed landing. Bob Simkins, who, in addition to his other duties, had taken on the role of First Lieutenant, was still on the foredeck with his little crew of seamen in charge of the anchor cable. She could see him casually leaning against the mounting of the fearsome-looking missiles, as he waited for the bridge to make up its mind what to do next.

As she was looking at him, the Brig turned round.

'The book. That book. Have you got it?'

Chris, who'd been lurking at the back of the bridge keeping out of the way, jumped forward. 'The Pilot? Yes, sir! Right here, sir!'

He darted across to the chart table in its little protective hood, and turned to find that his CO and the Brigadier were on his tail. 'Here you are, sir. A hundred and twelve, I think the page was.'

The Brig took it and riffled through. Sarah sauntered across and did her best to peep past his arm as he found the page.

'Yes, here it is,' he said. 'I thought so. There's a sketch map as well as a drawing of what it looks like; and it shows the other landing place. Look here, Andrews. See it? An opening in the cliffs. I know that it's only rough, and it was drawn in nineteen thirty-three...'

'Nineteen twenty-three, actually,' said Chris.

'Whatever. And they were Swedish...'

'Norwegian, I think.'

'Pipe down, Chris,' said his Commanding Officer.

'Sorry, sir.'

'Not British, anyway,' went on the Brigadier. 'But it does show that there's an alternative route, which is pretty clear of scrub, up to where the spring comes out. And that's at the foot of the hill. We'd be foolish in the extreme to attempt a frontal assault up the road...'

Sarah frowned. That's just what he'd been planning to do before the mist changed everything, wasn't it? Oh, but of course, then it was just a matter of arresting some men and women. Now they were actually going to attack a gang of alien monsters.

'Lord alone knows what sort of weaponry they'll have,' the Brig was saying, 'so we need to take them by surprise.'

Pete Andrews took the book from him and studied it. 'Mm. And with any luck, they'll see us leaving the lagoon, and take it for granted that we've sailed back to Bombay.'

'Exactly. But we have to get a move on. Okay?'

'Come in, Doctor! I was half expecting you.'

He paused in the entrance to Dame Hilda's room. No longer the marble apartment, albeit small, that would have graced the palace of a Roman emperor, its rough walls of volcanic rock enclosed a space that was more homely and snug than luxurious. There was a couch piled with cushions, which probably served as a bed, a small table and a couple of easy chairs (made well enough from the local bamboo), with more cushions.

Did the Skang need such comfort, or was it pandering to whatever was left of the human she had once been? It seemed impossible that he'd seen the white-haired old lady sitting a few feet away turn into a grotesque alien.

'Sit down. Have you hurt your leg? You must be tired after that exhausting climb.'

Could she read his mind?

She laughed as she saw his face. 'No, not telepathy – more's the pity – just simple logic. There is no other way you could have got into the temple without meeting a guard.'

After the cremation of Will Cabot's Skang body, and a repetition of the unearthly chanting that had heralded the first bodily transmutation, the gathering of Skang had resumed their human shape; and as they did so, the rest of his empathy for the warmth of their oneness fell away. They were now no more than a bunch of disparate human beings going about their business as casually as a bunch of aldermen at the end of a local council meeting.

Most, the Doctor gathered, were going to prepare their flocks for the coming ceremony – so it was not so imminent after all. Watched somewhat quizzically by Hilda, Brother Alex, practically unrecognisable in his recovered human form, had gone through the slowly dispersing crowd like royalty on a walkabout, receiving congratulations and giving thanks to his supporters, exiting through the front to a light scattering of applause. Dafydd, after a moment's hesitation, scuttled after him.

The Doctor, having marked where Dame Hilda had gone, had realised that the only way for him to get down to the gallery where the living-caves were was to jump.

Thirty feet.

If he had been regenerated into a younger body, there would have been no concern. Or if he'd kept in training. But this incarnation seemed to prefer riding on various forms of mechanical transport to exercising. Indeed, it seemed disinclined to do more than break into an occasional gentle jog. Perhaps he should take up some form of sport. He'd always fancied cricket.

Still, once the amphitheatre was clear, there was nothing for it but to have a go.

Which is why he was limping slightly as he arrived in Hilda's cave.

'Will you have a drink?'

'Thank you, no.'

She smiled again. 'Do you know, I had a strong suspicion that might be your answer. I think we need to talk.'

'I quite agree,' replied the Doctor, sitting down opposite her.

Hilda leant back with her elbows on the arms of the chair and put her fingers together, her forefingers lightly touching her lips, in the age-old gesture of a university don in a tutorial waiting to listen to the lame excuses of a benighted undergraduate for a missing essay.

'I saw everything,' said the Doctor. Straight to the point. Get her off guard.

'Of course you did.'

A perfect parry.

There was a moment of silence.

'The question is, why have you come? You're not a foolish man, and yet it seems a foolish thing to do.'

She was as ready as he was to speak plainly. Very well, he'd match her directness.

'I hope to persuade you to abandon your enterprise, Dame Hilda,' he said.

Again she laughed. 'You'll have a job!'

'We'll see. But first, I need to ask you some questions.'

She settled back into her armchair. She was enjoying herself.

'Fire away,' she said. 'I'm willing to tell you anything you want to know.

'You don't believe me,' she went on, seeing his slight frown. 'You think you'll get the edited version, the one for public consumption.'

The Doctor nodded. 'As in our last conversation,' he said.

Dame Hilda shrugged. 'The circumstances are somewhat different, I'm sure you'll agree. There's no reason any more for me not to be frank. You see, you'll never leave the temple alive.'

As he'd expected. But was she aware of the corollary of that statement? 'Then you'd better be careful, Dame Hilda. If that's the case, I've nothing to lose.'

'I can see that. Nevertheless, it's the truth.' She hesitated. 'Unless, of course...'

Again the hesitation.

'Unless what?'

'Unless, Doctor, you're willing to become a Skang yourself.'

Dafydd had been quite proud of the way that he'd garnered support for Brother Alex. But when he saw the master himself at work, he had to acknowledge that it was only right that he should take second place in the coming reign of the Skang.

'I already have the promise of more than seventy per cent,' Alex was saying to Brother Joseph.

Seventy per cent? So far it couldn't be more than forty... Ah, but Brother Joseph didn't know that, did he?

'But the last thing we need is another visit to the talking shop. The time has come for action, direct action.'

'I'm listening,' replied the man from Poland.

'If we leave it until after the Prime Assimilation, it will be too late. We'll be stuck with Nanny Hilda in the foreseeable future. Is that what you want? Or would you rather be in charge of your own destiny?'

In charge? Joseph wouldn't be in charge, thought Dafydd,

with a shiver of satisfaction. Thank goodness he'd gone along with Alex. It was working out for the best after all.

On the other hand, Joseph had been near the top in the secret police before he'd defected to the West. He knew all the tricks. Yes, it might be a good idea to consider putting him in charge of security.

Alex, another scalp in his belt, strode on through the gathering groups of the faithful, seeking out especially those amongst the teachers and organisers who had the necessary ruthless streak, with Dafydd trotting happily after him.

'To be truthful, I've been wondering why you are not one of us already. You're not a human being, are you?'

She really was a remarkably astute woman, thought the Doctor. 'I'm a nearer cousin than the Skang,' he said, 'but no, I'm not human.'

'That would explain it.'

Was she making him a real offer? And did she expect him to take it seriously? He remembered how he had felt only too recently, and shuddered. It would be easy to be seduced. But how could such a thing be possible?

'How can I even consider such a thing unless I know every-thing about the Skang?' he said. 'Every detail. You fobbed me off once before. How do I know that you won't try again?' How indeed?

'I told you no lies, Doctor. It was nothing but the truth. Not the whole truth, I admit. But when can anybody know the whole truth of any matter?'

The Doctor reminded himself again that the being he was dealing with was not only a professor but the recipient of the recently introduced Nobel prize for philosophy. If he could make her angry, perhaps she would give herself away.

'That, my dear Hilda, is as neat a bit of sophistry as I've heard for years.'

'Touché!'

She was taking it all far too lightly. He must bring her down to earth… 'I remember what you said verbatim. "The Skang pierces the very heart and mind…" But it's not only the mind that is pierced, is it? The Skang are space parasites. Isn't that right?'

Hilda was no longer smiling. 'It might seem that the Skang is parasitic. I would prefer to see its life process as symbiotic. What, after all, is the purpose – the most sublime aim – of a human, of any life beyond that of the mere animal?'

'The "good life"? That will be debated as long as intelligence lasts,' replied the Doctor.

'To be free from suffering, to be happy in this existence, and ultimately to experience the joy of the unity of being that lies beneath the world of appearances. Would you disagree with that? And that's exactly what we offer.'

'If I were offered the *Mona Lisa* for a fiver, I'd know it was a fake. I can buy paradise on the street corner of any big city – yes, and end up as dead as your victims.'

He wasn't succeeding in making her angry, but her response was passionate.

'They are *not* victims! They die, yes, but who will not? Are you immortal, Doctor? You didn't finish your quotation. "…the devotee vanishes forever in the ecstasy of the divine union." Remember?'

Careful! He mustn't let her make *him* angry, or the advantage would swing to her side. 'How very uplifting! Presumably your prey…' He lifted a hand to stop her interrupting him. 'I presume that your prey – and I use the word advisedly – as they're injected with the digestive enzymes, also get their "reward" – a massive overdose of the hallucinogen you use to give them their earthly paradise. No wonder they die in ecstasy. And all to supply food – and a psychic orgasm? – for a tribe of interplanetary leeches. Or am I wrong?'

For a moment he thought he'd succeeded. A flash of something very like anger passed across her face. But it was instantly replaced by her usual expression of calm and equanimity.

'A most unpleasant image, Doctor. May I offer you a more wholesome one? A swarm of bees. It's difficult to tease out whether the swarm itself is the individual or whether it is the particular bee. But each bee gathers the honey to feed the hive – and in return gives life to the next generation of the flowers it visits.

'In return for what is taken, the Skang heals the wound in the human spirit. All those born on this planet know only too well the emptiness that lies beyond their deepest yearning. The Skang fills that gap. Perfect symbiosis. My students would probably have called it a win–win situation.

'Let me explain. I don't know whether the Great Skang... and of course this is merely what it is called on Earth... I don't know whether there are a lot of them out there, or if it's a solitary mutation. I would suspect that there are countless examples, otherwise I can't see how it could have evolved in the first place. But I know only the one. It has drifted through space for ages past.'

'Aimlessly drifting? That hardly fits the facts.'

Dame Hilda nodded. 'You're right of course. It controls its path by the interaction of gravity and its own psionic energy. You might call it a colony of proto-Skang, with one conscious-ness and one purpose – to search out planets with intelligent races, which can feed its need for the psionic energy that keeps it going.'

The Doctor was beginning to understand. 'And when it chances upon a possible world,' he said, 'some scouts leave the swarm and fly off to make sure that the honey exists and can be gathered?'

'That's right. And the colony waits. It's waiting now. The Great Skang himself is in orbit, just beyond the moon.'

'...and I feel sure that there'll be many opportunities. With the colossal task that lies ahead, I shall need your help, my dear. There has been far too little female input so far. Mother Hilda's unconscious jealousy, perhaps, of those who are younger and... let's be frank... more attractive!'

Sister Till, from Holland, blushed. But she didn't take her hand away from Alex's.

Silly old bat, he thought. Fifty plus and counting, with the face of a frog and a figure to match. 'In any case,' he went on, with a twinkle and the suspicion of a wink, 'it'll give us an opportunity to get to know each other better.'

She opened her eyes very wide. Had he gone too far?

She took a deep, visibly shivering breath. 'Oh! I'd like that,' she murmured, when she managed to speak.

Alex, with a hint of the famous smile so beloved by his caricaturists, moved on through the gathering disciples. He'd spotted another possible.

Alex turned, as he felt Dafydd at his shoulder. 'Shouldn't you be gathering up the Celtic fringe?' he asked irritably.

Watching him leave with his tail down, he shook his head. If anyone qualified as a loser, Dafydd was out in front. The sooner he got rid of him the better.

'Ah, good, I was hoping to bump into you,' he said to his next target, the teacher from Madrid. 'I expect you've heard that I've been asked to lead the New Council.'

Brother Manoel frowned. 'There have been all sorts of rumours, yes. And I must say that I'm not at all...'

'I just wanted to assure you that I shall say nothing about the unfortunate business of the...' he lowered his voice, '...the Ronaldo legacy.'

The blood drained from Manoel's cheeks. 'But... I told you about that in confidence!'

'Exactly. That's why I'll keep quiet. Unless, of course, it really becomes necessary.'

'Necessary? What do you mean?'

'But of course it'll never come to that. Great to have you on board.'

With a smile, and a light touch to Manoel's upper arm (a

reassuring technique he'd learned as a junior whip), he moved away.

The time for the Prime Assimilation was fast approaching. He shut his eyes as the craving swept through him once more, and he remembered its clandestine gratification on Hampstead Heath.

Just a few more steps, and there'd be nothing between him and a future of endless bliss.

CHAPTER TWENTY-SIX

'Why hasn't the colony been noticed? Is it hiding behind the moon?'

'No, no. There's no need. It's far too tenuous for it to be detected from the surface.'

The confrontation between them had lapsed. The Doctor was too interested.

'Well, at least I know now how the Skang arrived on the Earth. It has been a puzzle, I must admit, as there was no record of any landing.'

'Nothing so simplistic, Doctor. The colony – the Great Skang – releases a small cloud of... of spawn, I suppose you could call it, which floats down through the atmosphere and automatically gravitates towards the most vital of the dominant species.'

'I see. And each... each "egg"...? Each one hatches out in a brain, I suppose, and takes control of it. But...' He stopped. It still didn't make sense. The dead Will Cabot was visibly a creature unlike any human, not an ex-champion boxer who'd been the puppet of an alien master. And the woman sitting in front of him... 'But you're still Hilda Hutchens, the Hilda Hutchens I met in Oxford, and it's quite plain that you're in absolute control of what you're doing. And yet... I saw for myself... What are you? A Skang who can fool me by taking on the shape of an old friend? Or a human being called Hilda, who willingly becomes something else?'

'Neither. Both,' she answered. Getting up, she started to pace up and down as she must have done when she was lecturing her students, trying to get across to them the concepts that were so clear to her. 'I told you earlier that I can't read your mind. That's true. It wasn't necessary for survival, so it never evolved. But that's not to say that my mind can't impose a thought, a perception, onto yours. Natural selection has made sure of that. But it happens without any volition from me. What you're looking at is a telepathic illusion of the original Hilda Hutchens. And yet, in a sense, it's still me.'

The Doctor frowned. 'I think you must be mistaken...'

Hilda laughed. 'Recognised code for "You're talking balderdash!" Right, Doctor?'

'When I met you in Bombay, I shook hands with you...' He stood up and took hold of her arm. 'You're as solid as the floor we're standing on.'

'I've seen many a deep hypnotic subject who would have said the same about an induced hallucination,' she replied. 'And this is a thousand times more powerful than hypnosis. If I were to scratch your face with these fingernails - these fingernails that exist only as an idea in my mind and yours - believe me, you would bleed real blood.'

'I'll take your word for it,' said the Doctor. 'You were saying...?'

'You could take the total process as the physical analogue of a spiritual conversion,' she said. 'But I'm not just metaphorically born again. I've been remade. Literally.'

If a professor of philosophy uses the word, she means it. Literally.

'Each "egg", as you call it, is breathed in by an individual and enters the bloodstream, and settles in the brain - to be exact, in the hypothalamus. As it grows, it takes over the host body cell by cell, starting with the brain itself. So, although the body gradually takes on the form of a Skang, it automatically uses this massive telepathic power to fool any observer that the original human still exists. And perhaps it does.'

Not balderdash. But surely illogical... 'But you've just described a physiological take-over that would destroy the very structure of the human being, cell by cell,' the Doctor said.

'Not destroy. Transmute, change. Where does your identity lie? What makes you the Doctor, rather than Joe Bloggs the dustman, or the next president of the United States?'

'I see what you mean,' said the Doctor slowly. 'You're saying that as the Skang grows into the brain cells and their neural pathways, it also takes over the memories and so on – the conditioning, the attitudes... The whole personality, in fact.'

'Exactly. I never felt that there was something gradually possessing me. I just became more and more aware of this inner core of experience and knowledge that was growing inside me, which was the collective mind of the Skang itself.

'At first I thought I was going mad; and then it seemed that I must be having some sort of a mystical experience. But in a very short time – just over six weeks it took – everything became clear. I was a Skang – and it seemed as if I always had been, and had only just found out; and more than that, when I made contact with my fellows and discovered how to become the real me, I found that I was nothing less than the Great Skang himself! And that... that wasn't an experience, something to categorise as good or bad. It just was. An utter liberation.

'I didn't give a damn whether I was Hilda Hutchens or not. She went on existing as the complex of processes she'd always been, with all the likes and dislikes, all the opinions and beliefs and prejudices that she'd developed over the years.

'She never stopped knowing that she was Hilda Hutchens. And I'll tell you something else. When I'm presenting myself as her, I'm as subject to the illusion of my physical solidity as you are. It's another evolutionary necessity. We'd never get away with it unless we believed it utterly. So, does the "I" that was me before still exist? If you can answer that, Doctor, you deserve to win the next Nobel prize!'

* * *

Jeremy was feeling far from chuffed. In fact he decided that he was definitely unchuffed. Or should that be dischuffed?

After all, you would think that twenty grand would make sure you didn't find yourself shoved into the middle of a mixed bunch of scruffy hippy types – yes, of course he felt full of loving-kindness towards them and all, but there were limits. They'd been pushed and pulled around like a herd of cows.

At least he was standing near to Emma. Though she hadn't talked to him much today. She just sort of looked through him.

Even when he was in the sixth form at Holbrook, Jeremy hadn't managed to get the respect he deserved. Nobody asked him to be in the first eleven, for instance (or the second, for that matter), and when he sort of hinted at it, everybody fell about laughing. You'd never think that Mama was in the prospectus as one of their patrons; and that hadn't cost a bag of salted peanuts either.

And there was that time he'd tried to go to the front of the queue at dinnertime, and all those fags, a bunch of little blighters from the third form for crying out loud, they'd just crowded him out. Giggling too. Admittedly he wasn't a prefect, but whose fault was that?

'You know,' he said to Emma, who'd been jostled into a position right next to him, 'I was really pleased when we first arrived on the island and we found that our lot from London were in the chalet thingies down at the bottom, near the sea. I mean, for swimming and all. And sunbathing and stuff.

'I didn't realise it would mean being right at the back of the flipping queue. With my luck, by the time we get up there, they'll have run out of rewards. It jolly well isn't fair.'

Emma at last deigned to look at him. 'Oh, for God's sake belt up, you little twit,' she said.

'Ingurgitation?' How disgusting. I much prefer the word we use, "assimilation". But whatever you want to call it, Doctor, you'll have to make up your mind by the time it starts. You haven't very long. The time for the Prime Assimilation is non-negotiable, I'm afraid.'

Should he pretend to go along with her extraordinary offer? It might give him a little more time to try to convince her – though his tactics so far had been a shameful failure.

'Why is that?' he asked. The information could be useful.

Dame Hilda didn't answer at once.

'I suppose there's no reason why you shouldn't know,' she said, after a moment's consideration. 'It's a plain matter of fact, as you'll see for yourself. This island wasn't chosen at random. It lies between the Tropic of Cancer and the Tropic of Capricorn, and...'

The Doctor interrupted her. 'And today is the day of the equinoctial spring tide!'

She looked at him in amazement. 'You astonish me, Doctor. How did you know that that was relevant?'

'You told me that the Great Skang uses gravity to help navigate space. The influence of the gravity of the sun and the moon will be greater here, today, than anywhere else at any other time. So if the Great Skang is to descend to Earth...'

Dame Hilda was smiling with delight.

'I knew you should be one of us!' she said. 'You're quite right. To use psionic energy alone would be far too costly. He will use the gravity waves to come down from the heavens to receive the... er...' She paused.

'The sacrifice?' said the Doctor.

'If you like. I was about to say, the glad offering of his disciples. It would be more accurate.'

He was starting to feel angry again. 'The Inca virgins were equally glad to allow their priests to butcher them. They ended up equally dead.' That must have blown it. Too late to pretend to be persuaded now.

'You can't do it, Doctor. You can't rile me no matter what you say. I notice within a nano-second when Hilda's reaction starts, and it's gone in another.'

So much for that. He wasn't doing very well.

Hilda continued, 'The trigger for his coming is the Prime Assimilation, which I shall carry out myself. So you see, the timing is crucial.'

Indeed it was. Unless he could do something about it pretty soon, this gentle, white-haired old lady was going to stab a weapon sharper than any dagger into the throat of one of those youngsters out there, inject a noxious fluid, and absorb into herself the liquefied (and to a Skang, no doubt quite delicious) guts.

The message from the Doctor was quite categorical. They had to be stopped *no matter what it cost*.

The Brigadier shook his head to clear it. His headache had long gone, but it must be that he was still under the influence of the Skang drug to a certain extent.

From what Sarah had told them, and from what they had seen on the beach and the road before they left the lagoon, it was plain that nothing was going to happen while the teachers were down in the hut village, among the Skangite devotees.

The plan was to get into a position where the teachers could be ambushed as they returned to the temple, where the vital ceremony was to take place. Once they were inside, it would be impossible to surprise them. As long as the ring-leaders were taken in good time – could they really be disguised bug-eyed monsters? – there should be no need for any bloodshed.

Though there might be some.

'Lower away... Handsomely, handsomely!' It was the voice of the Cox'n.

The original landing parties were being mobilised anew; two boats would carry eighteen seamen, Petty Officer Hardy, himself and the two senior officers. Twenty-two armed men to arrest as many Skang, it seemed. Would it be enough?

His internal chuntering was interrupted by Sarah's voice.

'They'll all be out of their huts about now,' she said in a worried tone. She glanced at her watch. 'Must be getting ready to go up to the temple. Can't we get a move on?'

The Brigadier didn't answer. These things took time. It was a rhetorical question in any case. It was just her anxiety talking. After all, she was very young, with little experience of things like this.

He took another look at the temple, and the path outside. There was no sign of the disciples. But she was quite right. It couldn't be long before they all started trooping up. And once they were inside, and they started the ceremony, according to the Doctor it would be too late.

What were the crew doing down there? Surely they must be ready by now?

Pete Andrews came up the ladder onto the bridge to take a look at the shore in his turn.

The Brigadier glanced at him. 'Can't we get a move on?' he said.

'But you don't have to have a reason, a purpose, for showing mercy. There is a natural moral law that demands it.'

Knowing that time was running out, the Doctor was making one last effort.

'Well tried, Doctor. But you're forgetting that I'm a Skang. To fulfil our purpose is not just a categorical imperative. It's the essence of our survival. Everything gives way to that.'

Mother Hilda glanced at her watch and stood up; and then she tilted her head on one side and gave a little laugh. 'There you are, you see, Doctor,' she said. 'A perfect example of our dual existence. Hilda Hutchens has to run her life to a strict timetable; she has done for years, so why should she stop now? But I don't need a mechanical gadget to tell me that we have to bring this discussion to an end. I can feel in my real body that it won't be long now before the sun and the moon will have aligned themselves with the Earth. The gravity waves are as palpable to me as a breeze on the cheek is to you.'

So. All that was left was the hope that Sarah had managed to warn Lethbridge-Stewart.

'What are you going to do with me?' he asked.

'You'll be confined in here until after the ceremony. I can't make the decision on my own. It may be that the Great Skang will decide to seed you whether you want it or not. I hope so, Doctor. I've enjoyed our talk. It would be pleasant to think that we might be able to continue it at some time in the future.'

A voice came from from the doorway. 'There you are, you see. I told you she wasn't to be trusted!'

They both turned. Alex Whitbread was standing in the opening, flanked by half a dozen or more of the teachers and a couple of brawny guards.

'Here's clear evidence of her treachery,' he went on.

Dame Hilda's years of authority came to the fore. 'What the devil do you think you're doing, Alex Whitbread?'

She might have been talking to a bolshie undergraduate.

'You've been deposed, *Sister* Hilda. You are no longer the leader. I have been asked to take over.'

She looked at him over her glasses. 'Leader? What sort of talk is that? When have I ever called myself a "leader"?'

'Silence! You've had your say for too long. Guards!'

The two men stepped forward. Unlike any other of the protectors of the Skang the Doctor had so far seen, they were carrying what appeared to be primitive but deadly spears of thick bamboo, with wickedly sharpened points.

'You will be kept in protective custody until the New Council decides your fate. I have no doubt that they will agree with me that mere dissolution would be too good for you.'

'Meaning?'

'You showed me no mercy. Why should I show you any? You called yourself Mother. Very fitting. You sentenced me to excision as casually as Mummy used to force her children to swallow tablespoonfuls of castor oil...'

'In the hope that it might do them some good, yes! I can see that in this case the medicine has failed to do its job.'

'Well, Daddy Alex has your best welfare at heart. We'll see how you like the taste.' He turned to the Doctor. 'As for you,' he said, 'it's merely a matter of deciding the most satisfying way to rid our world of you. It was plain to me all along that it was you who was really the one in charge of the feeble attempt to hunt us down, not that fool of a soldier.'

'You'd be well advised not to underestimate the Brigadier, Mr Whitbread.'

'Is that so, Doctor? Maybe you're right. The point is academic. HMS *Hallaton* has sailed out of the lagoon. Your friends have gone home and left you. What a pity you'll have no opportunity to say goodbye.' He turned to the guards. 'Helmut, stay at the door – and Hank at the window. Come along, the rest of you. We have some mopping up to do before the ceremony.'

He stalked away, followed by his little retinue. As they disappeared, his voice floated back. 'If they try to escape, kill them.'

CHAPTER TWENTY-SEVEN

There were different sorts of fear, thought Sarah, as she kept watching the path up to the top of the mountain. This wasn't the old butterflies in the tummy bit. This was more the solid lump rising into the throat that you got when you were ludicrously late for work, and you'd been warned, and you might get the sack, and you were so out of breath it hurt, and there wasn't a hope in hell of making it.

What would happen if they were too late to stop the Skang?

At last! The rattle of feet up the metal steps, and Bob Simkins' head popped up. 'The landing parties are embarking now, sir.' He disappeared.

'About time,' muttered the Brig as he turned to go. 'Come along Miss Smith. But remember, keep your head down, and don't get in the way.'

Cheek! You'd think he'd know her better by now.

Her choking apprehension had vanished in a moment. She started to put down the borrowed binoculars. But she couldn't resist a last check.

A flash of white.

Oh no! A stream of long-robed figures nearing the top of the path! The teachers were going into the temple... and, yes, at the bottom there was a less orderly line of figures in the mixed bag of white clothing that showed them to be the queue of disciples, marshalled by the recognisable tall figures of the guards.

'Brig! I mean, Brigadier! Come back, it's too late!'

'What?' He was back beside her in no time, almost snatching the binoculars from her hand.

After a quick look and a muffled exclamation (a Gaelic oath?), he turned and ran, literally ran, to the side of the bridge and leaned over.

'Andrews! Up here! At the double!'

This was clearly not the way to address the Commanding Officer of one of Her Britannic Majesty's warships. Pete Andrews arrived as fast as the Brigadier wanted, but with the obvious intention of making this quite clear. 'Who the devil do you think you're...?

'Yes, yes. Sorry and all that, but the landing's off!'

'What?'

'Take a look for yourself.'

Andrews seized the glasses and raised them to his eyes. There was a short pause, while he realised the implication of what he was seeing.

'Shit!' said the Commanding Officer of Her Majesty's Ship *Hallaton.*

'Exactly. There's only one thing for it. Bombardment.'

Pete stared at him. 'We're not a bloody battleship, man. What sort of damage do you think we could do with a forty-millimetre Bofors?'

The Brigadier was in full fighting mode, unstoppable. He had a job to do and he was going to do it no matter what, thought Sarah.

'With one of your missiles you could blast a hole in the Great Wall of China,' he said.

What? But they were just for show. Pete had said so himself.

'But we've never even...'

'I presume they've been kept in good order? Do you know how to fire them?'

'Are you suggesting that...?'

'Good. These things might possibly be impervious to bullets, but half a hundredweight of high explosive... They'll wish they'd stayed in outer space. We'll lob one into the crater and get rid of the lot of them in one go. Right?'

But... but that must be where the Doctor had gone. And she'd told the Brigadier as much. 'Brig...!'

'Not now, Miss Smith.'

'But the Doctor!'

He turned on her angrily, fiercely. 'Whatever the cost! Isn't that what he said? What choice do we have?'

He'd already thought of it. And was still going ahead.

Dame Hilda's philosophical selfless equanimity seemed to have been severely dented by the current turn of events.

'Brother Alex has no idea what he's getting into, with this ridiculous coup,' she said to the Doctor, as agitated as any mother whose family was being led astray. 'It was no accident that I became the "leader". Horrid word. He might as well call himself "der Führer". It was to avoid anything of the sort that I set up the Skang cult – so that I could be the "Mother".

'It's not just a job, a position to be handed over, or snatched. Once the web of interconnection has been established, it's sacrosanct.'

This didn't make sense. Hadn't she said that the Skang had only one consciousness? Presumably they were all part of it... 'Surely he must be aware of that? If you share a consciousness...'

'No. Unfortunately. Our connection with the Great Skang is limited. As I told you, our existence on Earth is mediated through our human neurological structure. His being highly intelligent doesn't mean that the original Alex Whitbread wasn't stupid. If he hadn't been totally lacking in common-or-garden nous, he would never have let himself run into the trouble he did when he was in the government. He'd have been prime minister by now.' She lowered her voice, checking to see that the guards outside the gaps in the rocks that did service as door and window weren't listening. 'Please help me, Doctor. I have to get out before the Prime Assimilation brings the Great Skang to Earth. If this is still the position when that happens, it may very well mean the aborting of the project on this planet.'

He looked at her in amazement. 'You seem to have forgotten that this is precisely why I came to Stella Island.'

'You don't understand. If the Skang makes the decision to terminate, it will be the end for everyone – and I do mean everyone. Giving my people… my children… granting them fulfilment – the fulfilment that every sentient being hungers for without knowing it – is one thing. A pointless massacre is quite another.'

'But why should there be anything of the kind? Just from mere pique? I don't understand.'

'Oh it'll be quite impersonal. The logic of the situation demands it. No trace must be left of the Skang's visit to this planet. There'll be nobody on the island left alive. Nobody at all.'

In spite of his private doubts that the firing of at least one missile was necessary in order to save *Homo sapiens* from a humiliating and ultimately terminal fate, Pete Andrews had soon been convinced that it was his duty.

This the Brigadier had accomplished with a good deal of biting comments about military efficiency compared with naval casualness, albeit sotto voce (which had the quality of shouting without the volume).

Pete could feel his face turning red as he listened to the Brigadier's remarks, but once he took on board the necessity of going along with his demands, he wasted no time. He'd show this arrogant brown job what efficiency was.

He picked up the microphone of the Tannoy. 'First Lieutenant to the bridge. First Lieutenant to the bridge. Chop chop!'

He glanced at the Brigadier, who had gone back to surveying the shore, to see if he'd noticed this lapse into decidedly unofficial slang.

It was over five years since the *Hallaton* had been equipped to defend Hong Kong from the might of Communist China. He just hoped to God they'd all remember the drill.

'Excuse me.' The Doctor was speaking to the sentry outside who was blocking the gap in the rocks that formed a window.

'Yeah?'

'Do you think it would be possible for you to stand a little to your left? A couple of feet would do nicely. If it wouldn't inconvenience you, of course.'

The giant guard grasped his home-made spear a bit more firmly. 'You trying to be funny, bub?'

Ah, a New Yorker. 'You're from Brooklyn, aren't you?'

He loosened his grip a little. 'What's it to you?'

'Used to be a haunt of mine, Brooklyn.'

In a sense, the Doctor thought. It was 1925, at the height of the disastrous experiment of Prohibition. He'd been there at least a fortnight – the time it had taken to ferret out Studs Maloney (an alias of course), who'd set up a lucrative business importing rot-gut hooch from the twenty-fifth century.

'Ma Goldoni's deli still going strong, Hank? Best apple pie in the US of A, Ma Goldoni's,' he said.

The big man beamed. 'You knew Ma Goldoni? She only croaked coupla years ago. Ninety-three, she was.'

Well, she would be.

'Madge took over. You know Madge? Her pie's even better!'

This was surreal, thought the Doctor. What a time to chat about apple pie. And what was he doing, colluding with Dame Hilda? She was the enemy, for Pete's sake! One step at a time.

The guard frowned. He'd remembered his duty. 'Don't try to get clever, sir.'

The Doctor held up his hands in mock surrender. 'I just want to see what's going on. Okay?'

He grunted. 'Mm. Okay.'

He moved out of the way, and the Doctor was able to see out. The first thing to catch his eye was the man who had been placed to guard the 'door', watching suspiciously. So there was no chance of any further action at the moment.

He looked down into the arena below. There was no sign of any of the disciples yet. But it did seem that all the teachers were assembled. Not bunched together at the front as they had been before, instead they'd spread themselves out amongst the extra seats, giving each a generous space, though there were several groups who had not yet settled down. There was a quiet hum of conversation, not unlike the sound of a concert hall or a theatre just before the house lights dim.

The newly imposing Brother Alex, restored to his former charismatic stature, a classic figure in his timeless white robe, was on the platform in front of the ceremonial throne. He held up his hand. The chatter subsided, and the groups dispersed to their seats.

He was standing as still as the statue of the Skang that Sarah Jane had described in London. Even with his diverse experience of decades of travel to some of the strangest civilisations in the farthest galaxies in the universe, the Doctor found it almost impossible to believe that this human being – whose face had at one time been on the front page of every tabloid – was nothing but an illusion, a mental image imposed by sheer psionic power.

Alex waited until the last of the fidgeting had stopped, and the murmurs had died down.

'It does my heart good to be standing here,' he said in the measured golden tones that had, on occasion, held more than six hundred MPs enthralled. 'It does my heart good to see my comrades in this great endeavour ranged before me, in unity at last. It does my heart good to know that the bad times are over, the shillyshallying is behind us. We can go forward together in strength to meet our destiny!'

At this, there was a tentative clapping, which was picked up and swiftly grew into a full-blooded round of applause.

A murmur from behind the Doctor's shoulder. 'Typical claptrap!' said Professor Hutchens.

He had to agree.

'And now... what we've all been waiting for. The moment fast approaches when our devoted followers...'

Was that the suspicion of a sneer?

'...and indeed we ourselves will get our reward.'

'Doctor!' An urgent whisper behind him. 'We must *do* something! They're about to turn!'

If he leapt through the opening in front of him, he'd have a javelin in his back. If he tried to mount a diversion while Hilda escaped, they would almost certainly both be killed. He shrugged. They were helpless.

The applause died away. As soon as there was complete silence, Alex indicated that they should all stand up. They rose as one, let their heads fall back, and closed their eyes. Once more the Doctor put his hands over his ears as he heard the alien voices, the crescendo of cacophony that had presaged the transformation before.

There was nothing to be done. Nothing that *could* be done. He had failed.

It was at this moment that the first missile arrived.

'Just over! And to the right. Shorten range by fifty yards.'

Pete Andrews stood up from the voice-pipe, which was always used in action, rather than a microphone, as the electrics could so easily be knocked out.

'Shorten range. Fifty yards.' Bob Simkins' voice floated back from the little gunnery control room deep below the bridge. From the radar scan in front of him, he would be able to confirm the CO's report, and make the necessary adjustments.

The Brigadier, surveying the plume of smoke from behind the volcano through his glasses – and the cloud of shrieking sea birds that had taken off from the cliff – firmly put out of his mind the thought that once they got the range they would in all probability be killing the Doctor, and allowed himself to feel a certain professional satisfaction.

This was the answer, without a doubt. That first explosion was enormous. Another like that actually into the crater would mean the end of the Skang.

Chris's voice came through from the foredeck. 'Number Two, armed and ready!'

This was the drill. Only one missile at a time to be fully operational. For safety, especially in a rough sea. Now, however, the *Hallaton* was almost as steady as she would have been in the lagoon. The sea was as still as glass, stretching to the horizon like a sheet of blue ice, with only the slightest of swells, very nearly undetectable.

'Steady on course,' said the Cox'n.

The engines were at minimum revs to allow the ship to creep along with just enough way for the rudder to take hold. The slightest swing to port or starboard would radically affect the aiming of the missiles.

'Very good... In your own time, Number One,' said Andrews into the voice-pipe, and lifted his glasses once more.

In the intensity of the stillness that overcame the ship as Bob swung the mounting fractionally to the left and waited for the precise moment to fire the second missile, the Brigadier heard a whisper from the corner of the bridge. He dropped his binoculars and looked over to Sarah. But she wasn't talking to him. Her eyes were closed. She appeared to be praying.

CHAPTER TWENTY-EIGHT

The Doctor's first response to the explosion was a surge of triumph. Lethbridge-Stewart had come up trumps! Time after time, they had disagreed fundamentally about the use of force. The Brigadier's instinctive reaction seemed to be that there were very few problems that couldn't be solved by blowing something up. But this time, it really did seem to be the necessary last resort.

There was only one snag. If the *Hallaton*'s aim improved, and Alex and his comrades were terminated, Hilda and he would certainly be terminated too, a consummation he devoutly wished to avoid. He *had* to escape.

But though the Doctor's American friend, like Hilda, had thrown himself to the ground at the sound of the explosion, and was only now picking himself up, his colleague at the doorway had swung round, spear at the ready, as though the ear-splitting noise had been nothing more than a planned diversion.

Nothing had changed. Even the Skang chanting had continued, almost without a break. Indeed, the clamour from down below was almost reaching its climax.

He looked down and, in the sudden silence, again felt the shimmering in his brain that meant the Skang were about to turn. He brought the utmost concentration to his watching, trying to seize the moment of transmutation. But again he missed it. It felt as if they'd always been there, these strangely attractive grotesques.

Standing proudly on the platform, where the photogenically well-favoured politician Alex Whitbread had been, there was the most impressive Skang yet: a bronze masterpiece almost as magnificent as the illusory painting; a figure to venerate, to worship.

Both the guards on the stage fell to their knees. Out of the corner of his eye, the Doctor saw Hank do the same, staring with adoration at the embodiment of their devotion, wonderfully incarnate... and this time, three yards away, his fellow followed his example.

Now! Now was the time to escape!

But the ground shuddered, the sound of the blast filled the sky, and the world collapsed. The second missile landed above their heads, just the other side of the makeshift perimeter wall.

Hank and Helmut disappeared, buried, broken, laid low by the rolling boulders from above; and the Doctor's cave was buried.

It felt as if she were being torn apart. The near-miss meant only one thing. The next one would be smack on target – and even if it wasn't, there would still be one chance left.

One more chance to kill the Doctor.

Sarah found that she was clutching her upper arms, trying to stop the violent shuddering that had overtaken her. This was what he wanted, yes, but it was unthinkable, unbearable, to know that the world – no, she herself – was about to lose this extraordinary figure, whose cranky intellect concealed a depth of compassion, and a more-than-human warmth that she'd never even glimpsed in anybody she'd ever known.

'Number Three, armed and ready!'

She shut her eyes. She couldn't bear to look.

'Very good. Okay, Bob, it's all yours.'

Again that moment when the world held its breath.

'Good God!' said the Brigadier.

'Hold it, Bob!' called the CO at the same time.

What?

For a moment, even after she'd opened her eyes, she had no idea why they'd stopped.

And then she realised. Rising out of the volcano crater was a flock of flying creatures like deformed giant bats.

The Skang had taken to the air, and were flying towards the ship.

The Doctor pulled himself to his feet and peered through the fog of stone dust. It wasn't quite dark, and that must mean that there was a gap for the light to get in. He half expected to see the figure of a Skang behind him but there, struggling to stand, was the frail woman who'd been his friend for a short time – no, who was still his friend, no matter what had happened to her since they met in Oxford.

He hurried over to give her a helping hand. 'Are you all right, Dame Hilda?'

'No bones broken,' she said, as she sat down heavily on her chair. 'I'm somewhat shaken, I have to admit. Your friends are more determined than our revered leader would have us believe. Curiously enough, I've never fancied being buried alive.'

A grim thought; and a real possibility if they didn't manage to escape before the next explosion; and that could be at any minute. He quickly turned towards the light. Yes, two of the boulders that obscured the window opening had a chink between them. He gave them a shove in turn.

The one on the left was immoveable, but the other rocked slightly as he pushed. Unfortunately it was the bigger, and seemed much too heavy to shift.

His mind flashed back to a beach near Athens, where he had been out for a walk with the leading scientist of his day, the Einstein of his time. It was only a few months ago – and yet, at the same time, it was some two centuries before the ships of Gaius Julius crossed the English Channel. It was always pleasant to listen to a mind like his.

'Give me a firm place to stand on, and I'll move the Earth,' Archimedes had said.

The Doctor was desperately looking round for something to use as a lever.

Grabbing the other bamboo chair by the leg, he raised it above his head and smashed it to the ground. It obligingly fell to pieces, leaving him with a length of bamboo at least as thick as the spears of the guards, and nearly three feet long. It fitted neatly into the crack beneath the stone, and the edge of the window – the corner, for stability – was the ideal place to provide a fulcrum. He had a mechanical advantage of nearly four to one.

But he still couldn't persuade the boulder to move more than a few inches, no matter how he heaved on the end of the chair leg... Until his hands were joined by the arthritic grip of his aged companion; and together they swung the lever down as easily as if he'd been joined by an Olympic weightlifter; and the light flooded in.

'The feeling in my body is that the strength of my muscles fits my appearance,' she said. 'But it's an illusion, like the rest. Whenever I've remembered, my real strength has turned out to be quite useful.'

The Doctor acknowledged her contribution with a wry grin.

'But not useful enough on this occasion, it would seem,' she went on dispassionately.

She was right. Though they could now see out into the arena, the gap was still far too small for either of them to climb through. The Doctor poked his head out to see if he could spot how to enlarge it – and was rewarded by seeing something very odd.

The assembled Skang, including the Alex figure on the stage, seemed to have lost it completely. They were tearing at their white gowns, frantically pulling them to pieces, and flinging them off. The sheen of the bronze bodies that were revealed was at the same time beautiful and shocking, even to the Doctor. In spite of their semi-humanoid shape, in the mass they seemed as utterly alien as any Dalek.

But a greater surprise was to come. As they became free of the trammels of their clothes, they unfurled smallish wings like those of a fairy-tale dragon, which had been invisibly moulded to their backs, and rose into the air, circling the crater as they waited for one another.

'I wondered if they might do that,' said Hilda, when he let her have a look.

'But... but it's impossible. Creatures of that size would need colossal wings – and a breastbone to match, just to anchor their muscles!'

'Not at all,' said Hilda. 'The Skang body is far less dense than the human. How do you think they... we... are able to grow so fast inside? Think of the pumice in your bath. It looks like a stone; it feels like a stone; and yet it floats.'

'Of course,' said the Doctor, remembering how light the Skang corpse at the bottom of the cliff had been.

As the last one joined them, the hovering, circling creatures came together and swooped into the sky like a flock of migrating swallows, with such a gust from their wings that it blew the dust from the second explosion right into the Doctor's face.

So they weren't to die quite yet, he thought, wiping his eyes. But what about the others, on board the *Hallaton*?

'Got him!'

Even as Sarah heard the cry of triumph from behind her, she saw one of the leaders of the flying pack seem to falter and drop, as ungainly as a shot pheasant, with a broken wing vainly grasping at the air.

As part of the drill for going into action, a machine gun was manned on each side of the upper bridge, as were a brace of them mounted outside the wing doors of the lower, covered bridge.

Sarah clasped her hands over her ears as a shield against the intolerable racket. Surely the sheer weight of bullets being thrown at the creatures would knock them out of the sky!

But no. The single hit was a lucky shot. She could see that it must be impossible to aim, the way they were flying: never on a straight course like an aircraft or a bird, but swerving and jinking in unpredictable zig-zags, which still took them towards the ship... Hang on, though! Maybe they'd been frightened off?

'Cease fire!'

Bert Rogers, the signalman, sounded the klaxon, which transmitted the Commanding Officer's order to the whole ship.

'What the devil are they up to?' said the Brigadier, squinting into the sun as the whole group soared up, way out of range, to hover for a minute or so...

...before closing in on one another to form a tight-knit circle, which fell with gathering speed towards the ship, as the Skang dived like a squadron of kamikazes from World War Two.

'Fire, fire, fire!'

Again the raucous tones of the klaxon horn, and the mind-battering clatter of the guns. Another Skang, and another, were jolted from the formation as the bullets found their targets. But still they came.

Had they got a secret weapon? Would some sort of death-ray sear the open bridge? Were they all about to be incinerated like the victims of a napalm flame-thrower?

The others on the bridge must have had the same thought, for, as their attackers swooped low overhead, both Pete Andrews and the Brigadier, who were standing in the centre, moved instinctively towards the side, as if it might afford some protection.

But it was Sarah herself who twigged what was going to happen. 'Get under cover!' she yelled, as she ran for the ladder that led to the bridge below.

She only just made it. The blue mist that was shooting from

the probosces of the flying Skang came swirling down the steps after her, almost as if she were being chased.

Nobody had followed. She slammed the door behind her. The wing doors, as always, were closed already. Would they keep it out? Or would it seep through the cracks, and make her a victim along with the rest?

Through the glass at the front, she could see that already the ship was entirely swathed in a thick cloud of blue, far denser than the one that had greeted them when they arrived.

Please! Please!

She had no idea who she was pleading with. All she knew was that if she were to be taken over too they'd be finished, the lot of them.

Not the smallest tendril of mist, nor the faintest sniff of violets, came through.

Thank God for Scottish ship-builders.

To say that Alex Whitbread was enjoying himself (though he wasn't quite sure whether *he* still existed) as the group took off from the temple, would be to understate the matter to a laughable degree. This was total rapture – a rapture of a different quality from the bliss of assimilation that he'd known in Hampstead, and even more overwhelming.

Until now he had never had the experience. To be one with the intention of the whole terrestrial group – to be, as leader, its very propagator – was to experience the ecstasy the word itself implied. He was standing outside himself, yet at the same time was more himself than ever before.

Once the intention was set, the process ceased to be voluntary. The hallucination to be generated by the enzyme grew organically from the combined background of the whole group.

He'd missed the creation of the island village and the temple, which had been settled as soon as *Skang* had anchored in the lagoon. If he hadn't been so obsessed with his own predicament when he arrived himself, he surely would have laughed when he saw the result. He'd always prided himself on his good taste and his appreciation of the finer points of modern art and architecture. What had emerged from the collective unconscious of the almost totally middle-class assembly of teachers was more like a Disneyland version of a classical temple – straight out of *Fantasia* – crossed with an ancient Greek theatre; a proper mongrel. And as for the village...!

Still, it had done the job. The disciples had thought they were in a paradise. Evidently the *Zeitgeist* of Western civilisation was irredeemably bourgeois.

As they arrived above the ship, he was seized by an additional glee that owed nothing to his new-found integration with his fellow Skang.

Nanny Hilda had insisted on a phony compassion for their victims when utilising the power of illusion, instead of admitting to herself that the whole Skang process was nothing but a cosmic con. Now he was going to use it very differently.

A short sharp burst of a high-strength dose of the hallucinogenic mist would have an immediate effect. It would last for only a short time, but it would be quite long enough for his purpose.

His treatment on the ship during the journey from Bombay had been beyond belief, culminating with his imprisonment. It had emanated from the Doctor and the Brigadier, of course, but the entire crew, from the Captain to the cook, had happily joined in.

If only he'd had the powers then that he had now! But the excision that the group had inflicted on him had put an end to them. To be cut off, not only from the others in the group but from one's own fundamental being, leaving only the dry husk of human persona, was to find oneself in an impotent hell. He'd just had to accept every humiliation they'd heaped on him.

But now it was his turn.

It was a pity that the enzyme would only produce euphoria as well as hallucination. If only he could have directly manipulated their minds. It would have done them all good to experience even a modicum of the mental torture that he'd gone through after his excision. Still, the illusion that he had planned for them, in spite of its only affecting the five senses, would be quite enough. The human mind would always believe what was before its eyes, and be only too eager to provide a rationalisation that would make sense of it.

He was going to take great pleasure in employing a Skang hallucination to destroy the *Hallaton*; and, with a bit of luck, everybody on board as well.

CHAPTER TWENTY-NINE

The arena was empty; now was their best chance to get out. It was easy to have the thought, but harder to put it into practice.

The doorway was utterly blocked by a pile of boulders. They hadn't a hope of getting out that way. Moving the loose stone in the window gap had revealed a number of other rocks of somewhat smaller sizes, and though they each proved to move slightly under pressure, they were locked together in an inextricable jigsaw that defied all their efforts to solve it.

They found a niche in which to put the end of the chairleg at the bottom of the mound, but it only shifted a few inches.

'If we get hold of the very end of the lever, and put all our weight on it, maybe it'll do the trick,' said the Doctor.

But even when they both hung onto it with their feet off the ground, it was still stuck. Hilda sank back into the remaining chair, out of breath. It was taking a lot out of her.

'We need a longer lever,' said the Doctor. 'We're just not strong enough to move the lot in one go. Or heavy enough, for that matter.'

Hilda gave him a startled glance. 'I can but try,' she said.

What did she mean?

'If I were in my Skang form, I could surf the gravity waves.' She gave a little laugh, and the pedantry of her former occupation briefly emerged. 'A metaphor, of course, and not a very accurate one!' she said. 'All the same, I can feel the gravity of the sun and the moon becoming stronger and stronger. I could make myself as heavy as a London bus.'

Again the Doctor felt a clash of motives; a dissonance created by his seeking the help of his enemy. And yet, what other choice did he have? 'If there's anything you can do, then please do it,' he said urgently. 'If they manage to stop the Brigadier, it could be our only hope.'

She shook her head. 'It takes a great deal of energy to turn by yourself. The human personality is incredibly hard to crack. The group chanting amplifies the psionic energy – like the body of a violin resonating with the vibrations of the strings, or the voice of a singer breaking a wineglass.'

But Alex Whitbread did it in London, thought the Doctor. And then he'd had a top-up from those poor kids on Hampstead Heath.

'It has been necessary at times, of course, to produce the serum we needed. But I doubt if I have enough energy left after these last few days,' Hilda went on. She shrugged. 'As I said, I can but try. But don't expect it to be quick.'

She pulled herself to her feet and threw her head back, closing her eyes. When she started chanting, the Doctor realised why the sound of the group had been so unpleasant. The strange articulations – you could hardly call them words – grated on the ear, and the musical intervals bore no relation to any scale he knew. This multiplied twenty times or more could tear the mind to pieces. And that of course was its purpose.

Pete Andrews sniffed the air. Bacon frying in the open. It had always been his favourite smell.

The Dartmouth summer camps, when the strict discipline of term time was relaxed – and even the Master-at-Arms became ninety per cent human – and you could put all your hard-won sailing expertise at the service of winning the regatta! Those were without a doubt the happiest times of his life. Until now. Until now?

He turned to share this surprising insight with the Brigadier, who was barely discernible on the other side of the bridge, through the thick mist. But the Brigadier spoke first.

'You know, Andrews,' he said, walking over with a broad smile on his face, 'if you'd asked me, I'd have said that the summer hols in India, up in the hills alone with my mother, were the jolliest times of my life. But do you know, I really think that our stay here beats them into a cocked hat.'

All over the ship, the crew had broken into a happy chattering. Their commanding officer heard it with a grin of satisfaction. The old saw, *An efficient ship is a happy ship*, was just as true the other way round.

He had a dim memory that they were at action stations. Some sort of exercise?

He glanced up into the mist. Even struggling to shine through, the sun was unquestionably way over the yardarm. Time to stop all this nonsense and have a snort. They were only showing the flag, for God's sake. A sort of pleasure cruise, really.

His order to stand down was greeted by a loud cheer.

'Good man,' said Lethbridge-Stewart.

A voice came over the intercom. 'I've already armed the third rocket, sir. Shall I abort?' It was Chris on the foredeck.

'Yes, abort, abort, abort! No! Hang on a minute...' Andrews turned to the Brigadier. 'Fancy a firework display?'

The Brigadier grinned and gave a thumbs-up.

'Hey, Chris! Set them both at five seconds, elevation at maximum, and fire the buggers!'

'What me, sir?'

'Yes you, sir. Fire 'em locally. About time we had a bit of fun!'

The *Hallaton*, still creeping ahead at minimum revs, had come to the edge of the small blue cloud that enveloped it, and in less than a minute, the bridge was clear, and it was possible to see again.

A few moments later, the ship was treated to an all-too-brief Guy Fawkes display, as the two missiles soared into the sky and exploded in midair with a satisfying display of smoke, followed by a couple of equally satisfying bangs.

This resulted in an even louder cheer than before. The Brigadier laughed out loud and Pete Andrews almost clapped his hands with delight.

He looked ahead. They could see the island quite clearly now. Funny. He could have sworn that when they'd been doing the missile drill... of course, that's what they'd been doing! A mock firing, just to keep in practice...

Then why had they actually fired them? If it was only a drill...

What the hell did it matter? After all, they could always get some more when they reached Chatham. The Irish Navy wouldn't go without.

He took another puzzled look at the island. Surely they'd been only a cable's length from the cliffs – two hundred yards. His memory must be slipping. The ship was at least four times that distance if not more; getting on for half a mile.

'Well, bless my soul,' said the Brigadier, gazing through his binoculars at the shore. 'How the devil did we miss that?'

What was he on about? Pete lifted his own glasses. How indeed!

Even at that distance – amazing how clear the tropical air was – he could see the little town, with its welcoming shoreline: the row of bars and restaurants; the beach with its thatched umbrellas and sun-loungers; and the tourists in their brightly coloured summer plumage.

Things were getting better and better!

'I think we all deserve a run ashore, eh, Cox'n?' he said.

'Count me in, sir!'

'Right! Full ahead, both engines. Steady as she goes!'

The sooner he was sitting under one of those palms, with a tall glass of gin-and-tonic tinkling in his hand, the better.

At first there was just surprise, and a babble of voices. But when the second missile landed, and part of the volcano wall collapsed not so very far away from them, the disciples at the front of the queue panicked, and tried to run for it, with catastrophic results.

Two young men from Cambodia, friends who'd joined up together, were thrown off the path by the sudden crush of bodies coming downhill. One landed on his head and was killed outright, and the other fell over two hundred feet, breaking an arm and three ribs.

A small girl of sixteen from Alabama, known to her friends as Little Nell, was near the bottom of the path. She didn't have time to turn as the tidal wave of bodies came down. She was crushed underfoot and died, her neck broken.

The panic, out of all proportion to the real danger, spread rapidly, in spite of the efforts of the guards in charge, and by the time all those fleeing reached the clearing at the bottom of the path to join the ones who were waiting, chaos had taken over.

To Jeremy and the others right at the back, the explosions had been remote enough to make the reaction of the others more of a surprise than anything.

But Jeremy had a strong sense of self-preservation, developed at Holbrook, partly from working out strategies to keep out of the way of the known bullies, and partly from learning how to avoid the more unpleasant demands of school life, such as the compulsory cross-country run.

So when he saw – and heard – the wave of terror coming towards him, he quietly moved away from the growing turmoil into the shelter of a group of shrubs nearby, and stood watching, poised to take off if it came anywhere near him.

In the event, the whole crowd streamed past towards the comforting familiarity of the village. He was left alone, apart from the dead, the injured, and some of the guards who'd kept their heads.

He came out of hiding. 'Excuse me...' he said to the nearest guard.

The guard, a tall Dubliner, who had been staring open-mouthed into the sky, turned to him. 'What?'

'Does this mean that we're not going to get our rewards?'

The guard stared at him. 'How the feck would I know?' he said, and turned away to survey the disaster left behind.

'Jesus, Mary and Joseph!' he said. At least five were lying on the ground, unmoving; one woman was sitting with her head in her hands, which were red with blood; another was wandering aimlessly towards them, her hands outstretched as if she were blind. A guard came up to her, and she collapsed into his arms, sobbing uncontrollably.

'You'd better come and give me a hand,' went on the Irishman, going over to the recumbent figure of a man who was gently moaning and had a trickle of blood coming from the corner of his mouth.

Well, really! Treating him like a servant! The guards were presumably paid for the job. Let them get on with it. What did he know about first aid, anyway?

It was then that he had his bright idea. This was his chance. The whole point of coming all the way from England, first to Bombay and then on the long voyage to the island, was so that they could get their rewards, whatever they were. And when they'd got things sorted out...

He walked across the clearing to the bottom of the path, and sat down on a convenient stone. When they queued up again, he was going to be right at the front.

Sarah's mind was working overtime as she peered out at the blueness that filled the windows at the front of the bridge.

Even if they came out of the mist, the assault was surely over. The others would be in no fit state. Or could she fire the missiles herself? No, no, no, that was a ludicrous idea. In any case, even if she could, would she want to, knowing the Doctor was still up there? For that matter, the Doctor wasn't always right. Maybe the world wasn't really in such danger.

But what was she going to say to the Brig? He'd be back in his way-hay playboy mode, likely, even without a bottle of whisky inside him.

She'd just have to play it by ear.

Her mind was still knitting itself into a ravelled mess when she became aware that the mist was fading. She could already see the cliffs, not so far ahead.

She jumped as she heard two explosions. What now, for God's sake?

She turned to go up top. But she paused at the door before she left the safety of the covered bridge, and looked for'd again. Had the mist absolutely gone? There'd be no point in going up if she was going to join them in la-la land.

No, it was all right. The cliffs were pin-sharp… A bit near, weren't they?

Out of the door. No smell. Up the ladder. Yes, there was the blue cloud well astern of them.

'Full ahead, both engines. Steady as she goes…'

The t-r-r-ring t-r-r-ring of the engine-room telegraphs, repeated back from the engine room.

It took a moment to sink in, what Pete had said, and what it meant. She could feel the wind in her face as the ship speeded up. What was he up to? He was heading straight for the cliffs! He'd have to give the order soon, or they'd…

She saw his expression as he leaned over the edge of the bridge, looking ahead: a vacuous smile of pleasure, of antici-pation, of…

'No!' she cried. 'Stop!'

They all looked round, even the Cox'n, who was steering. All of them on the bridge from the CO to the signalman had the same expression, an expression of glee. Small boys on a roller-coaster ride.

'Sarah! Where've you been?' cried the Brigadier. 'We're going to have a party! Tell you what, UNIT can buy us all a bottle of fizz. No, a case! I'll fiddle it on my expenses.'

By now, the ship was approaching its maximum speed.

HMS *Hallaton* was on course to smash straight into the cliff; and nobody was doing anything to stop it.

The Doctor didn't know whether to watch as Dame Hilda made the effort to 'turn' as she called it. Somehow it seemed an intrusion on a moment of extreme intimacy, a sort of voyeurism. But she didn't seem to mind one way or the other. She'd gone into another space entirely, a depth of concentration that quite removed her from the little rocky cell where they were imprisoned.

As she continued, her chanting became more intense, more passionate, but the volume didn't increase as it had when he was watching and listening to the whole Skang group.

Yet it seemed to be working. It took longer, as she had implied, but eventually her voice abruptly stopped and there appeared the strange shimmering that had heralded the moment of transmutation before.

But this time the process hadn't been nearly so overwhelming to watch. All the Doctor had felt was that his mind was going slightly out of focus, and as the image of Dame Hilda started to ripple he was aware that it was all happening in his brain, rather than a few yards in front of him.

But just when he expected the change (and he was determined not to miss the moment), the mirage effect faded away.

Hilda dropped her head. She was as out of breath as if she'd just run a champion's one hundred metres. She swayed, as if she were about to pass out, and gratefully accepted the Doctor's help as he guided her back to her chair.

'It's no good,' she said at last. 'I couldn't quite reach. It was just beyond my grasp – a few inches from my fingertips.'

This was a disaster! It was their only hope of escape.

She shook her head. 'I know quite well that this old body has no substance. I know that I'm not really an old woman. But knowing it with my mind – Hilda's mind – just isn't enough.

It has to be experiential. And after the last few days... Do you realise that if I lost my concentration, the village and the temple would disappear? I just haven't enough Skang energy left.'

The Doctor, who had squatted next to her, holding her hand, stood up and walked to the gap in the window they'd managed to make so far. He gazed down into the empty amphitheatre.

They weren't going to get out.

They were going to have a view from the royal box of the last act of this comedy – and the consequence would be tragic: the wiping out of everybody on Stella Island, if not the whole human race.

CHAPTER THIRTY

This was turning out to be one of the best operations he'd been involved in since he joined UNIT, thought the Brigadier. He hadn't taken enough time off in the past. Whenever he went on leave there always seemed to be some family duty to be taken care of. Things were going to change in the future!

His ruminations were interrupted by a shout behind him.

Ah, Sarah! To be honest, he hadn't even noticed that she'd disappeared. But he was glad to see her come back even if she wasn't a Betty Grable. Pretty enough, though, and the only female on board after all!

'Sarah! Where've you been?' he cried. 'We're going to have a party! Tell you what, UNIT can buy us all a bottle of fizz. No, a case! I'll fiddle it on my expenses.'

There was a general cheer from the others on the bridge, even Bert Rogers the signalman, and the two lookouts.

But Sarah wasn't even listening. 'Look! Look!' she shouted, pointing ahead. 'We're going to crash!'

What the devil was she talking about? He could see the seafront quite clearly now, with its row of shops and bars, but it was still a good six or seven hundred yards away.

Pete Andrews was actually laughing. Was it meant as a joke?

Evidently not. His laughter stopped and he watched open-mouthed as Sarah jumped forward and grabbed the brass handles of the engine-room telegraph, pulling them back to full astern.

This was beyond any sort of joke.

After an astonished moment, the telegraph answered. But by then Sarah had turned and launched herself at the Cox'n, who was so taken by surprise that he lost his balance and fell onto the deck.

But before she could touch the helm, Pete Andrews had leapt forward and grabbed her round the waist, lifted her bodily and swung her away from the wheel. She was frantic. She was screaming. She was kicking and beating at Andrews with her fists.

He was still laughing.

'God Almighty!'

What? What now? The Brigadier swung round. Bob Simkins had appeared in the doorway that led to the bowels of the ship.

The Cox'n was getting to his feet. Diving forward, Bob shouldered him out of the way, grabbed the wheel and spun it to starboard as far as it would go.

The ship had hardly slowed at all, and as it answered to the helm it listed to port, and the Cox'n, who had staggered back against Pete Andrews and his hysterical burden, fell over again.

The Commanding Officer had stopped laughing. He dropped Sarah, who was sobbing with rage and desperation, and charged across the bridge to Bob, and tried to pull him away from the wheel, watched incredulously by Bert and the lookouts.

The Brigadier found it equally incredible. The two most senior naval officers on the ship brawling like a couple of fourth-formers, for God's sake!

He almost lost his balance as he rushed to stop them before they could do anything they'd regret. But as he was trying to pull them apart, he felt a tug at his arm, and a voice screaming in his ear, 'No, sir! Look!'

It was the signalman, and like Sarah before, he was pointing towards the shore.

Despite himself, the Brigadier glanced round. The ship, still turning, was less than twenty yards from the black cliffs, and still slanting towards it.

Sarah and the Cox'n, just back on their feet, froze, along with everybody else. Nobody could move. They could all see it now; and there was nothing to be done.

They waited for a time out of time, an endless moment. Except for the rumble of the engines and the wind in their ears, silence...

The *Hallaton,* still travelling at disaster speed with her helm hard astarboard, reached the top of her turning circle, and started to swing away from the cliff.

It was so near, you could have counted the eggs in the boobies' nests.

Alex Whitbread, still in Skang form, looked out over his brothers and sisters (though the individual Skang were themselves sexless) as they took their seats, and revelled in his moment of triumph. The ongoing bliss of unity, controlled by his intention and his alone, was compounded with the deep satisfaction of his human persona at achieving his ambition.

They had overcome all the obstacles. He could feel throughout his body the rising force that told him that the optimum time was fast approaching for the descent of their parent swarm – the collective individual that was the Great Skang, at once the object of their devotion and the very core of their being. Once Alex's position had been ratified (he laughed to himself as the dry human term sprang to mind), nothing could stop him from becoming the de facto ruler of the world.

Everybody knew the form of the ceremony; it was so much part of their evolutionary heritage that it was as instinctive as the urge of a bird to make a nest. Their survival depended on it.

The first thing to happen would be the Prime Assimilation. This would be the sign, the trigger, that would bring down their Beloved, who would grace the Mass Assimilation of the rest of the faithful with the divine presence, absorbing the psionic energy of their vital young bodies, as a token of the richness that would be offered as soon as the Earth had become theirs.

And he, Alex, would be the privileged one. The first of the candidates lining up again outside the temple would be brought inside, and he, as leader (again the thrill as he relished the word), would be the first to taste the joy and the deep fulfilment he'd already sampled illegitimately in London.

He lifted his hands in the air to quieten the murmurs coming from the arena. In the silence he raised his voice and called across to the guard standing by the entrance. 'The time has come. Bring in the first of the faithful!'

At last he'd managed it! He was first in the queue. But Jeremy had found that it wasn't quite so simple as he'd expected.

He'd idly watched – to tell the truth, getting a bit bored after a while – as the guards, with reinforcements garnered by walkie-talkie, ministered to the injured and carried away the dead.

They did seem to be very slow in going about it. But there you were, it was the same all over. Mama was always complaining that you couldn't get the right sort these days. The faithful retainer was an endangered species, she often said, like the mountain gorilla.

He liked gorillas.

He didn't like being kept waiting.

He was seriously thinking of making his way down to the village to see what was going on when he saw them all coming back through the rocky bit into the clearing, shepherded by a lot of guards, who were being very officious, pushing people into line ready to go up the steps.

Including him.

'I was here first!' he'd complained to the big fellow who looked like a Red Indian, who'd manhandled him into the line about twenty from the front.

All he'd said was 'Tough titty' – which was hardly helpful – and turned away.

By the time he'd got to the top, Jeremy had slipped back another dozen places, and was as fed up as the day he'd lost his wallet in the Burlington Arcade and had to go home on the tube instead of taking a taxi as he usually did.

But then he remembered. Whenever he'd flown anywhere with Mama, she would never get to the check-in at the proper time, just to stand at the back of the queue. She'd arrive as late as possible, wander up to the very front of the line, and engage whoever was standing there in animated conversation, as if she was with them, part of their party. They always seemed a bit bewildered, but the rest of the people behind just accepted it – and only once had anybody objected when she stepped up to the desk first; and then she'd given him one of her looks, and he'd shut up.

Why hadn't he thought of it? It worked a treat. The faithful at the front were a couple of rather weedy females he'd never seen before. But when he started chatting about the guns and stuff, they just let him stay. As soon as they opened the big doors, he'd be in there.

Thank you, Mama.

'Why, there you are, Jeremy!'

He turned in surprise. Coming up the outside of the queue was his girlfriend – well, sort of – Emma.

'I've been looking everywhere for you, daarling,' she drawled.

Gosh! And there he'd been thinking that maybe she didn't like him after all.

Chummily taking him by the arm, she gave him a luscious smile. He could feel her body through the thin muslin. She wasn't wearing a bra!

Feeling wobbly in the legs, he opened his mouth to answer...

...but couldn't think of anything to say.

Luckily, at that very moment, one of the great doors swung open, and a guard appeared. 'First one,' he said, looking at Jeremy.

This was it! He'd made it!

'See you around,' said Emma sweetly, and walked inside.

No! He made to follow.

The guard put a hand on his chest. 'Just the one,' he said, and closed the door in his face.

'So what now?' asked the Brig, grimly.

Good question, thought Sarah.

'Half ahead together. Steady as she goes, Cox'n,' said Pete. 'Let's get away from those rocks.'

'Steady as she goes. Aye, aye, sir.'

Pete turned to the Brig. 'I was just about to ask you that. We don't carry any more missiles. That was the lot.'

Thank goodness for that, thought Sarah. At least they weren't going to kill the Doctor.

'We've got a few hand grenades...'

It was Bob Simkins joining in. A joke? Yeah, a joke.

They could all thank their lucky stars for Bob (and she didn't give a toss if that was a cliché). As he'd been down in Gunnery Control, he'd missed the blue fog entirely.

The silence had gone on for quite a few minutes after their narrow squeak. Once the *Hallaton* had come to a stop, Bob had cut the engines and brought the wheel amidships. The ship was rocking gently in the slight swell coming from the west. For the moment she was quite safe.

Bob had turned from the wheel and looked at his CO. At last he'd spoken. 'What the...?'

'Don't ask,' Pete had said.

Bob had turned to the Brig. He'd just shaken his head.

Sarah had come to their rescue. After all, they must be

feeling like a couple of right charlies. And yet it wasn't their fault. 'It was that mist, like before,' she'd said.

That had broken the dam, and Bob was swamped by words coming at him from every direction, even from Bert the signalman. They weren't just explaining to Bob, they were explaining to themselves.

When the torrent had dried up, there was another awkward silence, until Pete had realised that they were still nearer to the shore than he would have liked and did something about it, and the Brigadier had asked, 'So what now?'

After Bob's rather feeble joke, which made nobody laugh, there was another silence.

They were the experts, thought Sarah. Just because she was stumped that didn't mean...

'Revert to the landing party?' said Pete, at last.

'But it must be too late,' said Sarah.

'We can't know that. I don't see that we have any option.'

'And end up in another pea-souper?' said the Brig. 'They'll have us dancing a fandango before we're finished.'

There was a baffled silence.

Hah! Of course! 'Gas masks?' said Sarah.

'The time has come. Bring in the first of the faithful!'

The Doctor turned away from the window, where he had watched the return of the flying Skang.

Dame Hilda – Mother Hilda, as he had to think of her now – seemed not to have heard Alex. She was slumped in her chair, utterly defeated.

'There is a big enough gap for us both to be able to see,' he said.

Of course she knew that. But if she heard him, she gave no sign. The grief he felt as he turned back was not for her, nor yet for the stunning beauty who was being ushered in through the front entrance. It was for the world, for all the worlds, and the pain that lay at the heart of things.

He was about to see a ritual murder. Before his eyes, the perfect body of this trusting child would be reduced to nothing but a bag of bones.

And yet... there was no way that he could experience in himself the hatred that he knew his companions would be feeling for the Skang. They weren't fiends from some alien hell, but creatures with as valid a right to existence as humankind, or the natives of Gallifrey, or any other race from the kaleidoscope of living beings he'd met during his epic journeys through time and space.

The 'first of the faithful' had halted at the top of the steps leading down into the arena, a dismayed hand to her mouth as she saw the upturned faces.

But after the original hesitation, she drew herself up and, with her chin in the air, descended the staircase and walked down the aisle to the stage and the waiting leader of the Skang with a confident stride, the air of the high-couture catwalk, which said 'I'm-me-and-be-damned-to-you'.

Hilda's room, as befitted her position, was the nearest to the platform, so the Doctor had a profile view of the meeting, and was able to hear the murmured voices.

'Don't be afraid, my dear.' It was the golden voice of Alex Whitbread encouraging her as she hesitated once more at the bottom of the aisle.

Gazing up with the wide-eyed innocence of a neophyte at the living figure of the being who had taken possession of her mind and her heart, she slowly mounted the steps to the stage and gracefully knelt, bowing her head in submission.

A hand under her chin, gently lifting.

'What is your name, my child?'

'Emma.' There was no tremor in the voice.

'Are you ready to receive the reward your devotion so richly deserves?'

'I am.'

The Skang put his head back and closed his eyes, murmuring

some words. Was he praying? Or delving from the depths of their united being a structure, a ritual, which translated itself into human speech?

Emma's face was already blissful. She closed her eyes as the Skang took her lightly by the arms, and touched the nape of her neck with the needle tip of his proboscis. As it entered her flesh, there was a simultaneous sigh of satisfaction from every member of the watching group.

Emma didn't even flinch.

It wasn't plunged in like a giant dagger but glided through the satin skin as gently as the touch of a loving husband with his virgin bride.

At once Emma's peaceful countenance changed. She opened her eyes and, with a gasp, took a deep breath; and as the sharpness entered her further, she uttered a sound very like a moan, but expressive of a delight beyond imagining.

The Doctor dropped his eyes. If he'd been a near-voyeur before, now he felt that he was illicitly present at an intimacy deeper than any sexual encounter.

The sound of Emma's voice grew louder as the moan changed into a crescendo of ecstasy so exquisite it pierced the mind. At the very top of the cry, when it was beginning to seem that there was no limit to the exaltation that she could reach, her voice stopped.

Despite himself, the Doctor lifted his eyes to see. Sagging in the arms of the Skang, Emma's body was impaled as deeply as it was possible to be.

There could be no doubt of it. She was dead.

CHAPTER THIRTY-ONE

Everything stopped. The audience... the *congregation* - the Doctor found it difficult not to categorise the watching Skang in some such way - had all risen to their feet at the same moment, the moment that silence came, as if they were going to join in a standing ovation. But after a deep exhalation, they remained quite still, watching with their great eyes.

The waiting seemed to last only a minute or so, but with the utter lack of movement or sound it was difficult to judge, and afterwards the Doctor reckoned it must have been more like five minutes before he realised, with a gulp of nausea, that the dead girl was growing thinner, and that Alex's grip on her arms was tightening until the muscles on his arms stood out like a weightlifter's, and his Skang body was trembling.

A strange sound, like a sob from many voices, called his attention to the watchers in the arena. He could see that they were shaking too. Were they sharing the satisfaction, the consummation, they could see before them?

It didn't take long. In a matter of minutes, the proboscis was withdrawn, and the corpse, now no more than a covered skeleton, allowed to fall to the ground.

Alex sat down on the immense throne behind him, and the rest of the Skang also sat down. All remained quite still as two guards appeared and carried off Emma's poor desecrated body to the side and into one of the caves in the volcano wall.

A temporary storage place, a 'chapel of rest'? Or was it destined to become a charnel house for the victims of the coming massacre? How would they dispose of nearly two hundred?

The Doctor wasn't quite sure what would happen next. If the Prime Assimilation was to trigger the coming of the Beloved, he would have expected it to arrive within a few seconds. Nothing can travel faster than light, but even in those terms the moon was less than one and a half seconds away, and Hilda had said that the swarm that formed the Great Skang was on the other side of the moon. On the other hand, it couldn't be entirely composed of psionic energy; there must be a physical component, no matter how tenuous. That in itself would slow it down.

What actually happened was a surprise. As Alex Whitbread – the Doctor found it almost impossible to think of the thing on the stage by that name – as it sat there with its great head bowed, it started to sweat.

But this wasn't the glow of perspiration you'd see on an athlete who'd run his course. It ran off the Skang in streams, in rivulets, in waterfalls; so much that puddles were forming on the ground beneath.

Surely the act couldn't have been so strenuous? If it took so much energy, as the sweat implied, then it was difficult to believe that the absorption could be worthwhile.

But then the Doctor realised. The human body is about seventy per cent water. It had to go somewhere.

If all the faithful were to 'get their reward', each of the Skang below him would be ingurgitating the insides of some nine bodies. More if the guards were to be included in the final total. Each Skang would have to get rid of well over a hundred gallons of water... or burst.

The Doctor's thoughts were broken into by a new sound, like a distant wind. It was growing louder and louder, until the howl of a hurricane assaulted his ear – or was it heard only by the mind? Certainly the tops of the trees growing on the outer slopes of the volcano showed no sign of disturbance.

At the first murmur, all the Skang started to mutter in unison. It was impossible to hear what they were saying, but the Doctor turned in surprise when he realised that Hilda was joining in. She had her eyes closed, and her head bowed like the rest of the Skang, seemingly oblivious to her human form.

The noise stopped. All the Skang lifted their heads, stood up as one and raised their arms to heaven.

The Skang that had been Alex Whitbread did the same, turning towards the back wall of the arena and standing, like a priest, waiting for the descent of his god.

Pete Andrews was thoroughly fed up, but whether it was with the Royal Navy, himself, his officers or the Brigadier he didn't know. Or Sarah Jane Smith, for having had the idea in the first place.

He'd given the order to Bob, whose responsibilities would cover equipment like respirators, only to be greeted by a dismayed face.

Why did they have only five of them? It was okay if you were dealing with a smoke-filled engine room or something of the sort, but not much cop if the ship was facing a full-scale attack of nerve gas (or whatever). The whole point of their presence in Hong Kong had been to police the surrounding sea area, yes, but also to be prepared for any provocation the Commies might throw at them.

'Were you supposed to have them?' the Brigadier had asked, irritably and irritatingly, with a sub-text of Army glee.

That was the trouble. He had no idea what the regulation was; but it certainly had been his responsibility as First Lieutenant to make sure that it was followed.

'That's irrelevant, sir, if you'll forgive me,' he'd said. 'The fact is that only five of the landing party will be protected in the case of another gas attack. The question is, who?'

'Bags I have one!' said Sarah.

Oh God! That was all he needed. He'd read *The Famous Five* as well, but this was hardly the moment, now was it?

* * *

The Great Skang didn't come down from the skies like Peter Pan on a Kirby wire. Nor did it appear with a flash and a puff of smoke like the Demon King in a pantomime.

The first intimation that anything was happening at all, as the sound faded away, was a twinkling of sparks, which then multiplied and grew, tracing a three-dimensional outline of the now-familiar Skang figure in the space behind Alex.

This Skang was not a Gulliver, a living mountain seventy feet tall. It was little more than twice the size of its facsimiles on Earth. But it was no solid, bronze-skinned creature of muscle and sinew. As the hot-white scintillations increased in number, filling in the gaps, they expanded to such a splendour that at first the Doctor couldn't bear to look.

As his eyes became accustomed to the intensity of the light, he saw that the shape of the awesome figure wasn't fixed. It was perpetually melting at the edges, and forming its shape anew; a continuing reminder that this was a visitor from another realm of being.

When it spoke – and was he hearing it in his ear or in the depths of his brain? – the sound mirrored the form. It was a multiplicity of voices, as if blown by a gusty wind, at once coming and going, growing and fading; each separate, yet overlapping the next to speak as one, a great voice seeming to echo round the arena.

'Who are you?' said the Great Skang. 'You are not the Mother.'

The Doctor would have expected the voice to be detached, dispassionate. But here was an undertone of real emotion. It felt like the anger of a monarch faced with treachery.

How could this be? One might as well have expected a beehive to be jealous, to be proud. Ah, but a swarm of bees could certainly be angry – and for that matter, the Great Skang could communicate with the curious hybrid creatures standing before him only by sharing their human sensibility.

'By what right do you stand there?'

This was a question that could not remain unanswered.

'It was decided by the whole group that I should become their leader,' said Alex.

The Doctor found it difficult to believe what he was hearing. Was it bravery, desperation – or just foolishness?

The cold anger grew in the alien voice. 'You lie. There are many here that disagreed.'

'Then why should they have supported me?'

The arrogance of the man! Couldn't he see that he was digging his own grave?

'From fear. We can smell it, rising like smoke. Is this the unity of the Skang? Those we send are not mere messengers. They are torn from our very heart to become our children. Where is the Mother that we sent?'

For once, the royal 'we' seemed entirely appropriate.

Alex didn't answer at once.

'Well?'

'She's dead,' he replied.

Now the anger was very apparent, not only in the voice, but in the colour of the scintillations that made up the Great Skang body, which were rippled with deep reds.

'Again you lie! She is here – but she is not here! She is confined. She is imprisoned. We can see her buried in stone. *Where is she*?'

Would he answer?

But no. Even at such a time the pride of the man Alex Whitbread, the supreme conceit that had ruled his whole life, was greater than his fear. He remained silent.

'Very well,' continued the great shining figure, 'you have made our choice for us. This planet Earth will be remembered as one of the failures. We shall destroy all who know of our existence.'

Exactly what Hilda had warned might happen! But what to do? If the Doctor shouted through the limited gap in the window his voice would never carry; and it had been proved conclusively that he didn't have the strength to escape.

'But first,' the Great Skang continued, 'although it will pierce our heart with a wound that will never heal, we shall destroy you.' It raised an arm and pointed a finger at Alex.

As he realised what was to be his fate, his shell of arrogance cracked, and the power of words he'd lived by deserted him. He tried to plead for mercy, but all that came out was an incoherent babble of terror – which soon turned into a scream of the purest agony.

Again the Doctor witnessed an Incandescence. Again he had to cover his ears against the burning power of the sound, which this time came from the Great Skang itself. Again he saw the network of flame that fluttered over the skin and spread to become a white-hot blaze that blinded the eye; and again he heard the *swoosh* as it faded.

Only then did the screaming stop.

In the silence that followed, the Doctor realised that Hilda's murmured voice behind him had continued right up until that moment. Indeed, it was the fact that it was no longer there that called attention to it, like the sudden silence of an unwound grandfather clock. He turned.

But it was no longer Emeritus Professor Dame Hilda Hutchens standing behind him. It was a Skang.

It walked past him to the doorway, put out a hand and leaned on the pile of massive stones that blocked it; and the mound collapsed like a sandcastle when the tide comes in, leaving the way open to the outside.

There's very little that wouldn't collapse under the weight of a double-decker bus.

The coming of the Great Skang had been a conduit for the complex of psionic and gravitational energy that she'd needed.

At the door, the new Skang paused and looked at him. 'I'm sorry, Doctor,' said Hilda's gentle voice.

She went out onto the gallery, and the Doctor heard her

voice again, now clear and young, ringing out through the amphitheatre below.

'Here I am,' she said.

At least the threat of the immediate massacre of all those on Stella Island had been averted. But only at the cost of the greater danger: the continuation of the 'reward' ceremony and the mass ingurgitation of the faithful, which would provide the psionic energy for the seeding of the entire planet with thousands of Skang.

But if the Doctor showed himself, he risked incurring the fate of the late Alex Whitbread. He moved over to the door, where he could get a better view of what was going on.

The Hilda Skang had walked down and taken her place in front of the giant figure on the stage. At her feet, there was the small pile of dust, still smouldering, that was all that was left of the worldly dreams of Alex Whitbread.

The angry crimson streaks had vanished from the ever-changing carapace of light before her, giving way to a more gentle glow, a burnished gold that spoke of calmness and harmony; and the voice had lost its fury and become loving in tone.

'We give you our greetings, Mother, and the gratitude of our heart, which tells us you have gathered a cornucopia of plenty for our delight and nourishment...'

For a being that had spent thousands (if not millions) of years cruising through empty space, with only the occasional pitstop to replenish its fuel, the Great Skang seemed to be surprisingly articulate, thought the Doctor. Then he reminded himself that it was at one with the collective mind of the group below him, and *that* included some of the finest human brains the century had produced.

As usual, the Doctor's analytical faculties, which allowed part of him to stand back and watch without emotion, sat alongside his intense involvement in the fate of those he was trying to help.

He mustn't let himself be seduced by the ambience of warm-hearted amity. Just to be in the neighbourhood of these surprising creatures was to feel a kinship with them. But he'd seen what had happened to the unfortunate Emma; and if he did nothing to stop it...

'Now is the time for our banquet. Now is the time for us all to share the fruits of your labours, as a foretaste of the abundance yet to come. Let us begin.'

No!

The Skang that was Hilda turned and lifted its hand. But before she could speak, the Doctor shot out of the now open door onto the gallery.

'Stop!' he cried.

All the alien faces turned towards him. The Great Skang's body rippled with flashes like a sky full of lightning.

'Who is this? Who dares to speak so to the Great Skang?'

'You mustn't do this. Can't you see that it's wrong?'

'Wrong?'

The incredulity in the voice hit home. Of course it wasn't wrong to them. This was their life, as Dame Hilda had said to him. Like sentient beings throughout the universe, their only purpose was to survive.

He'd jumped out of hiding as unthinkingly as one who leaps in front of a speeding bus to save a wandering child.

But now... he could find nothing to say.

CHAPTER THIRTY-TWO

The pause nearly cost the Doctor his life.

The Great Skang lifted its arm and pointed. The Doctor heard the white-hot noise begin, and felt his skin starting to glow.

'Wrong for you, I mean! Can't you see that the Earth is the very last place for the Great Skang?'

The Great Skang paused. 'In what way?'

The thought had come instinctively, like a lifted arm to ward off a blow. But it was true. Of course it was true!

'You have already seen for yourself,' the Doctor said. 'No matter how intelligent or full of vital energy they are, human beings are flawed.'

'Explain.'

At least it was listening, he thought. 'By their very nature, they are always ready for combat. Their society evolved from tribes; and they've never stopped fighting since. Conflict is encrypted in their genes.'

Would it understand?

'Go on.'

'If you seed a thousand Skang, a hundred thousand, you're going to have a hundred thousand utterly different personalities scattered round the globe, all keeping their own self-pride and their own precious core beliefs – and willing to fight for them. And believe me, they will.'

The scintillations of its insubstantial body burst into a display of rainbow colours, changing and moving with streaks of fluid light.

'Hardly fits the image of the unity of the Skang, does it?' the Doctor asked.

'Silence!'

It must be considering the idea.

At last it spoke. The colours in its sparkling form disappeared. 'We can see that this was a danger. But not now, now that you have pointed it out. Thank you. But you yourself are a disruptive presence at this time of celebration. You must be eliminated.' Again it lazily lifted its arm.

'Wait!'

This time, it wasn't the Doctor who stopped the Incandescence.

'What is it, Mother?'

'The Doctor is one of the most intelligent, one of the wisest beings on this planet. If he were to be seeded, as a Skang he could give a lead, alongside me, that could help to sweep away the difficulties he speaks of; and I have to tell you they are very real.'

It would be difficult to believe that the Great Skang had a sense of humour, but when it spoke again, there seemed to be a hint of a laugh in its many voices. 'How fitting! What do you say, Doctor? It's a simple choice.'

Too simple. If he refused, in minutes he would be a heap of smouldering cinders. If he said yes to becoming the first of the new Skang, he would be losing the very thing that had motivated his life ever since he'd first run away from Gallifrey in the TARDIS: his ability to be his own master.

Had he escaped the veiled tyranny of the Time Lords, just to become the servant of an alien will?

He could pretend, of course, just to gain time. The seeding wouldn't start until the end of the Mass Assimilation. But then what? From Dame Hilda's explanation, it was quite clear that there was no resisting the implantation of the seed.

If he said no, he was dead, with no hope of regeneration, and it would be no help to the youngsters outside.

But saying yes wouldn't help them either, and he would be actively helping in the enslavement – maybe even the destruction – of the entire human race.

Round and round went his thoughts. A decision seemed impossible.

'Well, Doctor? Mother has offered you mercy. Do you accept?'

Round and round...

Round and round?

Of course! There was one last chance – a slender one, true but...

'I accept,' said the Doctor.

He was going to make jolly sure it didn't happen again. He had to admit a sort of sneaking admiration for the way Emma had made it to the front, though. Even Mama would have approved. What a wife she'd make!

They still had to hang around. Not very organised, this lot. After all, what did it take to sort out a few rewards?

He wondered what his might be. He'd always fancied a Merc, and Mama had promised him one as soon as he passed his test; and if he hadn't had such a wimp of a driving instructor, he'd have passed it and got one in the last summer hols.

But of course, they wouldn't have brought a Merc all the way out here. It had to be something more portable...

His ruminations were interrupted as the shining mahogany doors swung wide open.

'First sixteen only, right?' said the officious guard in charge.

Jeremy took great pleasure in giving him what he felt was a good imitation of one of Mama's looks as he marched through at the head of the column; but then...

He took it all back. This was a knockout!

He'd been pretty impressed when they'd had a guided tour round the temple after they'd disembarked from the *Skang*. All the white marble seats and stuff were really something.

And the enormous painting or tapestry or whatever it was, on the wall at the back, had made him go all goose-pimply.

But now, they'd managed to set up this colossal Skang figure, all covered with flashing lights! Sort of animated, too. He'd seen nothing like it since Uncle Teddy had taken him to Olympia when he was ten to see *Snow White and the Seven Dwarfs on Ice*, and the Prince's castle at the end lit up like a Christmas tree. And this was even better.

It had paid off, getting to the top of the queue, because he was escorted right to the front where he'd get a really good view of the ceremony. Probably a bit like Speech Day at school, only this time he was one of the prizewinners.

No sign of Emma. There must be a back way out.

And no sign of the teachers...

Ha! How stupid could you get? Obviously, it was the teachers who were all dressed up. Bit over the top, perhaps, but jolly good fun.

There was a lot of chattering going on as they sorted themselves out, with one of the faithful sitting next to each teacher. A jolly good way of doing it. So as you couldn't get things wrong. He wondered who he was sitting next to. Could be Brother Alex or anybody; there was no way of telling, with the masks and all.

The big doors had been closed behind them, and the teacher on the stage held up his hands – her hands? – to shut them all up.

'My children...' she started.

It was Mother Hilda! You'd never have guessed. Brilliant costumes.

'I think of you as my children,' she went on, 'even though I haven't met all of you face to face.'

He'd met her! Had a drink with her, hadn't he?

'I want you to know that you have my gratitude – and my love – for all your dedication, your commitment, your devotion. Now you are going to get your reward.'

Good-oh! About time too.

But then she started rabbiting on about the nature of reality and stuff, and how everybody was the same as everybody else deep down – and that just wasn't true. He certainly wasn't the same as some of the oiks he knew.

By this time he'd lost the thread, and just stopped listening; until the magic word 'reward' came once more.

'You may be surprised when you find out what your reward is,' Mother Hilda was saying. 'Don't be nervous. Just do as I say, and all the sadness, all the anger, all the loneliness in your life will be washed away; and the deepest longings of your heart... even if you've never recognised them... will be satisfied. The emptiness will be filled.

'You are about to have the most sublime experience a human being can possibly have. And you'll never be unhappy again.'

At these words, there flashed across Jeremy's mind a flickering picture show of all the times he'd hidden in a cupboard to escape the Bulstrode gang at Holbrook; and the times old Gaga got the class laughing at him; and the many times he'd huddled up in bed, sobbing, sobbing, sobbing until it hurt his throat, because Mama had been abroad for months, and Nanny had been so beastly; and the times that...

'Now I want you to stand up. The time has come.'

Jeremy stood up, with tears in his eyes.

Oh, please let it be true! Please, please, please!

The teacher next to him stood up too, and put out a gentle hand to turn him so that they faced each other.

He looked up into the strangely beautiful face.

What was going to happen now?

There may have been a way through in 1923, but it had long been overgrown. The jungle was as thick as when Sarah had made her way back to the ship by herself, if not thicker.

Fighting your way through the prickly, coarse undergrowth was bad enough, but trying to do it when you were wearing a gas mask was just about impossible. Apart from anything else the sweat couldn't get out, and it was like the steam room at a Turkish bath in there.

Sarah had at least made sure that this time she was wearing jeans, and a top with long sleeves. But this only made it hotter. She glanced up to nod a thank you to Bob Simkins, who'd chivalrously stopped to hold back a particularly vicious branch.

Well, really! He'd pulled his gas mask off his face so that it was resting on the front of his head.

And so had the others, Pete and the Cox'n... and the Brigadier had even taken his right off, and had got it hanging round his neck.

She promptly followed suit, and wiped the perspiration out of her eyes with her sleeve.

Just as well, otherwise she'd never have got up the slope of the volcano, especially as they were having to do the snaking bit again to keep out of sight. There were twenty-three of them, including the unprotected seamen with their automatic rifles, all trying to be as unnoticeable as possible in case they were seen by one of the guards. True, they were round the corner from the path, but you couldn't be too careful.

At last they reached the top, and the Brigadier motioned to them all to stop and have a rest before tackling the last bit.

'We'd have no hope at all in a face-to-face encounter,' he'd said, when he'd spoken to the little task force just before they embarked. 'Whatever weapons they have, we mustn't give them a chance to deploy them. Luckily, they've positioned themselves in a situation which would be very hard to defend at the best of times and, given our limited fire power, there's only one option. If we range ourselves round the top of the perimeter wall, we'll have them at our mercy, even if they try to take to the air. But surprise is of the essence. And nobody must fire unless and until I give the order. Got it?'

It was obvious, really, thought Sarah, as she got her breath back at the bottom of the wall. Like shooting fish in a barrel, as they said in America. Good old Brig.

As long as it wasn't too late.

At last he gave the go-ahead. Petty Officer Hardy and Bob Simkins led their men around the circle to the other side, while Pete and the Brig spread theirs at equal distances apart on this side. At a hand signal, they all started to climb to the top of the wall together.

'Stay with me, and keep down,' the Brig hissed to her.

A bit galling. Especially as they hadn't let her have a pistol, or even one of Bob's hand grenades. Still, war correspondents weren't armed, and they were always in the thick of it.

She didn't quite know what she expected to see when she crawled to the edge of the wall and looked down, but it certainly wasn't the stunning light display that greeted her.

It turned all her ideas upside down.

It looked as if the Skang cult wasn't a phoney after all. It wasn't just a front put up by a bunch of alien monsters to disguise their real purpose. There really was a being for the devotees to worship, whether it was divine or demonic.

The Brigadier was equally taken aback, she could see that.

At least they were in time. A line of disciples was only now being ushered in through the entrance, and... good grief, there was Jeremy, in the lead!

She watched as he was ushered into the front row, only a few yards from the... the god? Her mind refused to accept the idea. It must be as the Doctor had said, a thing from another world.

But where was the Doctor?

Ah, there he was, on the other side, leaning casually against the wall, with his hands behind his back, in the upper gallery, as if he was enjoying the show.

When the Skang standing at the front of the stage started to speak, Sarah realised with a shock of surprise that she was listening to Mother Hilda's voice. How clearly the words floated up! But of course, it was like the old Greek theatres. It was as if the speaker was at the centre of a gigantic loud-speaker.

But more to the point, it meant that the ceremony was beginning. This was what they'd come to stop!

She turned to see if the Brigadier was about to blow his whistle, which was to be the signal for the circle of armed men to show themselves.

But he'd gone; and she just caught sight of him, crouching down, making his difficult way over the rough piles of boulders, towards the top end of the perimeter wall.

She forced herself to listen to the words from below. The Skang with Hilda's voice – could it really be her? – seemed to be delivering some sort of sermon.

What on earth was the Brig up to?

And as for the Doctor...

But the Doctor was no longer leaning against the wall. He was peering intently at something in his hand, and seemed to be fiddling with it.

'... the emptiness will be filled,' the Skang was saying. 'You are about to have the most sublime experience a human being can possibly have. And you'll never be unhappy again. Now I want you to stand up. The time has come.'

Oh no!

All the disciples stood up and faced the Skang next to them. Each Skang took its partner by the shoulders and lifted their head.

She couldn't look. It would be too horrible.

But then, into the silence came a faint sound like a child's music box... and a long cry of despair from the Skang who had been speaking. All the Skang in the arena had let go of their human partners and turned towards the stage.

Briefly, the giant figure seemed to swell, and the stars that made up its tenuous ever-changing shape momentarily burned

even brighter. But then it began to come apart. A strange
voice – no, voices – came from the shining figure on the platform, with desperate words tumbling out that made no sense,
words not just foreign to the English ear, but alien to Earth
itself; and the form of the thing was writhing and turning…
and now it was shrinking, shrinking, shrinking as one by one
the sparkling lights that were its very substance went out.

But more than that. The creatures in the body of the
amphitheatre were also in distress, losing their balance and
falling to the floor; and cries of woe made a counterpoint to
the desolation of the voices coming from the platform.

The disciples were bewildered and scared. Some just
drew back, others tried to help the agonised Skang, others
clambered over the seats to get away from the distressing
scene.

For they were dying, the Skang. As their Beloved on the stage
was fading away, their substance was sinking into itself, melting, disintegrating, until, as the voices fell silent on the now-
empty stage, there was nothing left at the feet of the terrified
devotees but scattered dust.

Sarah, with such a relief coursing through her body that she
felt as euphoric as she had when they first encountered the
blue mist, watched the Doctor as he pressed another button
on the silver box in his hand.

The music stopped; and the Doctor sat down on the rocky
floor. He looked tired. Very, very tired.

'I think I must be getting old,' said the Doctor.

Sarah glanced round the wardroom. How surprised they'd
all be if she told them just how old he was.

There had been no time for asking questions; there was
too much to do. Quite apart from the sixteen traumatised
members of the faithful in the temple, the others outside
had suddenly found that their paradise had disappeared and
turned into an uncomfortable hell.

Pete Andrews and the Cox'n returned to the ship with a few of the men, to relieve Chris of his temporary command and bring the *Hallaton* back into the lagoon. If they'd left it much later, they would have missed the tide completely.

The others turned nursemaid, and shepherded the flock of bewildered youngsters back to their village, which they found somewhat less comfortable than when they had left it. But most importantly, apart from their being assured that a ship would be coming to fetch them home – and sending the necessary signal was one of the first things that the CO had done as soon as he was back on board – most importantly, they were told the truth about what had happened to them.

Except, of course, for an explanation of what the Doctor had done to save their lives, because nobody knew what it was.

Now he was going to tell them.

'That's the second time I've played brinkmanship in as many weeks,' he went on. 'It's not a game I enjoy.'

The Brigadier seemed a bit sniffy, thought Sarah. Nothing that a few drams wouldn't fix though. Pete Andrews had already poured him a whopper, and left the bottle near him.

The Doctor was enjoying teasing them.

'Come on, Doctor,' she said. 'Be a sport.'

'Now, Sarah,' said the Doctor, 'I'm sure you could give us the answer if you really thought about it.'

'Well,' she said, 'it was obviously something to do with the TARDIS circuit thing. And I'd guess it was a time loop.'

Bob Simkins looked up from the rum and peppermint that he was mixing for the Cox'n, who'd been invited to join them. 'Sorry love,' he said, 'but I haven't a clue what you're talking about.'

'Oh, I know that,' said Chris. 'A time loop...'

'Pipe down, Chris,' said Pete. 'Go on Doctor. Tell us.'

The Doctor thought for a moment. 'Not just one time loop. I set the temporal recursion circuit to operate recursively itself, so that it generated thousands of random time loops. That's why it took me so long. I had to get the dimensional co-ordinates exactly right. And I had to do most of it behind my back in case they saw me.

'Each time one of the elements that made up the Great Skang was hit, it was catapulted back to an earlier time in its existence; and there it'll stay, quite happily going round and round forever, without realising it. But, you see, they've all been sent to a different bit of their past. So that particular Great Skang can never be a danger again.'

'And the human Skang the same?'

'Of course. Why should they be any different? Their bodies were well over fifty per cent psionic energy deriving from their parent colony, the Great Skang. When that was withdrawn, there was nothing left but a few organic chemicals.'

The Brigadier poured himself another burra peg. 'Hmm. Well, Doctor, all's well that ends well, I suppose. Sounds a bit complicated to me. If you'd given me a few more minutes, I'd have dropped a hand grenade on the thing.'

'Ah,' said the Doctor, 'that would have been an interesting experiment.'

The Brig grunted. 'Much quicker. And I'd certainly have enjoyed doing it.'

'I'm sure you would, my dear fellow. If the only answer had been to destroy it – or should I say them? – I'd have done it too, if I could. But I'm glad I was able to do it my way. I gave them the respect due to them as another race of beings with as much right to existence as we have.'

The Brigadier shook his head. 'I shall never understand you, Doctor.'

'Since we from Gallifrey share your failings, I understand you – and the rest of humanity – only too well,' the Doctor replied.

The Brigadier didn't answer. He just grunted again and took an extra large swig of whisky.

I don't understand anybody, thought Sarah. But she wasn't thinking about the destruction of the Great Skang.

It was the Doctor – and the Brigadier as well – and the way they seemed to take it all so calmly, now it was over, as if saving humanity was all just part of a day's work. She'd never get used to it herself.

Her whole existence had changed since she met the Doctor. It wasn't just the adventures they'd shared – for that's what they were – it was that she found herself looking at life, her everyday life, in quite a different way. Sometimes, in the past, she'd felt like screaming with frustration when things didn't go right. Now, life was always worth living, even the infuriating and the boring bits of it. Somehow, everything was brighter and more colourful. It was as if a light had come on.

As for Jeremy, she understood him least of all.

When she'd found him, shaking and almost crying, and comforted him until he was in a fit state to learn what had nearly happened to him – and what had *actually* happened to his sort-of girlfriend – his reaction was not at all what she'd expected.

'I was at the front of the queue,' he'd said. 'Emma was the only one to get the reward. It's not fair. It should have been me!'

There's nowt so queer as folk, as her mum used to say.

ABOUT THE AUTHOR

I didn't appear in *Doctor Who* when I was earning my living as an actor in television, though my first appearance on the box – over half a century ago? It can't be! – was as one of the conspirators helping Guy Fawkes in his plans to blow up Parliament. So what's that got to do with the price of turnips, as Sarah Jane Smith might say?

Guy Fawkes was played by Patrick Troughton, that's all; and seventeen years later I was directing him, when he was the Second Doctor, in *The Enemy of the World*.

Since then, I've never really left *Doctor Who*. Within three years I was the producer, and was responsible for the show during the five years that Jon Pertwee played the part, sometimes directing and writing as well (including one book).

When Jon said that he wanted to leave, I had the job of finding his successor; and we all know who that was, don't we? My biggest claim to a sort of vicarious fame was undoubtedly my casting of Tom Baker.

I've had a great career (so far). I love books, and for over ten years, after handing over Tom and the show to Philip Hinchcliffe, I produced and sometimes directed the BBC ONE Classic Serial – the Sunday tea-time dramatisations of classic books, such as *Great Expectations*, *Pinocchio*, *Jane Eyre*. But even during this era I was in touch with the good Doctor, through conventions and so on. Indeed, this side of the connection has continued right up to the present. Who would grumble at all-expenses-paid trips to Los Angeles, or Florida, or a luxury cruise round the Caribbean, not to mention the innumerable opportunities to meet the fans all over this country?

Not only that: since I left the BBC staff in 1985, I've written two *Doctor Who* radio serials and two-and-a-third *Doctor Who* books (the last one, *Deadly Reunion*, I co-wrote with Terrance Dicks).

So here, in the year of the relaunch, which has already proved to be a thumping success, is another story about the Third Doctor. It's thirty-eight years since, at the age of forty-two, I found myself directing *Doctor Who*. I see no reason why I shouldn't be involved, one way or another, for the next thirty-eight years.

Coming soon from
BBC Doctor Who books:

Spiral Scratch
by Gary Russell
Published 1 August 2005
ISBN 0 563 48626 0

Featuring the Sixth Doctor and Mel

Carsus: the largest repository of knowledge in the universe –
in any universe, for there is an infinite number of potential
universes – or rather, there should be. So why are there now
just 117,863? And why, every so often, does another one just
wink out of existence?

The Doctor and Mel arrive on Carsus to see the Doctor's old
friend Professor Rummas – but he has been murdered.
Can they solve the mystery of a contracting multiverse
and expose the murderer?

With the ties that bind the Lamprey family to the past, present
and future coming unravelled around him, only the Doctor can
stop the descent into temporal chaos. But he is lost on Janus 8.
And Schyllus. And a twentieth-century Earth where Rome
never fell. And...

New series adventures also available from BBC Books

The Clockwise Man

By Justin Richards
ISBN 0 563 48628 7
UK £6.99 US $11.99/$14.99 CDN

In 1920s London the Doctor and Rose find themselves caught
up in the hunt for a mysterious murderer. But not everything
is what it seems. Secrets lie behind locked doors
and inhuman killers roam the streets.

Who is the Painted Lady and why is she so interested in the
Doctor? How can a cat return from the dead? Can anyone be
trusted to tell – or even to know – the truth?

With the faceless killers closing in, the Doctor and Rose
must solve the mystery of the Clockwise Man before London
itself is destroyed...

*Featuring the Doctor and Rose as played by Christopher
Eccleston and Billie Piper in the hit series from BBC Television*

The Monsters Inside

By Stephen Cole
ISBN 0 563 48629 5
UK £6.99 US $11.99/$14.99 CDN

The TARDIS takes the Doctor and Rose to a destination
in deep space – Justicia, a prison camp stretched over six
planets, where Earth colonies deal with their criminals.

While Rose finds herself locked up in a teenage borstal,
the Doctor is trapped in a scientific labour camp. Each
is determined to find the other, and soon both Rose and
the Doctor are risking life and limb to escape in their
distinctive styles.

But their dangerous plans are complicated by some
old enemies. Are these creatures fellow prisoners as they
claim, or staging a takeover for their own sinister purposes?

*Featuring the Doctor and Rose as played by Christopher
Eccleston and Billie Piper in the hit series from BBC Television*

DOCTOR·WHO

Winner Takes All
By Jacqueline Rayner
ISBN 0 563 48627 9
UK £6.99 US $11.99/$14.99 CDN

Rose and the Doctor return to present-day Earth, and become
intrigued by the latest craze – the video game, *Death to
Mantodeans*. Is it as harmless as it seems? And why are so
many local people going on holiday and never returning?

Meanwhile, on another world, an alien war is raging. The
Quevvils need to find a new means of attacking the ruthless
Mantodeans. Searching the galaxy for cunning, warlike but
gullible allies, they find the ideal soldiers – on Earth.

Will Rose be able to save her family and friends from
the alien threat? And can the Doctor play the game to
the end – and win?

*Featuring the Doctor and Rose as played by Christopher
Eccleston and Billie Piper in the hit series from BBC Television*

Was this what they'd come to worship?

The silence as the faithful drained their cups was broken by shouts of joy and wild laughter. Watched with benign equanimity by the guru (and utter astonishment by Sarah), they flung their cups to the ground and their arms round each other, giggling and chattering at the tops of their voices like a crowd of ten-year-old schoolgirls let out to play.

They were clearly as high as kites.

To Sarah's horror, Jeremy tripped his way through the swaying crowd, almost dancing, and threw his arms around her in an enveloping hug. This was a Jeremy transformed, very far from the usual reserved ex-public-school boy she'd always known.

'Come on!' he cried, pulling back and grabbing her hand. 'We're all going down to the garden. This is where the guests get to share our love-in!'

What!

'No, no!' said Jeremy, with a typical Jeremy chortle. 'Nothing like that! Just dancing and singing and stuff. Come on, Sarah, this is the first day of the rest of your life!'

Trust Jeremy to latch onto a new cliché, thought Sarah, taking back her hand. She lowered her voice. 'Jeremy, there's something not quite right with this whole set-up. Why don't we work together to find out what's going on? You could be undercover while I...'

'You've got it wrong, old girl! This is how life should be – loving everybody, sharing everything... Once you let the Skang into your heart...'

Sharing?

'You haven't given them any money, have you?' she asked.

He reddened slightly. 'Look, don't start that elder-sister stuff again. It wasn't much. Peanuts really.'

'Oh, Jeremy!'

'We're only talking about a measly twenty thou. Honestly, Sarah, you sound just like Mama sometimes.'

language, not even Finnish or Lithuanian – or Double-Dutch for that matter, even if it sounded like it.

As the voices rose in pitch and volume, she glanced over at the slight, curly-haired figure whose presence here was the reason she had come. The pale face of Jeremy Fitzoliver (her 'Hooray Henry' colleague on the *Metropolitan*) was ecstatic, with a wide-eyed vacancy that did it no favours at all.

Looks even more like an educationally sub-normal sheep than usual, thought Sarah, as her attention was caught by a movement.

Now what? The white-robed guru – if that's what he was. Where had she seen that handsome face before? – who was sitting at the front before a pair of ornate curtains, was pouring a colourless liquid from a handsome antique jug into a number of small plastic cups. These were then handed round by two helpers dressed like their master.

For a moment she was tempted to take a cup like the other couple of 'guests', as the newcomers like her were dubbed, but her journalistic caution prevailed. You could never be too careful. If she was going to discover what this was all about, she needed to keep her head clear.

As the chanting became more frenzied, rising in a crescendo of rapture, the guru, taking a larger cup in both hands, rose to his feet, turned his back on the gathering, and raised the chalice on high, quite obviously mirroring the actions of a Christian priest at communion.

Well really! At that moment, Sarah quite forgot all her reservations about the cosy version of faith she'd argued over in the vicar's confirmation classes. This was a sort of blasphemy!

But worse was to come. As the voices came to a climax with a resounding shout of 'SKANG!', the helpers pulled back the curtains to reveal a painting of a being: an Indian or Tibetan divinity it would seem; or more likely a demon. A horrific demon in the shape of a hideous insect with a needle-pointed snout... or... what was the word? Oh yes... a proboscis.

tight skin, made that quite apparent; her sojourn in the shallow grave on Hampstead Heath had been too short to affect the smooth complexion; and the fox that had revealed her to the early morning jogger had soon given up any hope of a decent dinner.

Doctor Prebble, the professor's assistant, peered at the body through his thick glasses. 'Could it be a virus?'

'When in doubt, eh?' said the professor. 'The all-purpose get-out! Where would the medical profession be without its pet viruses? I think not, Brian.' And he pointed to a mark on the base of the victim's neck, just above the breastbone. 'The skin has been punctured.'

Prebble whipped out his tape measure. It was a cut an inch and a half long. 'Doesn't look like a knife wound,' he said.

'Ah well, we're not going to find out by goggling at her like a bunch of tourists at Madame Tussauds...' The professor held out his hand, without looking, and as he expected his assistant placed within it the razor-sharp scalpel he would use to open up the chest and the abdomen. And, as was his wont at these moments, he abruptly burst into song. '*Che gelida manina...*'

And as suddenly stopped.

He would learn nothing from the internal organs of the deceased; nothing from the lungs, the heart, the liver, the kidneys; nothing from the gut, from the oesophagus to the rectum; and for a very good reason.

There was nothing there.

The dead girl's body was literally just skin and bone.

'Arimiggle arimoggle frendog Skang!'

At least, that's what it sounded like to Sarah Jane Smith, as she stood at the back of the white-clad bunch of about a dozen young people who were happily chanting the words.

Maybe it was Tibetan, she thought. Or Sanskrit. Judging by the images displayed on the walls, it wasn't any European

CHAPTER ONE

'Is it vampires, Prof? Or did she starve herself to death? Or what?'

Professor Mortimer Willow, consultant forensic pathologist to the Met in North London, grinned happily at the grizzly remains lying on the table in front of him. He loved a puzzle. 'What indeed, Sergeant. No, not vampires – for two reasons. One, vampires are a myth; unless you're talking about a member of the species *Desmodus rotundus*. I suppose one might conceivably have escaped from Regents Park, but it would have to have been a very large bat indeed to have done this to the poor lass. As for starvation...'

He leaned forward and picked up the bony hand. Anybody who had anorexia nervosa – or who had been deliberately deprived of food – would have been dead long before she'd reached this degree of emaciation.

'And the second?'

'Mm?'

'The second reason it's not vampires.'

'What are you talking about, Sergeant? Do try to stick to the point!' Glory be to Gladys, the man was a fool! Removing the entire contents of the circulatory system would merely produce a slightly thinner and extremely pallid version of the victim. The weight of the blood would be only about eleven pounds. Less than a stone.

The chestnut-haired young woman must have been quite a beauty: the structure of her skull, clearly delineated under the